PURPLE

by

Graham J. Sharpe

This book is a work of fiction.

All names, characters, places, organisations, businesses and events are either the product of the author's imagination or are used fictitiously. Any resemblance to actual persons, living or dead, is purely coincidental.

ISBN-13: 978-1475147001

ISBN-10: 1475147007

Dedications

Purple is dedicated to my mum and dad
and the loving memory of Rupert Marson

Special thanks to:

My partner Arnie for his never-ending patience

My friend Miriam for making me believe it was entirely possible

Jennifer Goehl at
Can't Put It Down ~ A Book Reviewer's Blog
and Extra Set of Eyes Proofing

My UK Edit Team Michael, Maddie, Janet, Angela and Stuart

Pauline Nolet ~ the best copy editor & proofreader in the business

Kitty Finegan for the amazing cover and art work

Finally, to all my other mates (too numerous to mention)
for their help and encouragement along the way

grahamjsharpe.com

Contents

~ One ~

Ellie's Leap of Faith

Ellie Arnold believes in reincarnation and thinks she may have been Marilyn Monroe in a previous life. When Ellie told her parents about this, they laughed out loud.

Twenty-three weeks later, June 22nd, one a.m. to be exact, Ellie tidied her freshly-bleached Marilyn Monroe hairstyle in the mirror. She applied a coat of red lipstick, pencilled in a beauty spot and blew herself a kiss.

She'd turned the light off at ten, but insomnia must be an eight-hour virus that lurks in toothpaste. As soon as she'd cleaned her teeth and put her head on the pillow, the symptoms appeared. Too late to prevent infection, she lay alone in the dark and imagined the blood rushing AWAKE round her system: *swoosh…swoosh…swoosh.* It made her feet burn, her legs restless and her shoulders ache. It caused a sudden onset of wriggle-squirm-roll-flip. When it finally reached her brain, triggering an explosion of thought, she gave up and trudged downstairs to the lounge.

Desperate to get on Facebook, Ellie opened her laptop and held her breath for an internet signal. No! Still nothing!

She flicked on the TV to watch *The Five O'Clock Announcement*'s midnight repeat. The usual, pinched and bespectacled face stared out from the screen.

"Welcome Golden Oldies and Bright Young Things! Thank you for tuning in. My name is Penny Treasure.

"Over five months have passed since Purple Monday, that horrific day in January…"

Ellie flicked the TV off. She'd already heard today's message and it hadn't brought her any comfort. "Penny Treasure…with her helmet hairdo…she's weird…she gives me the creeps. Looks like she's enjoying herself too much."

Frank purred and leapt up onto the sofa.

Ellie despaired that so much time had passed since Purple Monday because her memory still hadn't returned to normal. The past five months had drifted along in a blur. The details of *that* day remained a complete blank and the memories of her life before it seemed patchy and confused.

Yesterday, the smell of suncream triggered happy recollections from last summer: light glinting on ripples of water, Mum's laughter, Dad diving like a lunatic into the deep end, her brother George learning to swim. She remembered they used to go to the Lido in Brockwell Park. The flashback had stung her like an angry wasp, but determined not to let the tears leak out, she painted on a happy face. The unlocked staff entrance to Boots, the chemist on Clapham High Street, helped out with free make-up.

The basic facts had recently been established. On Monday, January 10th, a purple windstorm circled the planet in minutes and stole everyone between the ages of eighteen and sixty-five. No one knew what the purple storm was or where it had come from. No one knew if the missing were dead or alive. People worried it would return. Every other day someone came up with a new explanation, but nothing had been proved.

Ellie wasn't sure how she'd managed to keep her fears under control. Lately, usually at night, they'd started to niggle. For at least a week, she'd been troubled by an overwhelming sadness. Had post-traumatic stress disorder switched off her feelings? Had something happened to switch them back on? Ellie wondered why the pain had only just arrived.

The lucky ones received telephone calls from elderly relatives as soon as phone lines reconnected. Then, last week, when transport links were re-established, London experienced a mass exodus. Ellie's friends took trains to Runcorn, Llandudno and Leicester. George went down to Devon to stay with Great-Aunt Sarah, but Ellie refused the offer.

"I'm fifteen. There's a shortage of workers in the capital. I've got myself a work permit. I'm staying in London to do my bit."

"Oh, are you?" Great-Aunt Sarah said. "Well, I've heard it all now!" She omitted to say that George had always been her favourite and that, with her own grandchildren staying, she only had the space for one more lodger. "I'm not happy about it, but we'll see how you get along. Make sure you call me every Sunday for a full report."

"Will do," Ellie said through gritted teeth.

In the absence of people, Ellie had regular conversations with the cat. She scratched Frank's head and turned him to face her. "I've got this sensation in my stomach…it's like a physical pain. I've even given it a name. I've called it the Missing Feeling. I've been trying to get rid of it for days. I've tried deep-breathing exercises, indigestion tablets…I've even tried smiling for no reason."

Ellie lay back on the sofa and closed her eyes. Perhaps, if she dialled 999 and screamed for an ambulance, she would get rushed into the hospital and have the Missing Feeling removed. Perhaps, if she shoved her hand down her throat, she could remove it herself.

"Where did everybody go?"

Frank kept quiet.

"It's no use," Ellie said. "I'm going to have to call TIS again."

Frank blinked.

"Now, remember, this is strictly between us, it's our little secret. I don't want anyone to find out. I'm way too old for this kind of thing, but…well…I'm desperate."

Ellie reached over and picked up the phone. The number had been stored on automatic redial. She pressed the button and immediately the call connected.

"Hello and thank you for calling the Tucking-In Service," the recorded message said. "We are currently experiencing a high volume of calls. Your call is being held in a queue. Your call is important to us, so please stay on the line and we will be with you shortly."

Ellie put the phone on loudspeaker and tried to ignore the smooth jazz.

Maybe I need to eat something?

She made a piece of toast.

"You are now number one in the queue," the recorded message said.

I'm running short of ration coupons. Oh...what the hell...I'm having butter and jam.

"Hello, Tucking-In Service, Babs speaking," Babs said. "May I have your postcode and house number, please?"

Ellie grabbed the phone with sticky fingers and yelled the details.

"That's Ellie from Gauden Road in Clapham, isn't it? Trouble sleeping, dear?"

Ellie listened to the rasping flick of a cigarette lighter. She'd never met Babs in person, but she imagined high hair, glasses on a chain, chipped red fingernails and an overflowing ashtray. "Afraid so...could you send someone round as soon as possible?"

"I'll do my best," puffed Babs, "but you'll have to manage your expectations, it's busier than Trafalgar Square on New Year's Eve."

Fifty long minutes later and the customised Smart Car eventually appeared, its flashing orange light illuminating the street like a cheap school disco.

Ellie, peeking through the curtains, smiled at the sight of biker boots, camouflage trousers, cropped silver hair and earrings that resembled small chandeliers. "Thank God it's you," she said, opening the front door.

June dispensed one of her legendary hugs. "Ellie! It's great to see you again! How you doing?"

"Not good. I thought I'd be okay tonight, but..."

"You don't need to explain it, honey, I understand. We all feel miserable sometimes, no matter what age we are. Everybody has ups and downs. We're all muddling through."

"I suppose."

"No suppose about it. These past five months have been tough for everyone. I think you're doing a fantastic job living on your own."

Ellie closed the front door. She fiddled with her fringe. She tucked her hair behind her ears then pulled some free and twisted it round a finger. "I'm not so sure."

"Really? Why?"

"Honest truth...I've started to feel lonely. I've got anxiety. I can't get rid of it." Ellie put her hand on her stomach. "I've even given it a name, I've called it the Missing Feeling. Since George went to Devon, the house is like a morgue. I'm wondering if I should follow him down there."

"Well, there's no shame in that, honey, if that's what you want to do."

"What I want to do is brave it out. I want to stay in London. I'm doing really well with the business. I've even hired an assistant...her name's Ping...I think we could be friends. During the daytime, I'm fine."

"Well, why don't you set yourself a time limit? Give yourself a couple of weeks. If you still feel the same, you can pack your stuff and jump on the train."

Ellie nodded.

"Your eyes look red, honey. When mine feel dry and gritty I want to take them out and suck them."

"That's not helping," Ellie said.

They plodded up the stairs. Frank zoomed ahead.

"We've got to focus on the positive," June said. "Things *are* picking up. There's fresh food in the supermarkets and the new Drop-In Centres open this week...so we'll have somewhere to go, twenty-four seven, when we need help or just fancy a bit of company."

Ellie dropped into bed, running her hands over the cool, cotton duvet cover.

"Ooh, clean sheets!"

"Yes!" Ellie said. "Now that the water and electricity are on every day, I'm washing everything. The machine hasn't stopped. I even thought about giving Frank a quick spin."

They both laughed.

Ellie felt her shoulders drop. She sunk her head into the pillow and inhaled the familiar smell of June's coconut oil moisturiser. "I feel much better now. Must be because you're here. How come you manage on your own? Don't you get lonely?"

"No, to be honest, I don't. My husband died years ago, I suppose I'm used to it. And anyway, I'm not really alone; I've got all my animals."

"Oh yeah, I forgot, and I've got Frank...it's just..."

"It's just time, that's all. Give yourself a break." June pulled a chair over and made herself comfy. "Thing is, life does get better. The horrible Missing Feeling will fade away. Take it from someone who knows."

"But it feels worse than ever. For the first four and a half months I was fine. I managed. Maybe I was in a daze. Emotions are weird. I thought I had everything under control."

"Can you believe it, Ellie? There are 134 Tucker-Iners who work for the service?"

Ellie couldn't see the relevance of this statement, but if past conversations were anything to go by, it was bound to have significance. "Are there?"

"Yes, there are. So…don't you think it's funny that you always get me?"

"I suppose so. It hadn't really crossed my mind. I assumed this part of Clapham was your patch."

"Well, it's not. TIS HQ is the Telecom Tower in the West End, that's where we're all based. Although I tend to stick to South London, Babs can send me anywhere."

Ellie thought about this for a second. "Seems impossible."

"But it's happened," June said. "Here I am again."

"Wow…that's amazing! What are the chances?"

"I'd imagine the chances are slim. It's a massive coincidence."

"So, what does it mean?"

"Well, two things," June said. "Firstly, it suggests to us that anything is possible, and that's quite an exciting idea, don't you think?"

Ellie nodded gently.

"Secondly, and this is the really exciting bit, I don't believe in coincidences…I think everything happens for a reason."

In a desperate hunt for something, June began to remove several items from her backpack. Ellie smiled because it was a lot like watching a magician try to pull rabbits from a hat. Out came an iPod and speakers, some meditation joss sticks, an incense burner, a large bottle of lavender oil, an assortment of herbal tea bags, some sandwiches and a box of home-baked biscuits. Eventually, at the bottom of the bag, she found what she was looking for.

"I've been wondering why our paths keep crossing." June opened the small Tupperware container and broke off a thumbnail-sized piece. "It's been bugging me for a while. And now, after this conversation, I definitely know."

"Why? What's the reason?"

"I need to give you this."

"Oh," Ellie said, staring at the gnarled lump. "It looks like a piece of tree bark."

"Close," June said. "It's actually a piece of tree root. Remember I went travelling round South America on my motorbike? Well, I picked this up in Brazil."

"What am I supposed to do with it?"

"Chew it for a minute, then swallow. It'll put you into a deep sleep. You'll have amazing dreams…dreams that will help you find yourself."

"Are you for real? What do you mean find myself?"

"You're on your own and you feel lost."

"Oh, am I? That sounds serious. Maybe it's true. But…being free…it's what I've always wanted!"

"I know, honey, and there's no reason why you can't get what you want. But feeling free has nothing to do with other people; it's about finding that special part of yourself and being brave enough to let it shine through."

"I don't understand," Ellie said. "You're losing me."

"I'm talking about that part of you that's totally unique. Some people call it an independent streak. It's the voice inside your head that tells you to do things *your* way."

"You mean like staying in London on my own?" Ellie said.

"Exactly," June said. "It takes bravery to follow that voice and most people don't manage it for long."

"Why?"

"Because it's easier to conform. And if you stop to think about it for a moment, for the last fifteen years you've had a constant stream of information and instructions. It's come from parents, teachers, friends, books, magazines…the TV…the internet. Unless you're incredibly strong, all of that stuff will eventually cause you to lose sight of who you really are."

"I've never thought about it that way," Ellie said.

"The Purple stole so much…in a matter of minutes…you didn't get a period of time to adjust; you've been plunged in at the deep end. You're torn. Part of you wants to play it safe and head down to Devon, but there's another part that's desperate to do things your way."

"I see, I think I get it," Ellie said. "So, if I take this tree root and have the dreams, I'll find that special part of myself and feel instantly brave. Well...brave enough to follow my own advice. Is that what you're saying?"

"Almost," June said. "You'll be shown a path it would be wise to follow; a path that will lead you in the right direction. And the thing is, when you know you're on the right path, it'll be easier to ignore the unhelpful advice of others. I'm not saying you won't ever feel fear, it'll just be a lot easier to manage."

"Are you sure this...*thing*...isn't dangerous?"

"Positive. Members of a remote rain forest tribe have used it for centuries. It enables them to live the life they were destined to have. I've used it myself, so I know it definitely works. After taking this tree root, my dreams took me on the most amazing journey."

Ellie stared at the root in the palm of her hand.

"Do you trust me?" June said.

"Yes...yes, I do. Whenever you're here I feel calm and safe...I feel like I've known you for years. Does that sound silly?"

"No, it doesn't," June said, smiling. "It sounds perfect. You've got instinct, honey. You know much more than you realise."

Ellie placed the root on her tongue and began to suck. Seconds later she started to chew. Gradually, the flavours exploded...aniseed...tingling ginger ...fiery hot. "Ugh! Tastes like a burning cough sweet!"

Frank padded up the duvet, gave June the once-over and curled himself around Ellie's head.

"You've got a living, breathing, purring fur hat," June said. "Now, listen to me, your dreams may be a bit...strange tonight."

Ellie sat bolt upright. "What do you mean?"

"Well...the truth...it isn't always what you want it to be." June lit one of her meditation joss sticks and waved a stream of fragrant smoke above the bed.

"I wish you'd told me that a minute ago!" Ellie said.

"You'll be fine, honey. Just remember...fear needs to be faced head on...otherwise it paralyses you and you spend your whole life feeling small and insignificant."

Ellie opened her mouth to ask for a full explanation of that statement, but the words dissolved. Her elbows unlocked and she fell back onto the pillow. A haze clouded her vision, and she wondered how she would recognise the path of her life when she couldn't even distinguish her feet from the foot of the bed. The light in the bedroom faded. The walls closed in. A shudder of fear shook her awake. Her muscles tightened. "The day before Purple Monday I wanted to bleach my hair, but my parents told me I couldn't. My dad said I'd be in deep water if I did...my mum told me I'd look like a tart! Can you believe that?"

"Shhh, don't worry about that now," June said.

"I was glad the Purple took them...I *hated* them...I remember...I wished they were dead!"

Frank's gentle purring radiated down through Ellie's scalp, bringing a familiar reassurance. She closed her eyes and drifted. Her arms and legs lost the will to move, her breathing slowed.

"I'll sit here a while and finish my Sudoku…just relax and go with it…"

Before June finished her sentence, the insomnia virus died and sleep captured Ellie quicker than a crocodile grabs a paddling bird.

~ Two ~

The Journey Starts Here

Deep water. Ellie swam up through the darkness, towards the light.

The surface shimmered only two strokes away, so she relaxed. Her lungs prepared to release the old breath and take in a new one. The final reach up, arms down, fingers together, palms pushing water, head extended, mouth about to open...crack! Her head hit the frozen surface.

"Someone help me!" she screamed.

As if from above, Ellie saw her face squashed against the ice. Eyes wide in panic, water pouring in.

"It's me! I'm trapped under the ice!" she shouted. "Someone help me!"

Down below, in the freezing darkness, Ellie swallowed a mouthful of cold water. Skaters passed above her head, and she heard the muffled sounds of their steel blades crunching the ice. Her body started to drop. The sounds faded. Her head creaked like it would implode.

Standing on the other side, Ellie watched in horror as the shape below her feet grew smaller. She grabbed a skater. "It's me! Help me!" She pointed to the dark shadow moving under the ice. The skater pulled away.

Time's running out, I'm drowning! She wanted to cry. Life is happening only inches away, but something as simple as frozen water is preventing me from having it! She scanned the surface, but couldn't see a way through.

She fell to her knees and banged a fist on the ice. "Help me!"

"Just breathe," a woman's voice said.

Ellie turned and saw a hand, then a bracelet with charms: little shapes of gold twinkling in the winter sun.

"What?"

"Just breathe, dear, that's all you have to do."

Underwater, Ellie opened her mouth and took a breath. Glorious, pure, clean air filled her lungs. The hand grabbed her wrist and pulled her up through the ice. She felt herself rising out of the water, away from the clutches of something awful...death maybe?

And then, suddenly, she was flying through springtime with all its explosions, through bright light and colour, into summertime, into heat and life.

Deep blue blazed with the fires of the setting sun. Fingers of cloud, like sponges in a trifle, soaked up crimson, orange and purple, the colours brighter than Ellie had ever seen. Her bare feet reacted to the gravel by treading lightly. Small stones lodged themselves between her toes, but she didn't stop to remove them.

A bumblebee hovered at eye level for a second, swinging in the air like an obese trapeze artist, then it traced an intriguing figure-of-eight. “What’s your name?”

“Marilyn Monroe,” Ellie said.

“Honestly?” the bumblebee said.

“Yes,” Ellie said.

“Mmm? Well, maybe you are. Your lips look like hers.”

“Oh, do they!” Ellie lifted her fingers to touch them, but as she pulled them away, she heard a loud kissing sound and they came off in her hands. “My lips!” she cried.

Ellie’s bright red lips sat, like a butterfly, in the palm of her hand, and when she opened her mouth hundreds more fluttered out.

“Feels lovely, doesn’t it?” the bumblebee said.

“Mmm, yes,” Ellie said.

“No more butterflies in your stomach?”

Ellie chased her bright red lips along the path.

The butterfly led her to an archway with a heavy wooden door. A rusty key, made of elaborately-fashioned iron, protruded from the lock. Ellie turned the key, pushed the door open and walked through.

“Perfume!” she said.

Ellie stood in the walled garden, staring at the lush and perfect flowers.

Despite the fading light, the picture looked breathtaking. Thinking it couldn’t be real, she took a step forward. Cautiously, she reached up and grabbed a branch. Being careful not to catch her fingers on any of the prickly thorns, she pulled a stunning, purple rose towards her face. Now that she could see it up-close she knew immediately that it radiated with life.

Neat, brick pathways, without weeds, withered leaves or fallen petals, separated each flowerbed. Slowly at first, Ellie began to follow the pathway, pausing often to admire individual plants or simply to linger for a moment in a wave of scent. The huge walls held the air within them perfectly still. When she eventually stopped and placed her hands against one of them, she could feel the heat of the day that had been captured within its crumbling brickwork.

Ellie sat with her back against the wall and allowed the heat to radiate into every muscle. Above her, through the crowded canopy of leaves and petals, the first star flickered.

“Let them all out,” the bumblebee said, “there’s plenty of time.”

Nestled discreetly amidst the army of flowers, Ellie saw a tower. Distance had created an optical illusion and it appeared to be small enough to sit in the palm of her hand. The hands on the clock, at the top of the tower, said twelve. That’s odd, Ellie thought, how can it be sunset at midnight?

“Time is just an illusion,” the bumblebee said.

“What do you mean?” Ellie said.

“Well, you don’t have a past, do you?”

“Yes, I do. I have lots of…memories.”

“Aha! Got you!” the bumblebee said. “You’ve tried to forget everything. Every time you have a memory you push it away.”

“Some things are too painful,” Ellie said.

"You won't feel pain here," the bumblebee said. "This is paradise. Go on...have a go...think of something."

"I'm not sure..."

"Go on!" the bumblebee urged. "You can trust me; I make honey."

"Well, there was that time I ran into the lounge with a plate of spaghetti bolognaise and the whole lot slid onto the carpet."

The bumblebee made a high-pitched tee-hee sound. Ellie laughed too.

"See?" the bumblebee said. "No tears. What else do you remember?"

"Packing for a summer holiday," Ellie said, checking her eyes. "Washing the car and being told off for dropping the sponge on the gravel."

"Keep going."

"A Saturday morning shopping trip with Mum, George putting the gerbil down the toilet, burnt sausages on the barbeque, a wasp flying up my dad's shorts..."

"Ugh, wasps!" the bumblebee said. "They give us bees a bad name."

"Laughing at stuff on TV, raking up the autumn leaves for money, last year's wonky Christmas tree."

Ellie closed her eyes and thought about life before Purple Monday. Even though her parents had annoyed her constantly, she couldn't deny that the memories made her feel good.

When she opened her eyes, the bumblebee smiled. "Not so bad, huh?"

"I miss them; I know I do, but..." A squeaking noise interrupted the conversation. "What's that?"

"I have to go," the bumblebee said. "I've probably said too much already. Busy time for me...lots to do."

"Oh," Ellie said, standing up. She put her hand to her mouth and discovered her lips had flown back.

The squeaking noise grew louder then it stopped. Ellie turned. A tall, dark, hooded figure stood directly behind her. Long, bony, soil-encrusted fingers reached out.

"Let go of me!"

Ellie turned to run, her legs buckled and she tripped. She picked herself up and tried again. She started running. She gathered speed. Without looking back, she kept moving, faster and faster, deeper and deeper, her feet pounding the pathway. The impact of bare feet on fired brick sent shockwaves through her shins. She struggled on as best she could, but eventually, after less than a minute, she had to stop.

Confused and breathless, Ellie fell to her knees then slumped forwards. Trying to restore the blood supply to her brain, she rested her forehead on the ground. A solitary bead of sweat ran down her left cheek, circled the rim of her nostril and clung to the tip of her nose. Several more quickly followed, coursing across her scalp like tiny, creepy fingertips. They dripped onto the pathway releasing a smell like hot pavements after rain. Her vision blurred, failed completely and then returned.

Gulping for air, Ellie began to have the creeping suspicion that the flowers in the garden were stealing all the oxygen.

She lifted her head and stole a glance behind. Nothing. Relieved, she took another breath. Like a terrified fox hunted to the point of collapse, she began to crawl forwards. Still clammy and out of breath, with her hair stuck to her forehead, she tried to stand up. She did it. Fantastic! She managed a smile then wiped her face on her sleeve. A stagger became a jog, but the sight of something in the distance caused her to stop dead in her tracks.

With the sun no longer on duty, the black shadows of night were free to roam the garden. Ellie held her breath as two silhouettes crept out from a corner.

An intoxicating mix of fear and recognition caused her brain to release a stream of jumbled messages.

Compelled to run, her legs took her pounding heart along the path and into the embrace of her mum and dad. Arms reached around bodies, hands wrapped around hands, fingers interlocked with fingers and the smell of love, strong and distinctive like a favourite woollen blanket, enfolded all three of them.

Ellie clung on as tightly as she could, floating in the bliss of the moment, but when the old clock at the top of the tower began to chime, she felt herself falling. Tumbling through space, she grabbed for help, but found no one to hold. The sound became unbearably loud, until it mutated into something irritatingly recognisable: the buzz of her alarm clock. Ellie opened her eyes and banged her fist on the snooze button.

Morning screamed, like a lunatic, through the gaps in the curtains. Ellie stared up at the ceiling...What the *hell?*

Usually, her dreams faded upon waking, but this time the details sparkled in her mind like explicit memories of actual events.

She struggled to free her legs from the twisted knot of bed sheets. A circle of colour caught her eye. She turned her head and noticed a scatter of petals across the pillow, and then the long-stemmed, purple dream rose held tightly in her right hand.

June's words returned, bringing with them a devastating realisation: I know what I have to do! I have to free myself from the Missing Feeling. I have to discover what happened to Mum and Dad... I have to find them.

~ Three ~

Sad, Lonely Boy

Scott opened his eyes, closed them, and then forced them open again. "Was that you?"

Scott's brother Charlie sat quietly on the other side of the coffee table doing the weekly accounts. He looked up and smiled.

"Someone just shouted my name," Scott said. "It woke me up."

"It wasn't me," Charlie said.

Scott gazed around the lounge, but couldn't see a soul. "I'm hearing the voices again," he said. Slowly, he eased down the duvet and propped his head up on a cushion.

Scott had heard the voices many times before. In the beginning they were rare and infrequent so he'd paid them little attention, but lately, for at least a week, he'd heard them every day. "I wanted to have a lie-in this morning," he said. "I did a midnight dash to a stranded cyclist."

"Proper little businessman you've turned out to be," Charlie said. "Mum and Dad would be really proud. So would Lou."

Scott smiled. "I've had these cards made. Proper business cards." He stretched a hand out from under the duvet and lifted one off the coffee table. "Look!

They say Scott's Scooters Emergency Pick-Up and Repair, and it's got my telephone number."

Charlie carried on crunching numbers.

"I had to do something to earn money," Scott said. "For a few weeks, not long after you all went away, I helped to move the cars off the streets. It was spooky when the Purple cleared; they were all just sitting there. It was like you'd all calmly turned your engines off and walked away."

"Maybe we did," Charlie said.

"I was the youngest driver in the squad. They couldn't believe I was only sixteen."

Scott closed his eyes.

When he opened them again, Charlie hadn't vanished.

"Guess what happens in twelve days' time?"

"You and Lou will be nineteen," Scott said.

"Wow, you remembered! Wait till I tell Lou, she'll be impressed. How come you never remembered our birthday when we were here?"

"I dunno. I wish you'd tell me where you've gone. Give me a sign."

Charlie narrowed his eyes and shook his head. "Secret," he said.

"A man on the radio thinks you've all been abducted by aliens. He says they'll come back for the rest of us soon."

"Aliens!" Charlie laughed.

"Well, what is it then? It's got to be something huge. Freaky stuff is going on..."

Charlie picked up the calculator and waved it at Scott. "Freaky stuff? Are you sure you're not exaggerating? I know what you're like when you tell a story."

"No. Honest," Scott said. "Things have changed since you went away."

"What's different, then?"

"Well, for a start, no one's sick anymore, all the hospitals are empty and lots of old people are running around like teenagers. What else? Everyone's using pushbikes and mopeds, but," Scott said with a grin, "I've got a special permit to use my van."

Charlie didn't respond.

Scott had found the calculator down the back of the sofa last night. He'd thrown it on the coffee table. He should have known better. He should have hidden it immediately. He pulled the duvet up to his nose. "Is Mum with you?"

Mum disappeared nearly six months before Purple Monday. Scott glanced across the room at her picture. Frozen forever in time, locked within a shiny, silver frame, she never stopped laughing. The California breeze had blown several strands of hair into her mouth. In quiet moments, buried memories would spontaneously dig themselves up, allowing him to recall minute details about his mum: the scar on the bridge of her nose, the touch of her fingertips against his forehead and the smell of her hand cream. At the table in the kitchen, the taste of her special, creamy porridge made with maple syrup would fill his empty mouth.

"Why are you sleeping on the sofa?" Charlie said, avoiding the mum question.

"I like it down here," Scott said, suddenly annoyed. "I wish you hadn't shown up."

"I'll go if you like?"

"Suit yourself," Scott said. He pulled the duvet up and over his head and when he pulled it back down, a few seconds later, Charlie had gone. The calculator lay abandoned on the coffee table.

"Tell Dad I've taken down the old sign," Scott shouted. "It doesn't say Joe Bromley and Sons' Family Garage anymore. It says Scott's Scooters."

~ Four ~

Memories and Missiles

Seven in the morning on a deserted Clapham High Street and the promise of another hot day burned orange over the rooftops.

Ellie leaned against the bus shelter, whilst an eerie quiet tiptoed around. Breakfast had been a blur of blackcurrant squash and over-buttered toast: the thought of it mixing in her stomach made her feel queasy. Emotions woken by last night's dream had intensified the Missing Feeling. Directly across the road, a battered National Lottery pavement sign creaked on its hinges. Ellie stared at the words FEELING LUCKY?

A memory, like a solitary bat, flew out of a dark cave in her mind. Oh my God, she thought, I was here on this street when it happened. She closed her eyes. Several more bats fluttered into the light.

A ceiling of clouds dropped on the roofs of the houses, and then the colour purple began seeping through its cracks...that was the first sign something was wrong. I panicked. I sprinted across Clapham High Street. By the time I'd reached the other side, the wind had gone into reverse. Everything got sucked upwards and I felt my hair lifting off my head. There was a giant coil of purple, it looked like the tentacle of a jellyfish, it spiralled towards me. I turned to run, I got knocked down. The thing slammed my body against those railings...the pain...it shot through like a javelin. Something hit me in the face.

It's all coming back to me! And I remember what happened next...

I dropped to the floor and curled into a ball, my hands clamped tightly to my head. Howling wind engulfed everything. These weird things, deep purple...like...like...tangled of balls of candyfloss, they collided with me. I think they passed through me! I felt pins and needles in my flesh and my bones, burning hot then freezing cold. I saw flashes of blue and then something crashed down. It was that Lottery pavement sign! I remember those words *FEELING LUCKY?*

Oh wow! This is amazing! I remember it all...

I grabbed the sign with both hands and pulled it over my head. I used it like a shield. It protected me for a while, but then the wind got underneath it and lifted me off the ground. I freaked out. I wedged my flailing feet under the railings. The wind changed direction and blew me back to the ground!

And then what happened? Screaming? Yes, waves of screaming and it sounded like a crowd on a rollercoaster. I put my hands over my ears to block out the noise...it was a stupid thing to do...but...I couldn't stop myself...it was an automatic reflex. My shield flipped into the hurricane. I opened my mouth to shout for help, but the storm grabbed my voice and rammed it down my throat. I thought I'd been paralyzed. I wanted to throw-up but I couldn't even breathe! A fist of heat swirled under my ribs then surged upwards, filling my head with an explosion of white light. The howling stopped.

I stayed on the ground...I don't know how long I was there...maybe seconds, maybe minutes. I heard a dog yelping. I didn't move, I was cowering, and stuff crashed back to Earth...a mobile phone missed me by inches. I remember, I opened my eyes and stared at my fingers. There was no blood and nothing missing! The Purple...it swirled back through the cracks in the black clouds...it looked like...like the tail of a dragon. Thin, purple wisps snapped and cracked and popped and then there was total silence.

Ellie, still leaning against the bus stop, opened her eyes and stared across the road at the ghostly memory of her own self. The terrorised ghost spat out dirt. It pulled leaves and the front page of yesterday's newspaper from the hood of its sweatshirt. Debris fluttered down around the ghost, and it reminded Ellie of those ticker-tape parades she'd seen on old black and white movies. Briefcases and backpacks littered the pavement. A small dog shook itself then padded up the street, tail wagging, lead trailing. Most of the cars were empty; their doors were open and the drivers missing. She watched the ghost shove its hands into its pockets to stop them shaking.

The bus pulled-up, blocking Ellie's view across the road, so she stepped to the side and peered around the front of the vehicle. The ghost had vanished.

The doors of the bus squeaked opened. "Morning," the driver shouted, "you're the early bird."

Ellie picked up her bags, stepped onto the platform and attempted a smile. "I've got lots to do today."

"Don't go without me!" a voice screamed.

Ellie turned to see a girl rushing towards her, her tightly fitted dress forcing her to run like a Japanese geisha, her face obliterated by a mushroom cloud of curly hair.

"Stupid sandals!" the girl screamed. She hoisted up her dress then flicked them off her feet and into the air.

Ellie watched, open mouthed, as the girl leapt forwards, grabbing the handrail with one hand and catching a sandal in the other. It briefly crossed Ellie's mind that the other sandal must still be airborne, when a dark object filled her vision then whacked her on the forehead. The impact knocked her off balance. She stumbled backwards.

"Blooming heck, steady on!" the driver shouted.

The doors snapped shut. "I'm sorry! Are you all right? Did I hurt you?"

"You'll have someone's eye out if you're not careful!" the driver snarled.

"Yes! Okay! I *said* I'm sorry…really…I am." The girl dropped her briefcase and reached out a hand. "My name's Midge."

"I'm okay, I can manage," Ellie said. She stood up and brushed the dust from her dress. "I need to sit down."

"Yes, I expect you do," the driver said, rolling his eyes.

Ellie stumbled her way to the nearest seat and Midge followed with the bags.

"My hair…it's really getting on my nerves," Midge said. "It's Flaming Fox Red. I had it done yesterday." She searched her pockets, eventually pulling out an elastic band. "I need to get it out the way for a minute." She scraped it up. "That's better."

Ellie stared up at Midge's hair and grinned. "Looks like a bomb's gone off."

"We can't all be Miss Perfect!" Midge snapped.

Ellie instantly regretted the comment. Remembering Purple Monday – in all its glorious colours – had left her feeling elated and traumatised all at once. "Sorry…I'm not thinking straight…I didn't mean it…why don't you sit down?"

Midge dropped herself next to Ellie and stole a glance at her pony-tail-on-top-of-the-head reflection in the window. "Nightmare! You're right, it looks like a threat to national security," she said. She fiddled with the elastic band. "Hell…I've done it too tight."

Ellie decided not to stare. She glanced around the bus, but couldn't see any other passengers. She gazed out the window. Trying to ignore the uncomfortable silence, she scrambled a fake search through her handbag. She couldn't think what to say, so she asked a ridiculous question. "Going somewhere nice?"

"On my way to work!" Midge blurted. "It's really important that I'm not late. It's my first day at the DMC. I want to give a good impression…by arriving early."

“No way! You’re a member of the Decision Makers Council? I don’t believe it! I mean…I don’t think you’re lying. How exciting! Will you be making any of the announcements on TV?”

“Oh, I don’t know. I shouldn’t think so…I don’t know. I’ve got first-day-freak-out.” Midge held her hand out. “Look…can’t stop shaking.”

“You’ll be fine, don’t worry. We’re all muddling through.”

Midge hugged her briefcase to her chest. “Huh…yeah…muddle’s a polite word to describe it. What’s your work?”

“I run a property management business,” Ellie replied.

“Bloody hell!” Midge said. “All these jobs I’ve never heard of. Where’s a careers councillor when you need one. What do you actually do?”

Ellie shrugged her shoulders. “Well…it’s not as cool as the Decision Makers Council. Basically, I look after lots of flats where old folks live. I help to organise maintenance work, cleaning and decorating, that sort of stuff. Oh, and I have to make sure they pay their rent and service charges every month. It’s boring, really…but…well…the business used to belong to my parents. They told me at the work permit place I had to keep it running.”

“Doesn’t sound boring, sounds impressive.” Midge jumped up. “Westminster Bridge! This is my stop! Hello, driver! I need to get off here! Stop the bus!”

The driver waved his hand. “Keep your hair on!”

Midge turned back to Ellie. “Thinks he’s a comedian.” She leaned down and grabbed her briefcase. “You’re not getting off here?”

“No. If he gets me as far as Trafalgar Square, that’ll do.”

“Oh, right.” Midge tripped on her way to the exit.

The bus glided to a standstill. The doors squeaked open. The driver stared down the aisle and coughed.

That’s a hurry-up-and-get-off-the-bus cough, Ellie thought.

“Grumpy old git,” Midge said. “That’s a hurry-up-and-get-off-the-bus cough.”

The urge to jump up, grab hold of Midge, and blabber every detail of last night’s dream engulfed Ellie quicker than a pyroclastic flow. Fear of sounding like a lunatic kept her glued to the seat.

“Bye then.”

“Bye.”

Midge hesitated at the doors. “I’m all over the place…like an embarrassing dad on a trampoline.” She laughed. “It was nice to meet you…and I’m really sorry about…you know…the sandal incident.”

Ellie stroked her forehead. “Don’t worry, I’m fine. Good luck with the new job.”

“Thanks,” Midge said.

The driver coughed again, Midge stepped off the bus, and the doors snapped shut behind her.

~ Five ~

Rats and Freaks

Marty arrived in London three weeks after Purple Monday.

Alone, broke and low in self-belief, he made the mistake of accepting the first job that came his way.
"Where did they all come from?"

"Most of them were here already," Mr Clarkson the Rat Pack Chief, said. "But the rubbish hasn't been collected for weeks, and now they're out of control."

In the beginning, Marty did his best to make the most of a bad situation, but the novelty soon wore off. There's nothing joyful about laying poison or setting traps, and within six weeks he had become the longest serving employee. As the Rat Pack numbers dwindled, he found himself working the nightshift alone.

As an incentive to stay on, Mr Clarkson gave Marty his own van and allowed him to choose which district he wanted to patrol. Marty picked the West End because this area of London included all the famous sites and tourist attractions: the places he had only ever seen in the movies and on television. Trafalgar Square, Piccadilly Circus and Big Ben soon became familiar landmarks, and occasionally, he would take a detour off his path to check out somewhere new. One night, he even drove across Tower Bridge.

In order to escape the grim reality of his current situation, Marty took to fantasising. Draped in moonlight the capital appeared like a film set, and often, he would pretend to be Britain's most famous spy working undercover on a top secret mission to save the world. A black James Bond, he reckoned, was way overdue.

Every morning as the sun rose, Marty would drive back to the depot in West London and drop off the van. Usually, the cage in the back would be jumping with a dozen or so ill-fated captives, and these would be handed over to Mr Clarkson. Although the rats were clearly a health hazard, and breeding out of control, Marty always felt sorry for them: after all, they were living, breathing creatures just like him. He tried his best not to think about the grisly end that awaited them.

One morning as he deposited the night's catch, Mr Clarkson spotted his troubled expression. "Don't worry, son," he said with a wry smile, "we give them all a dangerously high dose of laughing gas...when the end finally comes they're too busy telling jokes to notice."

Of course Marty didn't believe this story, and by the time he'd reached the changing room his fake smile had disintegrated. Weighed down by fatigue, he lost the will to carry on. Feeling exhausted, he lay down on the bench and thought about his old life and the friends he had left behind. Sleep came sneaking up from behind and cracked him on the head with a mallet.

Marty woke to the familiar smell of disinfectant. He'd been having that dream again...running and searching...but as usual, he couldn't remember any details.

A reassuring patch of blue in the skylight told him it was still daytime and the absolute silence made him certain everyone had gone home. Marty rubbed his eyes and checked the time. "Twelve thirty! How could I have slept so long?" Quickly, he changed out of his overalls and grabbed his moped helmet; he desperately needed fresh air and the company of people. His empty stomach screamed out for food.

With no one waiting for him at home, Marty headed back into the West End. In the five months since Purple Monday some of London's shops and restaurants had re-opened.

"Hello, poppet-of-love," a voice said. "What can I get for you?"

Marty placed the menu on the table and stared up at the lady: Phyllis on the name badge, black mini skirt, fishnet tights and bottle-blonde hair that had been blown up into a shape. "Um, the all-day breakfast please. Bacon and sausage, eggs over-easy and a side order of mushrooms."

"Oh, you're American!" Phyllis shrieked. "I've just got engaged and Tony, my fiancé," she waved her pen towards the man behind the counter, "he wanted to take me to Boston. He wanted to show me New England in the fall." Phyllis giggled when she said the word fall. "But of course, we'll have to make do with a long weekend in Brighton."

"Cool," Marty said. "I'm actually from the west coast, San Francisco."

Phyllis stretched her hand out to show Marty the ring. "San Francisco! How fabulous...sounds like somewhere over the rainbow!" Marty took the waitress's hand in his and stared at the sparkly engagement ring. It hadn't occurred to him that some people were still finding happiness. Phyllis waggled her hips with delight. "Isn't love amazing?"

"Congratulations. I'm really happy for you."

"Oh, poppet," Phyllis said, "don't be sad." She squeezed his hand. "You never know what's round the corner."

Marty nodded his head and tried to think what would make him happy right now. "Don't suppose you've got any chocolate for dessert?"

"Oh, I'm sorry, poppet," Phyllis said. "I wish we did. Apparently, chocolate has sold out across the country. People are saying it's worth its weight in gold. How about jam rolly-polly and custard?"

"Cool," Marty said, trying to hide his disappointment. "Jam rolly-whatever-it-is sounds great."

By the time he'd finished eating, Marty's mood had lifted. He drained his teacup, left a generous tip for Phyllis in the saucer and, for the hell of it, took a saunter round the corner. Daylight and people conjured up exciting possibilities, and a sign in the window of a busy hairdressing salon that said APPRENTICES WANTED caught his eye.

A girl popped her head out. “Hello, are you Martin?”

Marty stared wide-eyed. No one had called him Martin for years, but it was his proper name. “Err, yes. I am...but...”

“Oh good, you’re a bit late, never mind, come in, I’ve got the paperwork all ready for you.”

Marty’s mouth failed to tell her she must have the wrong Martin. His feet followed her into the shop.

“My name’s Andrea, I’m the receptionist. Take a seat. If you wouldn’t mind filling out this?” Andrea handed Marty an application form and a pen then flicked her long, blonde, perfectly blow-dried hair over her shoulders.

Marty did exactly as requested.

“Would you care for a hot beverage of your choice?”

“Oh...no thanks...I’m good.”

“Mr Rupert will be with you in a minute, he’s just finishing Mrs Lewis-Brown, his two o’clock.”

A short distance away, on the salon floor, an elderly lady emerged from a thick cloud of hairspray. Dripping in jewellery and tottering in high stilettos, she tripped on the strap of her designer handbag. A jumble of arms and legs careered towards the reception and Marty watched in astonishment as something small, fluffy and yelping rocketed skywards. Without thinking, he dropped the pen, leapt to his feet, and did an amazing flying catch. Fi-Fi, Mrs Lewis-Brown’s toy poodle, was the exact size of an American football and Marty had practiced this move a million times.

Mrs Lewis-Brown landed safely on a pile of freshly folded towels and Marty, the hero of the moment, landed a new job. Returning the whimpering pooch to her grateful arms, he received a round of applause from the delighted onlookers and a start date for next Monday.

In the week that followed, Marty changed his mind every few hours. I'll take the job! I won't take the job! Frazzled anxiety caused sleepless days and a constant headache, but eventually, he made a decision.

Mr Clarkson had been reluctant to accept Marty's resignation and offered him a hefty pay rise to stay. Marty bravely turned it down. At the time it seemed like the right thing to do, but now he wasn't so sure. Panicky first day nerves had got the better of him.

Marty parked his bike outside the rear entrance and looked down at his newly purchased, second-hand, black shirt, trousers and shoes. The butterflies in his stomach had morphed into leaping frogs. He felt a bit sick. He knew absolutely nothing about hairdressing. A sign at the bottom of the stairs instructed all new apprentices to make their way up to the second floor so, reluctantly, Marty made the climb.

At the top of the stairs, a towering, orange hairdo and a thick layer of make-up appeared from behind a door. "You're late!"

Marty took a step back. "That's a crazy look, sister…it's like…whoa!"

The girl sounded irritated. "It's called a Beehive."

"A what?"

"My hair, this hairstyle, it's called a Beehive. And the colour, in case you're wondering, is a unique mixture from the shade chart. One part Pharaoh's Gold and two parts Satsuma."

"Satsuma? You mean...like...orange, huh?" Marty stared at the girl's green and blue eye shadow and wondered if she might be colour-blind. "Satsuma!" He laughed as he repeated the word.

"You need to get moving!" the girl snapped. "Mr Rupert and Miss Renee want to begin their welcome presentation."

Marty followed the girl into the training room and took an inconspicuous seat on the back row.

At the front of the room, on a raised platform, stood an elderly couple. The woman had an equally over-made-up face that reminded Marty of a circus clown. He wondered, for a second, where clowns go when they're too old to be funny. The image of a retirement home filled with pensioners making sausage dogs out of balloons swirled into his head. Old-lady-bright-blue hair rose steeply upwards from her high forehead then swooped down in waves and curls that stuck out in every direction. In spite of her erratic movements, the entire creation remained rock-solid.

Marty recognised the man standing next to her as Mr Rupert. Despite his advancing years, this broad-shouldered giant of a man boasted a full head of thick, dark brown hair and a smile that displayed a mouth full of shiny, white teeth. Around his neck sat a flamboyant, pink kerchief held in place by a glitzy, jewel-encrusted gold ring. “My name is Mr Rupert,” he said.

“And my name is Miss Renee,” the clown-lady said.

“Welcome to *our world*,” they said together.

You mean welcome to the freak show, Marty thought.

Mr Rupert turned his attention to the latecomer. “Marty! How lovely you could join us,” he shouted, “we’ve been waiting for you. Please come up here and join us on the stage”.

Marty’s scalp immediately started to itch: strong cheese and awkward social situations always had that effect on his body. He ducked down and stared at the floor. Perhaps, if he pretended not to hear, the old guy would pick on someone else?

“Don’t try and hide from me, rascal,” Mr Rupert said impatiently. “Come along, dear chap, quickly, quickly!”

Marty glanced up and discovered all heads had turned in his direction. “Oh man,” he muttered. He dragged himself up, shuffled to the front of the room and stepped onto the stage.

“Welcome!” Mr Rupert said excitedly with jazz hands. “Why don’t you introduce yourself to the group and tell us why you have chosen to study hairdressing?”

After an uncomfortably long silence Marty croaked out some words. “Hey, everyone…my name’s Marty…I’m fifteen years old.” He paused, desperate to think of something else to say. “I’m not sure why

I'm here...I caught a poodle last week...and...I've been catching rats for way too long."

A sea of bewildered faces stared up: this wasn't going well. He rubbed his forehead and stared back at the crowd.

"Well done, rascal, carry on!"

Marty puffed out a mouthful of air. "Well...I wouldn't mind doing something creative...I don't really know...I know nothing about hairdressing. I guess I enjoy a challenge."

"Ah ha!" Mr Rupert bellowed. "That's exactly the word I wanted to hear! You enjoy a challenge, eh? Well, you've come to the right place. Yes, indeed! You've certainly come to the right place. You see...here at Renee and Rupert's Salon and Training Academy we don't do average...we only do extraordinary." The old man thrust his arms out wide, as if to demonstrate the size of extraordinary, and Marty narrowly missed being knocked off the stage. "The shocking truth," he continued, "is that anyone can be an average hairdresser. Yes, that's right, anyone can learn the basic, technical skills, but that's not what we're looking for at Renee and Rupert's. In this salon we expect more from our staff than that. We expect brilliance. Our mission here at Renee and Rupert's is to make every customer feel fabulous...but remember...you can only make someone feel fabulous if you know how to bring out their inner beauty. Real beauty lies within. Real beauty has nothing to do with looks...it comes from the personality. A brilliant hairdresser doesn't just appreciate what's on the outside, he has the ability to go inside the customer's head and see what makes them tick. A brilliant hairdresser will then create a style that not only compliments the customer's physical features, but also matches their personality."

Marty stepped back in order to avoid Mr Rupert's flailing arms and silently wished he'd stayed at home.

"So," the old man continued, "in order to bring out that inner beauty we must be able to see it, and in order to see it we have to look inside. In order to create perfection on the outside of the head we have to know what is happening on the inside." Mr Rupert's face flushed pink with excitement. "FRIENDS! I CHALLENGE YOU TO LOOK INSIDE!"

Frightened bottoms jumped off seats, and a shower of saliva sprayed the front row. The clown-lady looked concerned, but the crazy man could not be stopped.

"How many of you are friends with *intuition*?"

Someone raised a brave hand, but it was totally ignored.

"If you have intuition," Mr Rupert ranted, "you will have immediate knowledge of something. Instantly, you will be able to sense what our customers are thinking and feeling. Here at Renee and Rupert's we will not only train you to sharpen your scissors, but also your powers of intuition!"

The speech came to an abrupt halt once again and the audience, frozen in a state of nervous anticipation, said nothing. Wary of another soaking, those nearest the stage closed their eyes. Convinced that Mr Rupert had finished, Marty clapped his hands together. Much to his relief, everyone quickly followed. Within seconds the entire room filled with rapturous applause and cheering. The clown-lady looked reassured.

"Oh, how marvellous! How wonderful!" a beaming Mr Rupert said. "Please, rascals!" he shouted, waving his hands in a downward motion. "Thank you! Thank you! There's no need for you to applaud my enthusiasm."

The clapping and cheering subsided.

"All I ask is for you to find an equal measure of your own enthusiasm. Arrive here, every morning, on time, with an enquiring mind and a hunger for knowledge. Never be afraid to ask questions, or worry about making mistakes. Work hard, seek perfection in everything you do, and remember…in *our world*…you must be prepared for the unexpected."

~ Six ~

Toilets and Teacups

Hopping off the bus onto stone-cold Westminster Bridge, Midge realised she only had one sandal. The other, she imagined, must be lost on the floor of the number four bus.

She stared down at her dirty feet and shook her head in disbelief.

After a thorough inspection, she noticed the tear in the hem of her dress: the stupid dress she had worn after trying on every item in her wardrobe at least twice. She pulled out the *what-happens-on-your-first-day-at-work* letter and realised she didn't have her glasses.

"Nightmare!" she said to no one. "This is all I need."

Have I got enough time to dash home, collect my glasses, and change?

Frenzied thoughts circled the inside of her head like badly driven rally cars. What she wanted was a second opinion, but at this precise moment, she had more chance of spotting a flying pig than getting one of those. In order to get a second opinion there needed to be a second person and the streets looked deserted. Midge tried to ignore the sinking feeling.

For her, the subject of second persons had long been a prickly one. Reliable second persons rarely swam in the waters of her world.

Once, two years ago, a stray sea lion swam up the Thames and everyone became hysterical. The people of London crowded bridges to catch a glimpse and film footage was shown on all the channels. The lady reading the news stated, matter-of-factly, that illness or global warming had caused the animal's inner compass to become confused, but Midge knew this was wrong. She alone knew that the sea lion had taken a deliberate detour to give her a secret message, which she received telepathically. The message was, *don't worry everything will be okay.* Midge knew for certain that he would have said more, but before he got the chance, a marine biologist shot him in the back with a tranquilizing dart then hoisted him onto a dingy. In a deep sleep he was whisked away to cooler waters.

Don't worry everything will be okay.

Midge repeated it to herself several times then scanned Westminster Bridge and the South Bank for a stranger: someone who might have an opinion or, better still, be in the mood for a conversation. She saw no one. After squinting across the Thames at Big Ben, she realised time was not on her side. Half blind and scruffy would have to do.

From here it was a short distance to the Decision Makers Council Headquarters, located at the old television studios on the south bank of the river. Midge ran down the steps and onto the embankment, but her momentum dissolved when she found herself standing in the shadow of the London Eye.

Before Purple Monday the giant observation wheel had been one of London's top tourist attractions but now, like so much of the capital, it had ground to a halt. Although it had been a year since Midge had taken a flight on the London Eye she remembered that day as if it were yesterday. She remembered the joy of spending the whole day with her dad, and the excitement they had felt as they boarded the capsule. She remembered the stomach-fluttery thrill as it lifted them high above the crowds. She remembered jostling for a good position, pushing past two nuns who giggled like schoolgirls and a boy who picked his nose and wiped it on the handrail. She remembered the amazing view from the top and how her dad had pointed out all of the capital's famous landmarks. She remembered where they had gone for lunch afterwards: to China Town for dim sum. She remembered saying, "Sounds like Chinese for basic arithmetic." She remembered her dad's smile. She remembered heated trolleys with windows that passed by the table dropping-off shrimp dumplings, spring rolls and spare ribs. She remembered sticky fingers and sesame seeds stuck in her teeth. But most of all, she remembered how much she missed him.

"I hate this bloody dress!" she blurted.

Exploding with rage, she grabbed the hem and ripped it off. After using it to dry her cheeks and blow her nose, she threw it into a rubbish bin. She wanted to chuck the sandal in with it, but an unfamiliar voice in her head convinced her otherwise. She put the sandal in her briefcase and began to stride with determination.

Tinted glass prevented passers-by from seeing inside the building, but Midge knew from previous visits that the DMC HQ always bustled with excited activity. Before entering she took a moment and a deep breath: "Calm…calm…calm." After a nauseating minute of hesitation, bravado shoved her up the steps. Nervous, uncoordinated footwork allowed the revolving door to hit her on the back of the head.

Midge stood, confused, in the foyer and surveyed the empty scene. "Where is everybody?" she whispered.

A faint clicking sound on the other side of the room answered the question. Feeling intrigued, she walked over to investigate. Sitting behind the reception desk, she saw two little, old ladies: their knitting needles moving at a frenzied pace. Bent double in deep concentration they failed to notice they had company, and it took two loud "hellos" to get their attention.

"OOOOH!" one said.

"Oh my lord, you scared us!" the other said.

"Sorry, I didn't mean to," Midge replied. "It's my first day here. My name's Michelle but most people call me…"

"We know who you are, darlin'," one of them said, "the boss called early this morning and left a message. We've been sat here for the past half hour waiting for you. My name is Pearl Moon and this is my sister Opal Heart. I'm the tea lady and she's the cleaner."

Before Midge could reply, Opal took over. "Now, dear, there's been a rather unfortunate turn of events and I'm afraid to tell you that no one else came in today. Last night everyone got together for Nadeem's goodbye dinner, Nadeem is the name of the boy you're replacing, he's gone off to live with his great-aunt in someplace with a strange name. Now where was it?"

"Newport Pagnell," Pearl said.

"Yes, that's right," Opal continued, "Newport Pagnell. Anyway, that's by the by, I'm losing the thread of the story. Now, where were we? Ah yes, last night they all had a celebration meal here at the canteen, and our resident chef, Leo, did one of his awful-alternative menus. Melon and Marmite Medley to start then Seafood Surprise for the main…and…then…what was it?"

"Spotted dick with angel delight," Pearl said.

Opal raised an eyebrow. "And I don't mind telling you…the Seafood Surprise…it really was a surprise."

"What was it?" Midge enquired.

"It was *baked* fish fingers with prawns in a *mustard-cream sauce,* and the prawns were rancid," Pearl said.

"Think he found them in the bottom of an old freezer," Opal said, "they'd probably been defrosted several times. Everyone's contracted food poisoning, I'm sorry to say, but that's what happens when you're daft enough to put a fifteen-year-old with dirty fingernails in charge of a kitchen. He's got no idea about personal hygiene." Opal shuddered, pulled a twisted face then shook her hands in the air: it looked like a tribal dance to ward off evil.

"The entire workforce has gone down with the splats," Pearl said.

Midge stared blankly at the two Eastenders. She couldn't believe what she'd heard or, for that matter, what she'd just seen. She'd noticed it immediately but, because it seemed implausible, instantly dismissed it as a trick of the light. For a brief second, in the mist of periphery vision, both Pearl's and Opal's heads appeared like light bulbs running on low power: light bulbs with brassy-blonde, bubble-perm hairdos.

When viewed straight on, however, Midge could see nothing but reassuring, wrinkly flesh and determined, steely eyes. Brash cockney accents made the two old ladies appear much taller than their four and a half feet. In traditional tea and cleaning lady style they both wore sky blue overalls and on their feet, in a colourful break with tradition, pink, fluffy mules.

"Cor blimey!" Opal exclaimed. "Me back's got stiff sitting there."

"Now, dear," Pearl said, "we've been asked to show you around and get you settled in. Your desk is upstairs in one of the offices on the second floor."

"Excellent! I've got my own desk already."

Opal butted in. "We'll show you everything: the offices, the discussion chamber, the broadcast room and the canteen. By the time we've finished with you, you'll know this place like the back of your hand. But, before that, we need to give the reception desk a quick polish."

In the corner of the foyer stood a large, four-wheeled trolley that had been dangerously overcrowded with a jumble of cleaning products. Opal shuffled over to it and grabbed some equipment. "Many hands make light work," she announced, distributing dusters.

With polish and duster in hand, Pearl burst into song. "There'll be bluebirds over the white cliffs of Dover…tomorrow…just you wait and see…"

"Come on, darlin', join in!" Pearl said.

"What, with the singing?" Midge said. "No thanks."

"Ooh la-de-da, Madame!" Opal said.

Midge felt her face redden. "I don't actually know the words."

"You'll soon pick them up."

"Well, at least squirt some polish, would you?" Opal said.

Lost for words, Midge picked up the can of polish and sprayed a cloud.

After several ear-splitting verses, Pearl and Opal agreed that the desk was "bright as a new pin".

Midge stopped twisting the duster and picked up her briefcase.

"No, dear!" Opal shouted. "Get the trolley, we're taking it with us!"

Before she had time to object, Midge found herself in charge of a heavy and awkward cleaner's trolley and she struggled to push it in a straight line along the corridor. The forward right wheel kept getting stuck, causing it to veer off and crash into the wall.

Halfway down, and much to Midge's despair, they stopped outside the ladies' loo.

"Right, Opal," Pearl said, "what do we use in here?"

"No way!" Midge exploded. "That's it! I've had enough! I'm not cleaning the toilets! That's not what I came here to do. I came here to be a member of the DMC. I'm supposed to be making decisions, attending meetings, making important phone calls. I've got a briefcase and everything. I want to see my desk. I want to speak to someone in charge. I'm not doing the bloody cleaning!"

The ladies, who had been rummaging through their supplies looking for bleach, stood in silence. After exchanging a dismayed glance, Opal shuffled over to Midge. "There, there, darlin'," she said, putting an arm around her shoulder. "Simmer down, simmer down."

"You'll have a heart attack if you carry on like that," Pearl said.

"Now then, missy," Opal said with a pointy finger, "you listen to me cos I've got something important to tell you. I'm very well aware that you came here to make decisions, attend meetings and talk to gaud knows who on the phone about heaven knows what and I'm not trying to tell you that running the capital ain't important, cos it is. Especially with everything that's happened lately, running London is a very, very important job. But let me tell you something, darlin', let me point something out...there is never anything more important than keeping a place clean and tidy. Nothing, and I repeat nothing, should go before dust-free shelves, smear-free windows, a sparklingly clean floor and a freshly bleached toilet bowl. You can't make clear decisions when you're surrounded by dirt and mess."

"A cluttered room creates a cluttered mind," Pearl chirped.

"I take pride in my constantly high and unrivalled standards of cleanliness and hygiene," Opal continued, "I work hard at my job, I never cut corners and I sleep well at night knowing that, if anyone chose to, they could at any time eat their food off any toilet seat in this building and not worry in the slightest about coming into contact with germs," she paused for a moment to draw breath before adding, "and if you don't believe me then maybe you should try it one lunchtime."

The ladies folded their arms and nodded their heads in agreement. Midge found herself disturbed by the vision of roast beef, Yorkshire puddings, gravy and all the trimmings served-up on a toilet seat.

"No, that won't be necessary," she said quickly. "I don't want to eat my breakfast or lunch or dinner off a toilet seat, thank you very much."

"Well, no one's saying you have to," Pearl said. "But you get the point, don't you, darlin'?"

"Well...yes," Midge said. She wiped her sweaty palms on her dress. "Look...I'm sorry...I didn't mean to be rude and I'm not for one minute saying your jobs aren't important. It's just that I'm nervous. It's my first day at work. I've been running late all morning, I've torn this stupid dress and...well...I've just been thinking about my dad."

"Oh, sweetheart," Pearl said, "we've all lost someone. I've lost me two sons, their wives and four grandchildren. And Opal, she's lost her daughter, her son and his family."

"But despite everything, darlin'," Opal said, taking over, "despite all of life's dramas, we've got to keep going. We've got to stay positive and believe that, whatever happens, everything will turn out fine in the end. Be grateful for what you do have and try to remember that every cloud has a silver lining. Go ahead and cry if you think it will make you feel better, but then take a moment to remember all the brilliant things in your life."

"Like what?" Midge couldn't think of a single thing to smile about.

"Well now, let's see..." Opal fiddled with her bottom lip. "There must be lots of them." Eventually, her face lit up. "The sun's shining, you're young and very pretty and you've got lovely hair and your arms and legs work."

"And you're not blind!" Pearl blurted. "Some people can't see a thing but they don't spend all day crying about it, do they? What you need is a cup of tea, that'll sort you out. You know what, dear? Every day I'm grateful that I can still enjoy a nice cup of tea and a biscuit. A plain digestive does it for me, but I'll tell you what, because it's your first day here, and because I want to put a smile back on that lovely face of yours, we'll open a packet of Caramel Wafers! How about that?"

"OOOH!" Opal said, and she raised her pencilled-in eyebrows inexplicably high.

For the second time in one day Midge found herself lost for words – partly because of the eyebrow manoeuvre but, mostly, because the incredible thought of eating something covered in chocolate had temporarily robbed her of the ability to speak. She nodded and attempted a smile.

Pearl picked up Midge's briefcase and placed it on the trolley. "It's time for a tea break! Let's go to Opal's stockroom and get you her spare pair of mules. Did you know, dear, you've got no shoes on your feet?"

Minutes later, at the end of a long corridor on the ground floor, Midge found herself standing in Opal's stockroom. Floor to ceiling shelves groaned with every kind of cleaning product you could imagine.

"Now, I've been meaning to do this for ages," a business-like Opal said. She pulled a red marker pen from her top pocket and wrote the words **REMEMBER STOCK ORDER FRIDAY** across the wall next to the phone. "Ordinarily, I hate graffiti," she continued, "but needs must. I keep forgetting to do the weekly order and, fingers crossed, this will remind me."

Meanwhile, in the far left hand corner of the room, Pearl turned sideways and did a vanishing act.

"Where did she go?" Midge said.

Opal pointed to a space between the shelves that had been cleverly concealed by black bin liners. "You're next," she said.

"Where am I going?"

"Through the gap and into the secret room, my darlin'!" Opal said.

~ Seven ~

Headline News

Everyday, Ellie would stare at the *Arnold Property Management* sign on the wall and groan that her parents hadn't come up with a more imaginative company name. This morning, however, she had something exciting to distract her.

Once inside, she made a beeline for the staffroom at the back. After checking her face in the mirror, she emptied the contents of her carrier bag into the cupboard above the sink. Before closing the door, she paused for a moment to marvel at her secret stash of treasure: a large jar of luxury hot chocolate drinking powder, three packets of chocolate-covered peanuts, one "creme" egg, two chocolate oranges, several small bags of chocolate coins, an out-of-date chocolate Santa and four boxes of after-dinner chocolate mints.

Back in the office, Ellie noticed Midge's sandal sitting in the bottom of the bag and its discovery made her laugh out loud. It must have bounced off her head and flown straight in there! An inexplicable desire to keep the sandal outweighed the urge to chuck it in the bin, so without further thought, she put it in her handbag. She checked the time. Ten past nine. Ping, her new assistant, was late again.

After interviewing ten applicants, Ellie chose Ping for reasons that had nothing to do with previous work experience or qualifications. In fact, on paper, Ping looked totally unsuitable, but on the day of her interview she tumbled into the office some twenty minutes late with an up-front honesty that Ellie had never witnessed before.

"One year before Purple Monday, my selfish cow of a mum ran off with the frozen food delivery man."

"I'm sorry," Ellie said.

"Don't be," Ping said. "I was glad to see the back of her. She never stopped moaning." Ping stood up and pushed her chair back. "I can't stand it anymore," she screamed in a hysterical mum voice, "I should never have married a man from China. I'm sick of the smell of fried food everywhere."

Ellie couldn't stop herself laughing.

"We could buy some air fresheners," Ping said.

"Sorry, love," said Ping's hysterical mum voice, "but I was meant for more than this..."

"More than what?" Ping said.

"Bringing you lot up and working in a Chinese takeaway. I need to spread my wings. I need romance. I need excitement. I need to be with someone like me...someone English!"

"You need a straight-jacket," Ping said.

Both girls roared with laughter, but the sadness in Ping's eyes threw out a cry for help. "So, what happened next?" Ellie said, grabbing hold of it.

"I realised it was pointless trying to stop her. I stared at my half Chinese reflection in the mirror then helped her carry the suitcase down the stairs. She didn't even turn to say goodbye...she just slammed the door shut."

The only words Ellie could say in response to this were, "You're hired."

Ellie had the key in the lock when Ping arrived at the office. "Going home? I didn't think I was that late!"

"Very funny," Ellie said. She glanced at her watch. "It's only twenty past nine...that's early for you." She dropped the keys into her handbag. "Can you wave us that taxi? We need to be somewhere ten minutes ago."

Ping launched herself off the pavement. "TAXI!"

The black cab screeched to a halt. "Morning, ladies," a small driver with a flat cap said, "it's a good job my brakes work."

"Never mind if they work," Ping said, "I'm more concerned that your feet don't reach them. I thought taxi drivers had to be sixteen. How old are you?"

"I'm small for my age, darling. Apparently, my mum was a heavy smoker...you know...when she was pregnant. But you know what they say? Good things come in small packages."

Ellie opened the door. "Obviously his feet do reach the pedals otherwise you'd be dead. Could we have this conversation on the way? We need to be at Drayton Court ASAP."

"I'll have you there in no time," the flat cap shouted. "It's a long ride, it's a fast ride and if you don't hold on it'll be your last ride!"

Ping jumped in behind Ellie as the flat cap revved up the engine. The taxi lurched then stalled. The girls flew forwards.

"Seatbelts!" Ellie shouted.

The flat cap re-started the engine. He revved it twice. The taxi hurtled along at high-speed, black smoke bellowing from the exhaust.

"Why are we going to Drayton Court?"

"We've got a major catastrophe at Mrs Mackay's…water's pouring through her ceiling…there must be a leak somewhere in the flat above."

"Hell!" Ping said, leaning forward. "You've got a lump on your head. What happened?"

"It's a long story. But if it were a headline in a newspaper it would probably be something like: *Girl On Bus Caught-Up In Flying Sandal Terror."*

"Oh, right," Ping said with a bewildered nod.

The taxi flew around a corner then came to a screeching halt at some traffic lights.

"Anyway, never mind my head," Ellie said, gripping the edge of the seat, "let's talk about your timekeeping."

"Yeah, let's," Ping said. "I bumped into someone from my past."

"Who?"

"A girl I used to share a room with in the care home."

"You don't sound over the moon about it."

Ping stared blankly out the window. "I'm not really. She used to get on my nerves. People like her remind me of a time I'd rather forget."

"Yeah, I can understand that."

"Thing is, I lied to her. I told her I was sleeping on a friend's sofa. I didn't want her knowing I've got my own place. She's looking for somewhere to live and..."

"You don't need to explain yourself, it's your flat. You can do what you like with it. After all you've been through, you deserve your own space."

The taxi lurched forwards again, mounted the kerb then reversed. Clouds of smoke flooded through the windows.

"This guy's a lunatic!" Ping waved her hand through the air. "And while we're on the subject of my flat, I just want to say thanks for letting me have it rent-free. I know I've said it already, but you've no idea how grateful I am. I owe you one."

"Well, you'd better not be late tomorrow," Ellie said with a wink, "or I might take the keys back."

Ping leaned her head against the window and closed her eyes. "I'll be on time tomorrow," she said. "I promise."

"I've got something I want to show you," Ellie said. She opened her bag, carefully removed a silk scarf then gently unfolded it to reveal a beautiful purple rose. "Last night I dreamt about a walled garden. It was full of amazing flowers, there was a creepy hooded figure...it chased me...I ran into the arms of my mum and dad and when I woke up I was holding this."

"No way!" Ping said. "Are you serious?"

"Totally. This is not a joke." The taxi crunched into gear. "What does it mean? This...*flower*...it could be a message? What should I do about it?"

Ping shook her head. "I've got no idea." Both girls stared at the flower. "Sounds more like a nightmare than a dream, and I'm not talking about the creepy hooded figure. I couldn't imagine anything worse than being stuck inside four walls with both of my parents. Within minutes they'd be arguing and I'd be looking for the door."

Ellie laughed. "Trust you to say something ridiculous." The Missing Feeling lurched in her stomach. She gave Ping's hand a squeeze. "It reminds me...well...it reminds me how much I miss them."

London flashed by without words: both girls lost in the madness of the past six months. In the last week, hundreds, maybe thousands, of people had plastered the streets with pictures of their lost family and friends. Ellie stared out at the blur of faces on doors, windows, walls and lamp posts: HAVE YOU SEEN THIS PERSON? HELP! MISSING! DO YOU HAVE INFORMATION?

The taxi came to an abrupt stop outside Drayton Court.

"We're here," Ellie said.

"Thank God," Ping said.

Ellie stepped onto the pavement and leaned into the driver's window. She stared down at the enormous flat cap. She wanted to give it a lecture on dangerous driving, but decided not to bother. She had more important business to attend to. She checked the fare on the meter and dropped the exact money onto the passenger seat.

"What? No tip!"

"Yes…I'll give you a tip…in fact I'll give you two. One, never stand on a swivel chair to change a light bulb, and two, please wait another four years before attempting to drive me anywhere again."

"Very funny," the flat cap said. "I think I'm stuck in reverse."

Mrs Mackay greeted them on the steps of the old mansion block in a smart tartan skirt and cream blouse. "Och, deary me, I canny believe what's happening to ma poor wee home," she squeaked, "there's water all over the place."

"Don't panic Mrs M, we're here!" Ping shouted.

Ellie gave the old lady an emergency hug.

"It's the strangest thing," Mrs Mackay said, "the flat above me has been empty since Purple Monday, but last night I'm convinced I heard footsteps up there. Then this morning, when I woke up, the water was pouring through my ceiling."

Ellie and Ping gazed up with troubled expressions.

~ Eight ~

Smile While You Style

Marty surveyed the hi-tech salon equipment and wondered how he would ever feel at home in such an alien environment.

"The blue-rinse-old-granny-look is now triumphantly back in fashion!" Mr Rupert bellowed. "And can anyone tell me why?"

No one said a word.

"It's because of us! Renee and Rupert's Salon and Training Academy are setting the trends! The Queen Lizzie is one of our most popular styles...even amongst you youngsters." Mr Rupert herded the new entrants across the room. "Now, before we begin, let me hand out your name badges. In order to keep with tradition here at Renee and Rupert's, you will be addressed as either Miss or Mr followed by your first names." The old man distributed the name badges. "Miss Charlotte, Mr Cormac, Mr Cassius, Miss Madeline, Miss Mabel, Mr Spike and last, but by no means least, Mr Marty."

Marty pinned the badge to his shirt, eyes darted round the circle checking out who was who, and Mr Rupert waited for a moment until, once again, he had everyone's full attention.

"We're going to start the day off by dropping you in at the deep end," he said with an excited grin. "I want you all to find a partner and then take it in turns to wash and style each other's hair. We'll be looking to see if you have read your pre-course workbooks and can demonstrate a solid understanding of the *Renee and Rupert Route to Success.* Remember, a cheerful gowning-up of the customer, a professional consultation, product knowledge, good scalp massage, effective use of conditioners and a confident attitude all play their part. Now, don't forget to relax and enjoy yourselves...and remember one of our favourite mottos...*Smile While You Style*."

Fear flashed across every face. In a tizzy, the seven new apprentices grappled for a partner but, inevitably, one of them stood alone.

"I thought it might be you," Mr Rupert said. "Never mind, rascal, you can work with Miss Jive."

Marty scanned the training room to see if he could find a face to match the interesting name. Slowly, as the newly-paired couples settled themselves into a workstation, the room cleared. The girl with the colossal, orange hairdo had an expression that could freeze hot tea.

"You must be Miss Jive," Marty said.

"Ten out of ten," Miss Jive said with a sneer.

Reluctantly, they made their way to the vacant section at the far end of the room.

Miss Jive dumped herself in the seat and there followed a brief, stony silence, punctuated by a defiant announcement. "This is all I need! Some idiot-new-recruit having a go at my hair! I'm the head apprentice here. Ordinarily, nobody touches it except for Mr Rupert or one of our other top stylists. My beehive is radical. It's the envy of everyone. It's my crowning glory, my trademark. It's a statement about who I am and it shows to the world that I know about style. I'm warning you, if you mess this up you'll wish you'd never been born."

Marty's *Smile While You Style* face did a runner. Cheerlessly, he tied the gown around Miss Jive's neck. She stood up, grimaced and marched herself to the backwash: the consultation over before it began.

The situation quickly went from bad to worse.

"You're burning me!" Miss Jive shouted. "The water's too hot!"

Marty fiddled with the taps and pulled down on the head apprentice's hair.

"Oww! You're hurting me."

"I can't help it," Marty said, "it's tangled."

"It's been backcombed, idiot!" Miss Jive yelled. "Anyone with half a brain cell knows that a beehive is backcombed...you'll need to brush it out first."

Marty attempted to brush out the knots, but they seemed impenetrable. He tried adding water.

"Arrrragh! It's freezing cold!"

On the other side of the room, Mr Spike had already given Miss Madeline her second shampoo.

A ball of fire ignited inside Marty's chest. He struggled to catch a breath.

"Two depressions of the pump dispenser," Miss Renee twittered, "will provide an adequate measure of conditioning product..."

What was that? Marty thought. What did she say?

"There's water running down my back!" Miss Jive screamed.

"What?"

"I said the water...you're soaking me..."

"Quit moving your head! You're doing it deliberately..." The ball of fire tripled in size, heat rampaged down Marty's arms.

I need to get out of this place, he thought. I'm gonna quit. I'll tell Mr Rupert on the way out that I've changed my mind...I need to be on the street...I need to be free. Marty turned the taps off, tipped his head back and snatched a breath. His feet remained bolted to the floor; their refusal to move screamed a warning: YOU NEED A JOB! YOU NEED MONEY! Marty's fist tightened around the showerhead. YOU'LL BE BACK TO CATCHING RATS AGAIN! IS THAT WHAT YOU WANT?

Miss Jive lifted her head up from the basin. "Finished, have you? Useless gay!"

The ball of fire detonated: an explosion of fury sending shockwaves through Marty's nervous system.

"Haven't even started!" Marty's hand reached out and grabbed a clump of hair. He heard a yelp, and then a thud. He leaned forward, staring into startled eyes. "I'm gonna say this only once Beehive Jive, so you'd better listen up. If you say another word you'll be the one wishing you'd never been born."

"Let go of me, idiot!" Miss Jive growled.

Reality congealed into a blur of noise and colour.

Marty spun the taps as far as they would go. On full pressure the hose buckled, straightened then lurched upwards, hissing like an angry snake. Using his other hand he pushed down onto Miss Jive's forehead, trapping her in the basin. She struggled and kicked so Marty aimed the jets into her mouth. Water shot up her nose and blasted its way under her eyelids, her hands reached up, grappling for help. Consumed, Marty held the showerhead directly over Miss Jive's face, but eventually, she managed to push his hand away and swing her legs back down. Desperate for oxygen she spat out a mouthful of water then gulped in some much needed air. With both feet back on dry land, and her body in forward motion, she sprang upwards as if from a pilot's ejector seat. Filled with rage and with her fists clenched, she came face to face with her reflection in a full-length mirror. The shock rendered her speechless. Her make-up now resembled an explosion in a paint factory: lips and eyelids impossible to distinguish, and mascara from her tarantula lashes running down each cheek creating long, black, hideous lines. The once impressively high, orange beehive was utterly flat, dripping wet and clinging to her head like radioactive seaweed.

Miss Jive's face crumpled. The fury that had engulfed Marty's senses dispersed in a second, leaving him with appalling clarity. He reached out a hand, but she pushed him away. Desperate not to be seen without her armoury of hair and make-up, she grabbed a towel, threw it over her head, and ran to the sanctuary of the ladies' toilet.

Left alone at his workstation, Marty surveyed the damage.

Grabbing a towel, he mopped up the pool of water. Anxiously, he gazed around. Miracle! Could it be true? Perhaps no one had seen! At the other end of the training room, a loud disagreement between Miss Charlotte and Mr Cormac had created a priceless distraction. Marty strained his ears to hear the details, but could only distinguish the words “wet-look gel” and “bum-face” above the whirring of hairdryer motors. It seemed that the rest of the crew were too preoccupied to notice his messy incident.

After a few minutes of anxious waiting, Miss Jive emerged from the toilet; the hair wrapped in a fresh, white towel and her face hastily reconstructed. Perhaps unwilling to start a fight she couldn’t win, she sat down.

“So, what do you plan to do with my hair?”

The softness of Miss Jive’s voice took Marty by surprise. He opened his mouth to reply, but the words didn’t come. He closed his mouth.

GO ON DO IT! Shouted the voice in his head.

Miss Jive stared up at him. “What’s wrong with you?”

“I have…an idea. Are these the smallest rollers we’ve got?”

Miss Jive nodded.

“And this setting lotion…is it the strongest?”

“Yes.”

“I’ll need you to pass pins and rollers up to me.”

“Yes…that’s okay…I can do that,” Miss Jive said.

Marty picked up a tail comb and began to work. It vaguely crossed his mind that something unusual had just occurred – was occurring – but the moment fizzled with energy, and the voice – the thing – in his head urged him to continue. Trusting his judgement, Marty used small sections of hair on each roller and, for maximum effect, two or three rollers for the longest bits. Within minutes, rollers and pins had been stacked one on top of the other. Marty's fingers soon began to ache, but driven on by an unseen force they wouldn't stop. The unseen force seeped out, tranquillizing the atmosphere. Miss Jive methodically passed up pins and rollers until, finally, every strand had been rolled away. Marty tied a hairnet over his creation and stared in wonder.

Miss Renee appeared out of nowhere. "Oh…my goodness! Good gracious! I've never seen anything like it!" she said. "With this number of rollers I don't know how it'll fit under the dryer."

"It will," Marty said. And then he wondered how he knew.

Miss Renee wheeled the dryer over and jiggled it in place. "When using these dryers," she twittered, "always ensure the hair isn't touching the inside surface, as this may cause the hair to burn. It could take up to an hour for this creation! Never leave the customer without offering a hot beverage and a magazine…some of our younger customers may prefer a cold beverage."

With Miss Jive safely under the dryer, beverage in hand and timer set to fifty minutes, Marty had time to reflect on the situation. His patience had snapped, he'd lost his temper, nearly drowned someone and then had a blinding flash of…inspiration? He paced the training room floor trying to make sense of it.

Every minute felt like twenty.

I'm out of control. I have no idea what's going to happen next. The sweat's running like Niagara Falls…at least this shirt's black and no one can see the wet patches. Keep busy. Yeah…try and look normal. The old dude's looking my way. I'm sure he knows. Head down…don't make eye contact. Fold some towels. Make some drinks…beverages…why does everyone keep using the word beverage?

When the timer on the dryer eventually pinged, the panic erupted.

Keep a lid on it…go with it…don't spin out!

Miss Renee fluttered out of the shadows, calling and waving.

"Yes, I'm coming!" Marty snapped.

Because Marty had read, and then re-read, his pre-course workbooks, he knew that, *"small amounts of dampness cannot be detected by using hands alone..."* He removed a roller and rubbed the hair against his chin. Miss Renee unrolled a section and did the same.

"Well done," she said, "you're the first and only new apprentice to have remembered the chin test. Very good."

With Miss Jive's hair now fully dry, Marty escorted her to his workstation and took out the remainder of the rollers. Once free, each section of hair curled back on itself to reveal a bald head strewn with orange springs. Undaunted, he continued. Using a wide-toothed comb he teased each section apart, and slowly, moment-by-moment, the head apprentice's hair ballooned in size. With each strand supporting the other it stood up and out from her scalp at a ninety-degree angle.

Marty ignored his racing pulse and cleared his throat. "I need you to swing your head upside down."

In silence, Miss Jive did as requested. Marty applied a generous cloud of extra-strong hairspray and gave it a long, wild blast with the hand dryer. After a few seconds of scrunching and tweaking, he'd finished.

"Oh…" Miss Jive said, standing up and facing the mirror, "it's…it's enormous. It's bloody brilliant. It's a gravity-defying miracle! I love it!"

Mr Rupert bounded across the training room, nearly knocking Mr Cormac into the dirty towel bin. "Well done, rascal!" he boomed. "This is excellent! The volume, the lift, the shape, the texture, it's outstanding! Look how the light catches the colour…deep orange at the roots giving way to a fusion of red, gold and yellow. It's pure fire and drama. An explosion of flames!"

Marty smiled, his cool exterior hiding his inner hysteria. "Thanks."

"And do you have a name for this most wonderful work of art?"

"A name?"

"Yes, rascal, a name. It's got to have a name. All of our styles have a name: there's The Flick, The Scoop, The Shag, The Queen Lizzy, The Beehive,

The Curly-Wurly Poodle, The Cocks-Comb, The Tuft…"

"Oh yes, of course," Marty replied, "a name." Out of nowhere, it came to him. "The Midsummer Sunset," he said proudly. "It's called The Midsummer Sunset."

~ Nine ~

Flood Damage

Once inside Mrs Mackay's flat, the girls realised the gravity of the situation: water pouring down the walls, an enormous, sagging bulge in the lounge ceiling and squelching sounds from the carpet.

"How can water suddenly be coming from the property above? I pounded on the door, but no one answered," Ellie said.

"Your flat looks like a stately home," Ping said.

"Sentimental value," Mrs Mackay said, wringing her hands. "I'm ninety-four, these are all my memories."

"They'll be washed away if we don't do something," Ellie said, frantically rummaging through her handbag. "Maybe we can move you and all of your things next door? I've got the key to the place across the hall…I know it's empty."

"How are we going do that?" Ping said.

Ellie pulled out a metal whistle on a purple string. "We're going to use this."

"That wee thing!" Mrs Mackay said. "What will that do?"

"It's the whistle-blowing scheme," Ellie said. "You blow it, people hear it and then, hopefully, they come and help. The DMC have sent one out to every house."

"Oh, that's what it's for!" the old lady said. "One came through my letterbox last week and I'd been wondering what to do with it. I'm a wee bit old to become a football referee, don't you think?"

"Don't you watch *The Five O'Clock Announcements*?" Ping said.

"No, not very often," Mrs Mackay replied.

"Why not?"

"Well, to be honest, I'm not that interested. I'd much rather listen to some music on my record player or read a book. I always assume, if there's anything really important for me to know about, someone will tell me. I do have a television set, but I hardly ever switch it on."

"How weird," Ellie said. "Well, perhaps this afternoon, just on this occasion, you should switch it on. Today's announcement is important because the DMC are going to give us a full update on all the developments so far. You'll probably find it useful."

"Water!" Ping said, squishing her feet into the carpet. "We need to get moving!"

"I know," Ellie said. "Wish us luck, Mrs Mackay. We'll be back in a minute."

The girls dashed outside and down the steps of the grand, old building. Ping lifted both hands to reveal crossed fingers. Ellie took a deep breath, put the whistle into her mouth, and blew. The blast reverberated along the street, skipped around the corner and vanished. Silence.

"Try again," Ping said.

Ellie re-inflated herself and blew out another scream. This time the sound bounced off the pavement, onto the rooftops and into the blue: more painful silence.

Both girls waited. No one appeared.

"Where is everybody?" Ping said.

"I've been wondering that for months," Ellie replied.

"Give it to me," Ping said.

Ping grabbed the whistle, placed it in her mouth and ran up the street, waving her arms like a lunatic, creating noisy, erratic bursts. Ellie crossed the road, but couldn't see anyone. How can this be? Surely someone can hear us? She leaned against the railings.

Ping ran over to join her. "What will we tell the old lady?"

"We'll have to tell her we tried our hardest to get some help. We should be able to rescue a few bits and bobs on our own."

"You're probably right…this is a nightmare…"

In the communal hallway Mrs Mackay greeted them with a chirpy smile. "Well done, girls!"

"Huh?" Ellie said.

"This is Big Bernard! He lives on the third floor, we hadn't met properly until a minute ago," Mrs Mackay said.

A shiny-headed giant with a scarred left eye, impossibly large biceps and shovels for hands stepped out from the old lady's flat. If pets look like their owners, Ellie thought, this man definitely keeps a bulldog.

"I like your tattoos!" Ping said.

"Thanks, treacle," Big Bernard said.

"Can you believe we've been neighbours for years, but never spoken. Apparently, he used to be a famous boxer in his youth! He heard your whistles and came rushing down to help. Everyone in the building heard the noise...there's three other people in there waiting for you."

"Phew!" Ellie said. "I thought for a moment we were on our own." She unlocked the flat across the hall. "Thanks ever so much. I thought we could move everything into here and then try to find a way to stop the water. You don't know who lives in the flat above, do you?"

"Some geezer who disappeared in the Purple," Big Bernard said. "I thought the place was empty. We'll start moving things across and then we can work out how to bust the lock."

Mrs Mackay and Big Bernard disappeared into the waterlogged flat.

"What seems to be the trouble?" a voice yelled.

Ellie and Ping turned to see a stranger on the doorstep.

"Ugh! That's all we need," Ping whispered.

"What do you mean? Who are they?"

"It's the Mum Police," Ping said.

"Mum Police?" Ellie vaguely remembered hearing Penny Treasure rant about them on an announcement: Attention all mums! The kids are running riot! We need some law and order in this town. Can you ride a mountain bike at breakneck speed? You'll be cruising the streets in groups of three or more and dispensing friendly but firm discipline!

"Yes! Mum Police!" Ping repeated. "Pensioner busy-bodies in purple track suits...but they've got the power to make an arrest!"

"My name's Deirdre. I'm in charge," Deirdre shouted. "Obviously I'm a mum, but I'm also an ex-police detective. We're out on a training exercise, we heard a whistle, what's the problem here?"

Deirdre had MUM POLICE written in bold, white letters on the front of her baseball cap. When she waved her colleagues up the steps, Ellie read the words TOUGH LOVE on her back.

"We need all the hands we can get," Ellie whispered. "Try and be polite."

Ping pulled a face then turned to Deirdre all smiles. "Well, are we glad to see you!"

"Here to help!" Deirdre barked. "This is Sonia and Brenda."

Sonia and Brenda puffed their way up the stairs. "Holy crap! I think my bike must be stuck in the wrong gear," Sonia said, her face red enough to stop traffic.

Deirdre frowned and cleared her throat. "So, come along, out with it, what's the trouble?"

"Well, if it were a headline in a newspaper," Ping said, "it would probably be something like...*Mackay Misery In Flood Fiasco*."

"What?"

"What she means," Ellie said, "is water's pouring into an old lady's home. We've got volunteers and they're about to start moving her stuff into this dry place across the hall, but we need to get into the flat above and stop the leak...or whatever it is."

"Someone must be in there," Sonia said. "It's not winter, why would a pipe burst on its own?"

Ping shrugged her shoulders. "Dunno."

"Ladies, we need to get into that flat now!" Deirdre pointed at Ellie. "You should come with us. You," she said, pointing at Ping, "can stay down here and help the others."

"Bossy old trout."

"What was that?" Deirdre snapped.

Ping shook her head. "Nothing...I said...yes, boss...over and out."

A scowling Deirdre ordered Sonia and Brenda up the stairs. Ellie did a muted laugh in Ping's direction and ran up behind them.

"Now, I'd like you to look away," Deirdre said. "I'm about to slip the lock with one of my tools and this sort of manoeuvre is top secret. It's certainly not for the likes of you to know."

"Whatever," Ellie said. She took a small mirror from her handbag, checked her red lipstick then re-applied the beauty spot. She heard Deirdre make a scraping sound then a click.

"See that, ladies? It's all in the wrist action. We're in! No time wasted when I'm on the job."

Ellie turned back in time to catch Sonia rolling her eyes.

"Hello! Is there anyone there?" Deirdre shouted.

No one answered.

"Phew! It smells a bit sour," Brenda said.

"You stay here," Deirdre ordered, obviously enjoying the drama, "we need to do a quick search."

"Suit yourself," Ellie said.

The Mum Police separated and returned within minutes.

"Come and take a look at this." It was Deirdre again.

Ellie followed the ladies into the kitchen, where dead blue bottles floated in a pool of water.

"It looks like it's been deliberately tampered with," Sonia said, pointing to a broken pipe under the sink.

"But we don't know how that's possible," Brenda added. "We didn't find anyone, or any evidence of a break-in."

"I hate to admit it," Deirdre said, "but we're baffled by this one."

"Oh. Maybe it broke on its own?" The mums nodded and hummed. "Well, can you at least fix the pipe?" Ellie continued. "It's vital that we stop the downpour as soon as we can."

"Yes, absolutely," Deirdre said, "give us ten minutes and it'll be right as rain. D'ya get it? Right as rain?"

Ellie smiled at Sonia and Brenda's forced laughter and went for a walk.

More dead bluebottles and cobwebs suggested the flat had, indeed, been empty for the past five months. On the table in the lounge a half-eaten piece of mummified toast, a dried up coffee cup and a newspaper dated January 10th provided more evidence. Ellie sat down at the table and stared at the newspaper; several programmes on the television page had been circled. She picked up the pen that lay discarded nearby and twirled it through her fingers. The man who lived here didn't survive to watch these programmes, she thought.

The words melted and jumbled and lost all sense. Nothing made sense. The Missing Feeling lurched in her stomach once again. Where is everybody? What happened? Her mind skipped backwards, back to that exact, horrifying moment on Clapham High Street: the howling wind, the colours, the noise, the flying debris, the panic and the suffocation. The invasion?

Disconnected from the present moment, but anxious to leave the past behind, Ellie forced herself onto her feet. "I'm responsible for these flats," she mumbled. "I need to find out what happened here."

She stared around the room looking for information, evidence, anything to provide a clue but, just like the Mum Police, saw nothing suspicious. A normal lounge with normal furniture, books on the shelf, a rug on the floor, some magazines, a TV, a remote control, a brass Buddha, a framed poster of the trees at Kew Gardens and a plate with a doily and some biscuit crumbs.

Deirdre's voice pulled Ellie into the here-and-now. "Right, that's us all sorted. You won't have any more trouble from this pipe."

"I'm on my way!" Ellie shouted.

Back in the kitchen, the Mum Police had made a great job of the repair. They'd also mopped the floor and emptied the smelly bin.

"I'm going to put some crime scene tape across the door," Deirdre said. "I'm not convinced this was an accident. When you've been in this business as long as I have, you develop a sixth sense."

"I expect you do," Ellie said. "I mean thanks. Mrs Mackay will be really grateful you've stopped the leak."

Back downstairs, Ping had a lampshade on her head. "We've got loads more volunteers! Another two Mum Police in the new flat, one's up a stepladder fixing a curtain pole, a lady from across the road donated the curtains. Someone else brought a rug and we've taken the lounge carpet into the courtyard to dry out."

"Wow! This is amazing!" Ellie said.

"Also, an old bloke from across the road came over with a great big tin of biscuits and a pot of tea! We're doing tea break in rotation."

Less than one hour later, everything had been moved.

With everyone next door, Ellie found herself alone in the wet flat; she wandered through making mental notes. Empty of belongings, the decorating appeared worn and every room needed a lick of paint. Ellie fancied herself as an interior designer and had often laughed at her own mum's curtains-should-match-the-bedspread sense of style.

The bulge in the lounge ceiling looked dangerously pregnant.

During a final check of the bedroom, Ellie noticed an old black and white photo that must have spent several years hidden behind a piece of furniture. Intrigued, she picked it up and blew away the dust.

The image registered in her brain immediately, but logic screamed “impossible!” She felt her back slide down the wall, the base of her spine bump over the skirting board and her bum hit the floor. She slumped to the side, her hand resting in carpet fluff.

Ellie stared at the picture and tried to make sense of it. How could she be holding a picture that had been taken in last night’s dream? A photo of her standing in the walled garden, surrounded by flowers!

“What are you doing down there?” a voice said.

Ellie looked up to see Mrs Mackay standing in the doorway. She held the photo up. “This…picture…who does it belong to?”

The old lady tottered forward and peered down. Her eyes widened. “Oh!”

“You have to tell me, I need to know where it came from!”

“It’s mine!” the old lady said, her bottom lip shaking. She snatched the photo from Ellie’s hand. “It’s private. I don’t want to talk about it.”

“But…”

A familiar voice making an unfamiliar sound interrupted Ellie’s sentence. Following the scream, Ellie jumped up and darted into Mrs Mackay’s sodden lounge.

Ping stood in the middle of the room holding a broom above her head, the bristly bit pushing up against the bulge in the ceiling. *“CHINESE ORPHAN DODGES DEATH IN DOWNPOUR DRAMA!”*

“What shall I do?”

"I don't know!" Ping yelled through anxious laughter.

In a panic, Ellie grabbed a mop and swung it upwards.

"It's going to split any minute!" Ping shrieked. "I heard it creaking!"

"Push up a bit, maybe we can relieve the pressure?"

Ping pushed the mop into the bulge and a crack sped from one end of the ceiling to the other.

"RUN!" Ellie shouted.

~ Ten ~

The Lion and the Deal

The Midsummer Sunset caused a sensation on the salon floor, and Mr Rupert announced it would be named as Style of the Month.

"From tomorrow, a larger-than-life picture of it will be placed in the reception area, and promotional flyers handed out to passers-by on the street. Well done, rascal, this is an unheard of achievement for a brand new apprentice!"

"Without the watchful eyes of parents, you youngsters probably change your hairdos more frequently than your underwear," Miss Renee twittered, "and it's imperative that we keep up with the permanent demand for original and outrageous styles."

The remainder of the day passed by in a haze of glory for Mr Marty, and at three o'clock in the afternoon it came to an earlier than planned conclusion.

"Gather round!" a still-energetic Mr Rupert shouted, his white teeth flashing in the spotlights. "We're handing out some freebies!"

The new apprentices fluttered into the centre of the training room wide-eyed and expectant.

"You're all going to be given some equipment. There's a pair of scissors, two combs, a gown, a dryer, some setting lotion, hair gel, wax and mousse, a mixed bag of rollers and three different brushes! Not bad, eh?"

"We want you to take these things home with you," Miss Renee said, "and practice what you've learnt on any surviving friends and family."

"We'll see you back here, bright-eyed and bushy-tailed, at nine thirty tomorrow morning, rascals," Mr Rupert interjected. "You've all done very well today and don't forget this evening to have a good read through book one, chapter twelve. It tells you all you need to know about head lice and dandruff…there'll be an exam first thing."

A hubbub of goodbyes headed for the stairs. Marty had his foot on the top step when he felt a hand on his shoulder; it belonged to Mr Rupert. "Before you go, Mr Marty, I'd like a word with you in my office."

On the way through the salon they passed a flustered Miss Renee, who'd skidded on a stray squirt of hair mousse. "These youngsters need to learn to clean up," she muttered. Under normal circumstances Marty would have laughed.

Inside the office, Mr Rupert closed the door. He pulled out a seat for Marty before sitting in a large, swivel chair behind his desk. "Well, rascal, it's been quite a day, hasn't it? Have you enjoyed yourself?"

"Yes…I've…had a great day," Marty said. Hell! I'm about to be nuked, he thought.

"I saw it all, you know, what happened between you and Miss Jive. And although I'm delighted with your achievements, I have to say I'm a little concerned. What on earth made you behave in such a way? What if Miss Jive had been one of our paying customers?"

"Oh…there's no way I'd do anything like that to one of our *proper* customers."

"Well, I have to be sure of that. Here at Renee and Rupert's we have very high standards of customer service. And even though we've only been open for a short time, we have an excellent reputation to maintain. What you did today, covering Miss Jive in water, is not acceptable behaviour from any of our staff…no matter how talented they may be."

Marty's high came crashing down. Anger boiled upwards from deep inside. "But she called me a useless gay! From the moment I arrived here this morning she's had it in for me. You don't know it, but she's your worst nightmare!"

"Steady on!" Mr Rupert said, his tone sufficiently curt to silence Marty. "I'm well aware that she can be difficult and, for your information, I've already spoken to her. I don't tolerate that kind of language from anyone. But what I'm interested in right now is your behaviour."

"You're gonna fire me, aren't you? This is so unfair…I…I quit!" Marty stood up, slamming his chair against the wall.

Mr Rupert placed his hands on the desk and gave a friendly smile. "Let's both calm down for a moment, shall we?"

Marty took a breath.

"I think I know what's happening here, rascal." The old man pointed at Marty's chair. "There's a lion inside of you and he's been disturbed."

Marty sat back down.

"Yes, my dear fellow, inside of you is a very dangerous lion and he's awake. He wants revenge. He's ready to rip someone apart. He wants to taste blood."

Marty stared blankly across the desk at Mr Rupert. Mr Rupert stared back, scratched his head, and took a deep breath of his own. "I'm going to explain this in very simple terms because, well, to be honest, it's quite a simple hypothesis. In fact, I made it up. Some people have to put up with a lot of crap in this life and, after a while, all that crap starts to get them down. I know this is true because I'm speaking from personal experience. Through no fault of my own I had to deal with some terrible…experiences. Experiences that left me feeling very unhappy, and that's putting it politely. I'm not sure how it happens exactly, but these unhappy feelings bury themselves deep down inside of us, and if left to fester they grow into anger. The anger that grew inside of me was enormous, it had the ferocity of a wild animal, and at times, I found it impossible to control. The slightest thing would cause it to roar."

"Like a lion?" Marty said.

"Yes, exactly," Mr Rupert said. "Like a lion. Well, at least, that's how I imagined it. And it helped me to think of it that way because, once I could picture it as a living entity, I was able to do something about it. It wasn't easy and it didn't happen overnight but, in time, I found a way to calm it down."

Marty nodded, pulled his chair forward like he might stay a while longer, but didn't speak.

"Now, I haven't known you for long, rascal, but my instincts are telling me you have a similar problem, and here's the thing: Miss Jive may be a foul-mouthed, attention-seeking nuisance who rattled your bars, but we can't blame her for putting the lion in the cage. Can we?"

Although he hadn't expected to understand a word that Mr Rupert was saying, Marty was surprised to discover that this old man's jibber-jabber did make some kind of sense. Deep within Marty anger had been seething for months.

"Young man," Mr Rupert continued, "I believe you have a wonderful talent for hairdressing and I know that with hard work you will make an excellent stylist. But talent and hard work are nothing without the right attitude. If you want to make a success of yourself, and if you want to keep your job here at Renee and Rupert's, then you will have to learn how to control your temper."

The old man paused. In the unexpected silence, you could have heard a hairpin drop.

"I'm going to make a deal with you," he said eventually. "You get to keep your job and in return you must agree to meet me here in my office every morning so that we can talk. Within the safety of these four walls we can scream our heads off if we want to. It will help us to release our frustrations. I believe I can show you how to tame your lion and harness your talents."

Marty sat for a moment and tried to take it all in. He'd been preparing himself for the worst or, at the very least, an argument. "Why...why would you do that?"

"There are two reasons why I want you to stay, rascal, and I'm going to tell you about them. The first is straightforward: your talents impress me, and I have no doubt that you will be an enormous asset to the business. The second reason is not so obvious, and what I'm about to say may come as a complete surprise...when I look at you I see myself."

"Really? You're kidding me? We don't look much alike, do we?"

"Well no, of course not, rascal," Mr Rupert said, laughing. "We don't look alike at all. You're as black as I'm white, but the colour of our skin has nothing to do with it. Your creative ability, your drive and determination and your quick temper all remind me of myself when I was younger. Also, there was a time in my past when I was scared and angry and had no one to turn to and, what's more, I can clearly remember how that felt. So, you see, I think we may have more in common than you realise."

Marty felt an air of comfortable familiarity, the kind that's normally reserved for old friends, settle in the room. His story came tumbling out in a relentless stream. "I moved to this country eight months ago because my dad had been given a two year posting. He is, sorry, I meant was, involved in research with the U.S. Military. I didn't want to leave San

Francisco…it's where my friends are. I pleaded with my mom and dad to change their minds, but they didn't listen. We moved to a small village in Cheshire and I hated it. People made fun of me. My American accent and my skin colour made me an easy target…anyway…a group of boys started picking on me, there were six of them. And one day, when I was walking home, they attacked me. One of them punched me in the face and when I was on the ground, they kicked me. It was agony to breathe. I think one of my ribs got cracked. I told my mom I'd fallen off my bike. Sixteen days later the Purple came. It left me on my own. I put some stuff in a backpack and hitchhiked my way to London."

"Well, well, rascal, no wonder you're angry. I'm sorry for your dreadful ordeal. Just as I said, life can be unfair. But even though it may seem like an impossible task, do not allow your mind to dwell in the unhappy past. Do not allow the misery of yesterday to pollute the joy of today. Focus on the fact that you are a brave and resilient young man. Remind yourself that you are a survivor! You know…I have a feeling your life is about to take a turn for the better…I think it's high time you started looking forward to a glorious future here in the big city. And remember, at Renee and Rupert's Salon and Training Academy everyone is equal and treated with respect."

For the first time in ages, Marty suspected he'd made a connection with someone. Deep within him, not far from his prowling lion, a flicker of hope caught light. The heat from it drifted upwards, filled the empty space in his heart and lifted the corners of his mouth. "So, what happened to you?"

Mr Rupert stopped rummaging through a drawer. "Me?"

"Yes, you. You said there was a time in your past when you were hurt and angry and had no one to talk to."

"Ah...yes...the story of me and my lion." The old man's eyes opened wide. "It's getting late, probably best if we leave that one till tomorrow. For now, let's just say that many years ago I did a different job to the one I'm doing today...and because of it...I found myself in a very difficult situation."

Marty desperately wanted to ask more questions, but a gut feeling kept his mouth shut. Together, they sat in silence: both of them lost in totally different yet strangely similar worlds.

"Some memories are like another lifetime," Mr Rupert said eventually. "I can't believe I'm so old."

Mr Rupert's words jolted Marty back to life. "I don't think you look that old."

"Well, thank you for the compliment, young man. Flattery will get you everywhere. But...don't be fooled...appearances can be deceptive." Mr Rupert smirked then spat his teeth out into the palm of his hand.

"Arrrrghh, that's gross!" Marty shrieked.

The lower half of the old man's face collapsed in a gummy, open-mouthed roar of laughter. He threw his head back and lifted his hair into the air.

"Arrrrghh-ha-haaa! Dude, you're bald!"

Mr Rupert slipped his dripping dentures back into his mouth and replaced the wig. At first, the glossy hairpiece sat back to front, and this caused another explosion of laughter.

"Now, rascal, don't forget our agreement," Mr Rupert said after a few minutes of adjustments.

"I won't forget anything," Marty replied with a snigger. He knelt down to pick up his new hairdressing equipment. "I don't suppose you have a backpack I could borrow; it's just that I'm on my moped..."

"No, I don't, rascal...but I do have something...give me a moment..."

The old man disappeared and Marty walked back into the empty training salon; after the hullabaloo of the day's events it seemed eerily quiet. Within a minute Mr Rupert returned and in his hand he had a basket – the sort that attaches to the front of a bicycle. "Now, I know what you're thinking. You're thinking how ridiculous this basket will look stuck to the front of your bike; you're worried that people will laugh."

Marty nodded. "Yeah...kind of."

"Well, let me give you another piece of advice, don't be. Don't worry what other people think. I wish someone had told me that when I was your age."

There seemed little point in objecting to this statement, so Marty shrugged his shoulders. Together they made their way downstairs to the car park. Once the basket had been attached and loaded, Marty pulled on his helmet. He mounted the bike, turned the key and revved up the engine.

"Now, remember, it takes practice," Mr Rupert shouted over the noise.

"What does?"

"Controlling your temper, finely tuning your instincts, not worrying about other people's opinions. All these things take practice, so be patient. It's worth the effort. Practice makes perfect."

"Sure thing," Marty shouted. "I hear you loud and clear."

"Drive carefully," Mr Rupert shouted, waving. "And don't forget…chapter twelve, head lice and dandruff!"

Within seconds, Mr Rupert shrank to a dot then vanished from the wing mirror.

Cruising on a high, Marty allowed the bike to speed up and his mind to wander. Apart from a taxi in the distance, the road ahead looked clear.

The shouts from panicked pedestrians must have made it through the noise of the engine and into Marty's brain because something seized his attention.

The taxi…no way! It's reversing towards me!

The space closed in seconds. In a desperate, last minute attempt to avoid the collision, Marty slammed on the brakes then steered to the right. The wheel locked, and the bike, his most prized possession, the thing that had cost him nearly all of his rat-catching money, crunched into the back of the taxi. As he somersaulted through the air, above the screech of rubber on tarmac, the cloudless blue of the sky replaced the face of a horrified pedestrian. After a second of silent, weightless bliss, his stomach lurched upwards. The rays from the afternoon sun caught the visor of his helmet, splitting the light into every colour of the rainbow.

Marty stretched his arms out hoping they might save him from breaking every bone in his body.

Red, yellow, pink, green, purple, orange and blue went black.

~ Eleven ~

Love Comes Quickly

Scott had planned to spend the majority of the day in the workshop fixing a bike, but the voices and the ghost of his brother Charlie had knocked him off track.

The second incident had an explanation. Objects belonging to loved ones, when stumbled upon, usually by accident, have the ability to cause shock and emotional disturbance resulting in uncontrollable floods of memories. That, according to Scott, was the definition of a ghost. In the immediate aftermath of Purple Monday it happened all the time. If he came across a wallet, a purse, a hairbrush, a bunch of keys, a mobile phone or a calculator, he would be haunted.

To put a stop to it, Scott moved everything high-risk upstairs. The lounge, the kitchen, the hallway and the workshop became the Safe Zone, and the only time Scott ventured out of it was to make an essential journey. Taking a shower and finding clean clothes were considered essential.

Scott lived in a rambling, three-story Victorian building on the edge of Clapham Common, which had belonged to his family for generations. Before his mum went away it had been the perfect family home, but now it looked neglected. All housework and maintenance had been abandoned and the dust on every surface sat thick enough to host limitless games of noughts and crosses. No use though, because that activity required two people.

The word cataclysmic best described the kitchen. Used dishes, saucepans and utensils covered every work surface and had been stacked so high in the sink they almost blocked out the light from the window. The bin resembled a mini volcano, but instead of rocks, ash and lava it spewed out eggshells, tea bags and potato peelings. In order to get from one side of the room to the other, Scott did a leaping, U-shaped manoeuvre.

The state of the kitchen did, at least, provide evidence of Scott's culinary efforts. For the past five months food had been his primary comfort, and he'd cooked himself regular, decent meals.

"You're a pernickety little eater," his mum once said to him.

"What does pernickety mean?"

"Difficult to please," she had replied with a smile on her face.

Scott closed his eyes and thought about the last time he had seen his mum. For nearly a year the images of that afternoon had played in his brain like a never-ending horror movie. They had driven him to the brink of madness. "I wish I could go back in time," he heard himself say out loud. "I wish I could change things."

By midday, Scott hadn't moved from the sofa. Soured by anger, grief and guilt, he half-heartedly threw back the duvet and forced himself onto his feet. "I need to tidy this place up," he muttered.

On the way to the kitchen, a stranger's face popped into the perimeter of Scott's vision. Fascinated, he walked across the room and stared into its emotionless eyes. The eyes stared back. A wave of confusion ripped through Scott's brain, before realization pooled. I'm staring at my own reflection! How shocking! I don't even know who I am anymore.

Scott didn't look like anyone else in the family, and on the day he came into the world there had been lots of jokes about the milkman. His appearance caused constant amusement and wonder, but the explanation was straightforward: a forgotten ancestor from Delhi and, generations later, tall, dark and handsome simply re-emerged from the gene pool. His hair, blacker than the bike tyres he regularly repaired, could now touch his shoulders. In the past five months it had been totally ignored; wild and scruffy, it desperately needed cutting.

Distracted by thoughts about his down-at-heel appearance and overwhelmed by the amount of housework that lay ahead, Scott lost the motivation to do anything. He threw himself back on the sofa and pulled the duvet over his head. Eventually, he drifted off.

In the middle of the daytime, in his creaky, old house, Scott lay alone and asleep, but he wasn't alone for long.

Down the stairs came the translucent shape of a woman. Her golden hair flowing behind her, her every move shrouded in silence. Her bare feet scarcely touched the steps as she travelled. Maybe she floated above them. She cast her spell in peace, and all about her the light sparkled and flickered. Scott fell deeper into sleep. She smiled. She barely paused, barely breathed. Oxygen swirled into the magnetic field of her presence. She moved with the speed of sound and completed her task in seconds. She vanished.

For the second time in one day, Scott woke with a jolt.

Frustratingly, he could only remember a few disconnected details of his dream. In the small gap that exists between sleeping and waking he could recall the setting sun, a garden filled with flowers, the glorious smell of perfume and a strong sense of peace. His mind tried to cling on to these comforting remains, but to his despair, the images slipped away faster than a raw egg running through open fingers.

Scott desperately wanted sleep back so he could return to the blissful place. He rolled onto his side and tried to make himself comfortable, but sleep wouldn't return. He sat up and opened his eyes. In his right hand he held a purple rose, but that wasn't the strangest thing. What really disturbed him was the state of the lounge: it was absolutely, perfectly clean and tidy.

Scott leapt up. The sudden movement nudged his brain into gear. He wobbled into the hallway and waited for his vision to refocus. The hallway too looked immaculate, and even his dirty work boots, the ones that got shoved off at the front door every night, had been polished. The kitchen gleamed: every pot, pan and plate washed and put away, the bin emptied and the floor scrubbed. Scott rushed upstairs to find clothes tidied away and beds re-made with fresh linen. Curiously, a clean, neatly folded towel had been placed on the foot of each bed with the top corner of every duvet turned down. The bathroom was squeaky clean.

Scott froze on the landing, heart pounding, head spinning. He swallowed hard and dropped to his knees. Better put myself there before I fall, he thought.

What seemed like an injection of blue ink flooded his brain then swirled into his eyeballs. He managed several shallow, rapid breaths. The carpet pressed rough against his lips.

It started small, like the disturbing buzz of a thirsty mosquito, and Scott flapped his hands over his ears. "Leave me alone!" he shouted. Seconds later it mutated, now a wasp in a jam jar. I know what's coming...but I don't want it! Rumbling and buzzing became high-pitched whistling. He closed his eyes. The pitch shot up in frequency. "Argh! You're hurting me! There's too many of you!"

The bombardment ceased.

"Scott?" the voice said.

A rush of emotion surged upwards through Scott's chest and he automatically thrust out an arm. He felt his mouth smile. A hand grabbed his.

"In the circus under the gaze of ear ross." The words soft, like cotton, danced across his cheek before slipping into his left ear. A gentle whistle faded to silence; the signal lost, the trance over.

Something damp pressed against Scott's right cheek, he lifted his head and saw tears on the carpet. His hand, still outstretched, lay empty.

Desperate not to forget, Scott heaved himself up, bolted downstairs and scribbled out the message. He stared at the words on the notepad.

in the circus under the gaze of ear ross

He read the words over and over again. What did they mean?

Scott paced the hallway, relentlessly repeating them out loud, until he came to a standstill at the front door. His newly blackened boots sat on a copy of London's daily newsletter After Purple, and a picture of one of the capital's most iconic landmarks caught his eye. The memory of a long forgotten afternoon with his brother Charlie filled his mind.

He remembered them sitting to eat slices of pizza on the steps of the Shaftesbury Memorial Fountain. Charlie's head had always been crammed with a million fascinating facts, and as he shoved the last piece of food into his mouth, he told Scott about the statue that stood above them. Made entirely from aluminium, it was the figure of a winged boy holding a bow and arrow and his name was Eros. Scott realised immediately that he had written the message down incorrectly: it wasn't ear ross, but Eros. Eros was the name of the statue that stood in the middle of one of London's most famous traffic intersections.

The circus under the gaze of Eros had to be Piccadilly Circus!

Scott grabbed his keys, pulled on his boots and dashed out the door. With luck and a foot hard on the accelerator he would be there in less than fifteen minutes.

~ Twelve ~

A Nice Cup of Tea and a Sit Down

Pearl and Opal's secret room looked like biscuit heaven.

After squeezing through the gap, Midge gazed longingly at shelving jam-packed with packets of jammy dodgers, gypsy creams, chocolate digestives, ginger snaps and caramel wafers. Family photos in gleaming frames, well-dusted ornaments and china collectibles competed for space. An open window on the far wall allowed the tangled foliage and flowers of a rambling rose bush to peek inside. Two bird feeders crammed with nuts and seeds swung in the summer breeze. Against the other wall, three upturned wooden tea chests created an ideal sideboard. On top of this sat all the apparatus required to make the perfect cuppa: various types of tea in tins, a teapot and cosy, a silver plated milk jug, several china cups and saucers, numerous teaspoons with fancy handles and a tea strainer. Next to the teaspoons Midge could see an old transistor radio, and next to that an even older-looking record player. She smiled at the artificial Christmas tree with multi-coloured, flashing lights, and the two pairs of tights that appeared to have dried hard on a makeshift washing line.

"It's always Christmas in here!" both the old ladies shrieked.

The back of the metal shelving unit that created the fourth wall had been plastered with faded black and white portraits of yesterdays Hollywood heartthrobs. In the middle of the room stood two well-used, emerald green, velour armchairs, a matching footstool and a small, round table.

After the ladies had plumped up the cushions, Midge sat down in one of the armchairs.

Pearl put the kettle on.

After searching through an extensive stack of records, Opal removed an album from its cardboard sleeve and placed it on the turntable. Singing along, she busied herself at the sink filling a bucket. "Start spreading the news…da-da-da-da-da…I'm leaving today…I want to be a part of it…New York! New York!" When it was eventually full, she carried the bucket to the middle of the room and placed it on the floor. "For your tootsies, darlin'."

"Ooh, for me? Thanks!" Midge eased her tired and mucky feet into the hot, soapy bubbles and a delicious wave of loveliness washed through her body. "Ooooh, I feel like I've died and gone to heaven." Not only did the dirt on her soles begin to disintegrate, but so too did the frown on her forehead. It wasn't until her face began to relax that she realized she'd been carrying a scowling expression with her for most of the morning.

"That's better…ain't it?" a grinning Opal said.

Midge grinned back, wriggled her toes and sank her feet deeper into the gorgeous water. Pearl appeared from behind with a fully loaded tray, which she carefully placed on the table. Each of them helped themselves to a Caramel Wafer from the neat display that had been fanned out on a doily and the tea was ceremoniously poured in silence. For a good few minutes nothing could be heard but the tinkling of teaspoons on china, the rustling of wrappers and the whistley-slurpy-hissing sound that cautious lips make when they're negotiating hot liquid.

In between sips, Midge told the old ladies about herself. "I'm a single child from a one parent family. My mum was a nurse and she worked twelve-hour shifts. The early ones started at seven, the late ones at three in the afternoon and nights were from seven till seven. Usually, when I came home from school, the flat was empty and I'd have to cook my own tea."

"Oh," the old ladies said.

"Occasionally, my mum would arrange for me to go and stay with friends, but most of the time I was left to fend for myself. To be honest it didn't bother me because I quite liked it when she wasn't there. I had my own routine and it worked better without her. I had *me time*."

"*Me time*?" Pearl said. "What the heck's that?

"Time for me," Midge said, her cheeks warming. "When my mum was home she was always knackered and grumpy and bossing me around. And then, when I was at school, every minute was accounted for. My life was ruled by timetables and ringing bells, it was really irritating. Even lunchtime wasn't *me time*. I wasn't where I wanted to be, doing what I wanted to do. I was stuck outside, in the freezing cold, with a load of people I didn't really like."

"Where did you want to be, darlin'?"

Midge folded her arms then unfolded them. "I don't know exactly. Sitting on my own reading a book, I suppose." As soon as she'd said the words, Midge regretted them. They made her sound like a friendless freak. She decided to change the subject. "My dad left when I was two, but he turned up once in a while to take me out. He drove around the country fixing photocopy machines. My mum hated him. He spent lots of money on me and I think that made him feel better, you know, about his irresponsible behaviour."

The old ladies smiled and nodded.

"For ages I've wanted to leave school and get a job, and now...well, now...I've got what I wanted."

"Are you sure about that?" Pearl said.

The water in the bucket had lost its magic. Pearl tidied up the wrappers and Opal lovingly dried Midge's feet on an old tea towel before slipping them into a spare pair of pink, fluffy mules. A delicious, empty-teacup-silence, broken only by the occasional cheep-cheep of a bird on a feeder, numbed the moment. Midge struggled to keep her eyelids from closing. Her head wobbled like a balloon on a stick. She tried her hardest to fight off sleep, but the fight only lasted for fifteen seconds.

Midge woke up gradually. She began by wiggling her toes in her pink, fluffy mules. She recognised the feel of the patchy fabric on the armrest, and the lumpy cushion tucked beneath the small of her back. After a short while, hearing returned. She noticed the sound of her own breath moving in and out of her semi-conscious body. Groggy fingers played with something long and thin in her right hand. A cool breeze wafted through the window and flicked her eyelashes. Suddenly, something sharp pricked her thumb. “Ouch!”

Midge opened her eyes and gasped at the immaculate, long-stemmed, deep-purple rose. “What’s this? Did you give it to me?”

The birds on the feeders stopped nibbling.

“No, darlin’,” Pearl said, perched on the small table next to Midge’s empty teacup, “I’ve got no idea where it came from.”

Midge placed the flower in her lap and sucked the droplet of blood from her thumb. “It’s a bit chilly in here…can we shut that window?”

“NO!” the ladies screamed.

“We like lots of fresh air,” Opal said.

“Before I begin, would you like a sandwich?” Pearl said. She lifted Midge’s cup and studied the tea leaves in the bottom. “You’ll soon warm up once you’ve eaten.”

“I was having this amazing…dream. It’s all a bit hazy now. I thought it was real.” Midge stared down at the rose.

“Never mind, dear,” Pearl said. “It won’t stay a dream forever.”

“Won’t it?”

Pearl ignored Midge's question. "Now, before I begin reading your tea leaves, would you like a sandwich or not?"

Opal crossed the room and settled herself into the other armchair. Midge felt as if she were in two places at once: her physical body here in the room with the old ladies, but her mind off someplace else. She couldn't recall specific details, only vague memories of a divine garden filled with beautiful flowers and the secure, joyous feeling of being in the company of best friends.

"Hello! Sandwiches!" Opal said, waving a hand through Midge's vacant stare.

"I thought we were going to the canteen?"

The ladies pulled a face. "Well, sweetheart," Opal said, "I thought cos we were having such a lovely time in here we might as well stay for a while longer. And anyhow, in case you've forgotten, there's no one else in the building today and that includes all the canteen staff."

"You'll get nothing to eat in that place unless you fancy munching on a paper napkin," Pearl said.

"That might be preferable to the food," Opal added. "To be honest with you, we don't care for the muck they serve up in there. If I had the choice between the chef's dish of the day and a paper napkin, I'd choose the napkin every time."

"What's wrong with the food?" Midge said.

Both Pearl and Opal opened their mouths to speak, but Pearl got there first. "Well, for a start, half the dishes have ridiculous names we've never heard of. And secondly, we don't like the way it's served.

You get everything piled up in the middle of an enormous white plate with a miserable dribble of sauce around the edge. Apparently, it's called nouvelle cuisine."

Opal interrupted. "We've already told you about Leo, the head chef, remember, he's the one who managed to poison everybody last night! Trouble with him...he's all gold-bracelet-and-suntan...spends too much time showing off and chatting up the ladies and not enough time cooking sensible food."

"Anyway," Pearl said, "this is all by-the-by. We ain't got time to be twittering about the canteen food, I was about to give you a reading. So, before I start, would you like a sandwich or not?" Pearl leaned forward, took the flower from Midge's hand, and carefully tucked it into one of the teenager's buttonholes. "That looks pretty on you, my dear, brings out the colour in those lovely cheeks."

I haven't got purple cheeks, Midge thought. I don't want to start an argument...best I ignore that remark. "Well...if we're not going to the canteen then...yes...I'd love one...thanks very much...what are my choices?"

"Brawn or tripe," Opal said.

"I don't know what those things are."

"Honestly," Opal tutted, "you youngsters, you don't know nothing. Brawn is pressed meat from a pig's head and tripe is the lining of a cow's stomach. Now, what's it to be?"

"Oh," Midge said.

"Why don't you try one of each?" Opal said. She handed Midge a plate.

"That would be…lovely," Midge said.

The sandwiches had been neatly cut into triangles and the crusts removed. Midge didn't want to appear ungrateful so she lifted one to her mouth and took a bite.

"Mmm", Pearl said. "Lovely, ain't they?"

"I mashed them up," Opal said. "Both the tripe and the brawn then I mixed them with other things…tomatoes…bit of cucumber…grated carrot…salad cream."

Pretend they're roast chicken with mayonnaise, Midge thought. Chew fast! Swallow quickly! Don't breathe! Try not to retch! Eeee…werrr…yuuuk! My eyes are watering! "Gosh, I'm full!"

"Full already?" Pearl said.

"Yes. Sorry. Thank you. Completely full."

Pearl took the plate, passed it to Opal, then looked down at Midge and smiled. "You did very well," she said.

"Yes, I did," Midge said. "I think I deserve a medal." She sucked bits of tripe from the gaps between her teeth. "Sorry…I mean…they were very nice."

Pearl chuckled then turned Midge's cup upside down on its saucer. Following instructions, Midge tapped the bottom of the cup thirteen times with a teaspoon.

"I don't believe in this kind of mumbo-jumbo. I'm a career girl. I prefer to deal with facts."

"Really?" Pearl said. She studied the inside of the cup for several minutes before speaking. "I see you will be going on a long journey."

"Will I?" Midge said.

"Yes, darlin', you will. I see you going on a long journey north. Do you know anyone in Scotland?"

"No, I don't think so."

"Well, you soon will, sweetheart. In Scotland you can find all the answers you seek."

Midge leaned forward.

"You are poised on the edge of an incredible adventure. Ahead of you lies a voyage of discovery and I see you forming new friendships, travelling on unfamiliar paths and bravely stepping into the unknown. Deep within you lies all the wisdom and courage that you need. You have enormous power, darlin', power you're not even aware of."

"Have I?" Midge said. She leaned forward a bit more.

"Yes, darlin', you do. Ooh, now what's this I see? The leaves are telling me you have already crossed paths with an important stranger. I'm seeing some kind of collision. The leaves strongly advise that you make contact with this person again. There must be a coming together of gifted minds if you are to fulfil your destiny."

Midge pulled a face and Pearl continued.

"Like the pieces of a jigsaw eventually come together to reveal the whole picture, so must new friends unite in order to solve the puzzle."

"New friends?" Midge said. "How many new friends?" Pearl stared into the teacup and Midge suddenly remembered her journey into work. "I know who the stranger is! I bumped into a girl on the bus this morning…but…but…now that I think about it…I don't actually know the girl at all. We didn't swap names. I wasn't wearing my glasses."

"Trust that luck is on your side and that fate will bring the pieces of the puzzle together," Pearl said.

"Trust?" Midge said.

"Yes, trust," Pearl said. "There is a path running through all our lives and the leaves point in its direction. The leaves also suggest that next time you come to work, you wear the jeans you want to and not the dress you think you should."

"Crikey," Midge said, "how do they know about that?"

Midge perched herself on the edge of the seat desperate to hear more. Unfortunately, the cushion could no longer support her full weight and it slipped forwards. On the way down, Midge knocked the teacup from Pearl's hands and it flipped into the air. After spraying everyone with wet leaves, the cup hit Midge's head and smashed into four even pieces.

Unruffled by the calamity, Pearl picked up the remnants of the cup and laid them out on the table. "The message is clear," she announced, "these four pieces represent the four minds that must come together."

It occurred to Midge that four minds must mean four friends, but she was too busy feeling clumsy to give this information her full attention.

"I wish to conclude my reading by giving you a very important piece of advice," Pearl said. "You have been blessed with the gift of extra special vision. You can see things that other people cannot. Always remember this."

Because Pearl had dispensed a lot of information in a short space of time Midge struggled to remember every detail. She sat on the floor in silence and willed her brain to soak it up. All attempts to look sophisticated had gone out of the window, and in an effort to check for teacup damage, Midge managed to snap the elastic band from her crazy-curly hair. Her Flaming Fox fringe fell down faster than the final curtain at the theatre.

"You could do with a trim and tidy," Pearl said.

A shriek ended the short-lived silence. "Aghh!" Opal cried. "Look at the time!"

"Cor blimey, saints preserve us!" Pearl shouted, checking her watch.

Midge jumped in her skin. "What's wrong with the time?"

"What's wrong with the time?" Opal screamed. "I'll tell you what's wrong with the time."

Pearl got there first. "We're running out of it, that's what's wrong with it."

"It's quarter to five!" Opal screeched.

The horrified tone of the old lady's voice nearly curdled Midge's blood.

"We've only got fifteen minutes!" Pearl yelled, leaping up from the table as if her knickers had caught fire.

Opal joined Pearl in the Flaming Knicker Dance and Midge felt the panic rising. It started in her toes, but within seconds had reached her stomach. "Will someone tell me what's going on?"

"*The Five O'Clock Announcement*!" the old ladies bellowed in unison.

"Oh…is that all?" Midge said.

"You're presenting it," Opal said.

"I'm what?" Midge said.

"Perhaps we should have told you this earlier," Pearl said. "Penny Treasure, the chief council member, she left you a message. She says it's unavoidable…you know…cos everyone's off sick."

"Sorry," Midge said, "did I just hear you correctly? Did you say I'm presenting *The Five O'Clock Announcement*?"

"Yes, darlin'," Opal said. "But don't worry, it's pretty straightforward…apparently. It's been put together by the movers and shakers in the Publicity Department, it's all typed it up. All you have to do is read it from the autocue machine into the camera."

"I don't believe this! Why didn't you tell me earlier? I need time to prepare. I can't do it." The panic rocketed to Midge's throat.

"Yes, you can," Pearl said. "Just stick to the script and make sure your voice is clear. You can read, can't you?"

"Yes, of course I can read!"

"Well then," Opal said. "The camera's easy to operate, there's an autocue machine and a remote control pad. It'll be a laugh."

Midge squeezed through the gap into the stockroom, grabbed her briefcase and chased the old ladies up the corridor. "Stupid, bloody, pink shoes!" she shouted. "I can't run in these!" She hoisted up her torn dress and flicked them off.

The Five O'Clock Announcements were broadcast from the main television studio, with the presenter's desk positioned in front of a large window that afforded a fabulous view of the River Thames. Before Purple Monday, this studio had housed a long-running daytime show, and so the setting looked familiar to many people. With only minutes to spare, Midge sat down at the desk.

"When the green light comes on we count down from ten to zero," Pearl said.

"Then the red light comes on and that means we're live on air," Opal said.

Midge cleared her throat and tried to make herself comfy. Nervously, she shuffled the papers on the desk. Her clammy hands shook. When she glanced down to read the blurred instructions she remembered she didn't have her glasses or anything to tie up her hair.

The green light came on.

"You've gone a bit pale," Opal shouted.

"Lick your lips and pinch your cheeks," Pearl shouted.

~ Thirteen ~

Giving

At five minutes to four in the afternoon, Scott parked his van in Piccadilly Circus.

Picking his way through the wreckage, he saw two brushes, a comb and an abundant scattering of hair rollers. A smashed-up moped with scuffed paintwork, a blown tyre and twisted handlebars rested against the Shaftesbury Memorial Fountain. Behind the throng of people, Scott noticed a black taxi and a boy in a flat cap sitting on the kerbside. A member of the Mum Police was making notes. An ambulance had arrived and its crew were kneeling on the ground treating a casualty.

The sight of the blue, flashing light caused a surge of haunting emotions to muddle his brain, but Scott found the strength to ignore them. Pushing unwanted memories to the back of his mind, he shoved himself to the front of the crowd.

The casualty wasn't moving and the ambulance crew were busy assessing his vital signs. Deep in concentration, but still able to talk to each other, they exchanged information about his pulse rate, breathing and circulation. Continually they addressed each other by name, and Scott almost smiled at the comical coincidence.

"His pulse rate appears to be normal, Dave."

"Does it, Dave? That's good."

"Also, Dave, his breaths per minute seem to be regular."

"Do they, Dave? That's a positive sign. There's some movement in his left hand, Dave...did you notice?"

"No, Dave, I didn't."

Dave may not have noticed, but Scott noticed the casualty's left hand immediately. Held tightly in its fist was a long-stemmed purple rose, and although not in full bloom, it looked bright and vibrant as if freshly picked. Dave tried to free the flower, but the hand wouldn't let go. It held onto the rosebud as if it were holding onto life.

"Dave, I don't think we should move the casualty in case there's an injury to the spine."

"Absolutely, Dave, I quite agree."

Horrified gasps emanated from the crowd.

This is serious, Scott thought. I'm here for a reason...but what should I be doing? If I suddenly announce that a mysterious voice told me to come to Piccadilly Circus people will think I'm a lunatic. He's holding a purple rose...it's the same as mine...what the hell's going on?

Without warning the casualty sat up and pulled off his helmet. His hair, twisted into mini dreadlocks, celebrated its release by springing upright. The crowd, like a well-rehearsed group of extras on a film set, took a sharp intake of breath and a collective step backwards.

Scott didn't move.

The casualty pressed the tarmac on either side of his legs, perhaps to confirm it existed. Droplets of blood ran down the rose stem and trickled onto his trousers. The gawping crowd mumbled, and Dave 1 scrambled with a tangled oxygen mask. Scott stared down at the boy on the ground, but didn't recognise him. The boy's gaze turned to Scott. Their eyes met. Dave 2 took advantage of the moment and unclenched the bleeding hand. The crowd cringed at several large thorns embedded in his palm. Dave 1 attempted to place the oxygen mask around the boy's face, but the boy pushed the paramedic's hands away and shook his head.

"Scott? It's me...Marty."

The crowd fell silent.

"Do you know this boy?" Dave 1 enquired.

"Err, yes," Scott said.

"Why the hell didn't you say something?"

"Sorry..." Scott lied. "I only recognised my friend when he removed his helmet."

Marty leapt to his feet in one agile, easy movement.

"The dead can walk," a member of the crowd said.

"Why don't you come and sit in the back of the ambulance for a moment and we'll put a dressing on that hand of yours?" Dave 2 said.

"Sure thing," Marty said.

"The show's over!" Dave 1 shouted.

Dave 2 noticed Scott's van. With SCOTT'S SCOOTERS – REPAIRS AND EMERGENCY PICK-UP painted in enormous letters on the side, it wasn't easy to miss. “That’s handy. Your mate can fix your bike for you.”

“Yeah,” Marty replied.

Dave 2 escorted Marty to the ambulance and Scott heard himself saying he would gather together Marty’s belongings. Some members of the crowd helped to pick up the rollers.

After a methodical search of the road, a lady called Doris located the wing mirror. “It’s a miracle, it’s a miracle,” she babbled. “I witnessed the whole thing! I don’t understand how anyone can survive such a terrible accident!”

After wheeling the bike into the back of the van, Scott guided Doris to the ambulance. “I think this lady may have shock.”

“Sit her down here,” Dave 2 said. He turned back to the Mum Police. “So, what happened?”

“He’s only twelve years old.” The uniformed Mum pointed to the boy in the flat cap. “He’s been driving without a licence. I’m afraid he’s in for it. He’ll be grounded for several weeks then join a Clean Team power-washing pigeon crap from Nelson’s Column.” Adjusting her cap, she marched across the road towards the already-troubled culprit.

Doris had gone from white to green, so Dave 1 grabbed a sick bag.

“Now, listen to me, sunshine,” Dave 2 said, busy bandaging Marty’s hand, “I’ve been doing this job for more than forty years and I know what I’m talking about. We need to take you to the accident and emergency department. You could have concussion or an internal injury.”

Scott found himself standing alone. The statue of the winged boy caught his attention.

"Most people think that's Eros, the Greek god of love," Dave 1 said, "bow and arrow poised to shoot us all in the heart."

Scott nodded. "Yeah...I know."

"I'm a self-confessed history anorak. The Romans named him Cupid...they believed him to be a symbol of life after death."

Scott stared up at the statue, but didn't reply.

"But if the truth be known," Dave 1 continued, "that's not Eros at all; it's actually a statue of Anteros. Anteros is the brother of Eros...he's the god of requited love."

"Requited love?"

"Yes, you know, love returned. We can't receive love without giving some of our own away...giving and receiving...that's what makes the world go round."

"Is it?" Scott struggled to control the anger in his voice. "It seems to me that...well...these days...everything's being taken away..."

"You could try giving," Dave 1 said, interrupting, "even though you don't think you should...and see what happens."

"Maybe," Scott said, doing his best not to scowl. He turned 360 degrees. Where did everybody go? Piccadilly Circus kept spinning. He tipped his head back. Way above, a flock of seagulls screeched and tumbled; it looked like the crowd had sprouted wings. Okay, Scott thought, I'm going to do it. I'll give this stranger a lift...offer to fix his bike. The words sprang out of his mouth, “Don’t worry about Marty, I’m sure he’ll be okay. I’ll keep a close eye on him. If there’s a problem, I’ll take him straight to the emergency department.”

“Well, we can’t force him to come with us,” Dave 2 said, “but you have to make a promise. Promise he’s not left on his own for the next twenty-four hours…”

Marty clambered down from the ambulance. “Hey, it’s cool.”

“I promise,” Scott said.

On cue, Doris produced something that resembled vegetable soup and neither of the boys missed the opportunity to make a run for it.

The van moved slowly, through theatre land, past musicals and plays closed down: the actors missing. I’ve got a part in something, Scott thought, but where’s the script? What are my lines? “What…what’s happening?”

“You’re asking me?”

“How do you know my name?”

“I don’t,” Marty replied.

“Yes, you do, when you came round you said my name, you said, hello, Scott!”

“Did I?”

Silence. The van stopped at a red traffic light.

“How do you know my name? How did you walk away from that accident without any serious injuries? And where did you get that flower from?”

“Don’t know. Don’t know. And don’t know.” Marty placed the rose on the dashboard. “I’m sorry, dude, I really am, but I can’t remember what happened.

There is something familiar about you, like maybe we've met before. I do feel like I know you…but I don't know how or why."

The van accelerated and Scott moved his line of vision to the road.

Marty rubbed his temples. "I picked that flower. I'm certain I picked that flower. This is weird, maybe I'm going crazy."

"I don't think you're the only one who's going crazy." Scott reached over to the glove box and pulled out a near-identical purple rose, the one he'd woken up with less than an hour before.

For the next twenty minutes the boys drove through central London and Scott told Marty everything. They talked about the voices, the mysterious house cleaner and the matching flowers. After passing Trafalgar Square the van went under Admiralty Arch and down The Mall. Then, after circling the Queen Victoria Memorial three times, it came to a standstill outside Buckingham Palace.

"Someone or something has brought us together," Marty said. "When I close my eyes all I can see is a sunset-coloured sky. Maybe…I can remember the smell of perfume…I don't know. Was I with you in a garden? The questions outnumber the answers."

"You're right about that," Scott said. "So, what happens next?"

"I wish I could stay and talk about it all night, but I'm training to be a hairdresser and I've got an exam tomorrow."

"Oh. What's it on?"

"Head lice and dandruff," Marty replied with a roll of the eyes.

Scott smiled at the absurdity of the situation. "I suppose I'm lucky. I work for myself…I get to do what I want when I want." He stared at the Palace then wound down the window, hopeful the late-afternoon thermals might lift his spirits. "The DMC will be doing *The Five O'Clock Announcement*."

"What's the DMC," Marty said, interrupting.

"It's the Decision Makers Council." Scott was taken aback. "Sorry, I thought everyone knew that. Anyway, we could go to a Booster Bar and watch *The Five O'Clock Announcement*. When it's finished, I'll give you a lift straight home."

"A Booster Bar?"

"Yeah," Marty said, "you know…Booster Bars…it's what everyone's started calling them." He waited for a response, but Marty said nothing. "The pubs, lots of them have re-opened, they're selling fruit smoothies and giving away vitamins. They get really busy just before five."

"Oh. I didn't know," Marty said.

"*Dude!* Where have you been for the past few weeks?"

"In the dark," Marty replied.

The Hounds of Love – a Booster Bar on the Kings Road – had several blackboards leaning against the wall by the entrance. WIDE TV SCREENS IN BOTH BARS said one. ELVIS LIVE ON STAGE TONIGHT said another.

The uproar on the other side of the door brought to an end all hope of a normal conversation. The boys pushed their way through the crowd and up to the bar. With only three minutes to go until *The Five O'Clock Announcement*, it seemed they were the only ones who hadn't been served. The landlord of The Hounds of Love, with an obvious sense of humour, had included blueberries, blackberries or plums in every cocktail recipe. Consequently, the name of every drink served started with the word Purple. The vast list of choices included a Purple Strawberry Swirl, Purple Apple Doom, Purple Berry Breeze, Purple Double Freeze, Purple Lemon Lovely, Purple Tangerine Terror, and the PurpleXXX, which, according to the menu, was guaranteed to put hairs on your chest.

Jostling at the bar, Scott noticed two girls in tartan hats, cream blouses and matching tartan skirts. The barman presented the girls with enormous frozen purple cocktails and held out his hand for the money.

"Oh!" one of them said. "We've just remembered, we've left our money in our wet clothes."

"I'll get those," Scott said. He leaned over and dropped some money onto the counter. "And we'll have a couple of your XXX's, please."

"Oh, thanks very much," the girls said and they smiled.

"Are you with Elvis?" Marty enquired.

"With Elvis?" one of them said.

"Your outfits. Are you the backing singers?"

The girls laughed.

"No. We had a bit of an accident with a burst water pipe and we've borrowed these outfits from an old lady," one said.

"It's a look that could catch on, don't you think?" the other said.

Before Scott could reply, the opening credits of *The Five O'Clock Announcement* burst onto the widescreen and a hush descended. Hideous classical music accompanied the usual, pre-recorded history of the DMC leader's life. Film footage of a younger-looking Penny Treasure, along with details of how many companies she'd owned, how many people she'd employed and how much money she'd made, flashed up on screen. As the music drew to a close, the regular close-up of Penny's mouth, with its unusually large gums, promised to serve the people of London with unwavering duty.

"Seen it a million times!" a voice shouted.

"Get on with it!" another shouted.

Needless to say, Midge's unexpected appearance took everyone by surprise.

~ Fourteen ~

A Star is Born!

"Hello, citizens of London! Penny is off sick today and my name is Midge!"

After sneaking a peek at the television monitor on the desk, Midge realised the top part of her head appeared chopped off. In an attempt to adjust the height of the seat she reached down and pulled the lever underneath, but it wouldn't budge. She continued to struggle with it, tugging as hard as she could, until the infuriating thing snapped off in her hand.

"NO!" she cried in horror.

After staring at the broken lever in disbelief she placed it on the desk then scraped the hair from her face. Terror took over. The words on the autocue became a blur because she couldn't decipher them without her glasses. In desperation she squinted and pushed her head forward like a tortoise, but it didn't help.

"I CAN'T SEE A THING...I'LL BE BACK IN A MINUTE."

Off camera, Pearl and Opal searched their overall pockets for anything that could be of help and, seconds later, after making some major adjustments, Midge dashed back to the desk. Her hair had been squashed into a food-handlers hair net, and on her face she wore a pair of old-fashioned ladies glasses (the kind that go pointy at the corners). In order to keep her head in line with the camera she pushed the seat back, leaned forwards from her waist, and rested her elbows on the edge of the table.

"Good afternoon, Golden Oldies and Bright Young Things!"

Midge felt her trussed-up tresses wobbling like a giant ball of wool, and her restored vision stole a glance at the instructions. She took a deep breath. In the background Pearl and Opal stood grinning with their thumbs up. Midge pressed the auto-focus button on the remote control pad and the camera made a whirring sound as it moved forwards. She took a second deeper breath and pressed the start button. The autocue machine began to roll.

"Thank you for tuning in. My name is Penny Treasure. Oh no! It's not! I do apologise! My name is Midge.

"A warm welcome to *The Five O'Clock Announcement*! Today's announcement is a special one because, over the next thirty minutes, I'm going to be highlighting our major developments so far..."

After taking a second to refill her lungs, Midge continued.

"...Yes, that's right, today I'm going to be sharing with you everything you need to know. New rules, new ideas, what's hot and what's not. What's in and what's out. The ups and downs, click, the highs and lows, clack, the thrills and spills, click, clack..."

Nerves had stripped Midge's mouth of saliva, causing her tongue to make irritating noises. She gestured to Pearl and Opal desperate for advice and then, without warning, her seat dropped. On the way down her nose clipped the edge of the desk.

"OUCH! THAT HURT!"

Midge staggered to the rear of the broadcast room, lifted her hand up to her nose, and felt a warm drip of blood on her palm.

"I'M BLEEDING!" She tipped her head backwards and pinched the fleshy part of her nose. *"DON'T PANIC! I'M OKAY! TWO MINUTES...I'LL BE WITH YOU."*

"Here you are, darlin'!" Pearl said, off camera. "Use some of this tissue paper!"

Midge careered back to the desk and threw herself in the seat. In an attempt to stem the blood she stuffed tissue paper up each nostril and then, when that was done to her satisfaction, readjusted her old lady glasses.

"That's better...please excuse my nose-blocked voice...and my ridiculous appearance...oh...and the blood."

I've got nothing left to lose, she thought. I've made a complete idiot of myself. I'll run out of time if I don't get a move on!

She patted her colossal ball of netted hair. "Do you like it? It's the very latest in sophisticated styles!"

Hurriedly, she scrabbled about with the control pad until the autocue was back on track.

"In the weeks and months that have passed, much progress has been made, but it's important for us to remain focused."

Phew! Keep breathing! I'm all right. I'm doing okay. Keep going. Keep going.

"First of all, let's talk rubbish...Although we've made great progress in several areas, many parts of the capital continue to be overrun with rats. Therefore, I'd like to make an urgent plea on behalf of the Rat Pack.

"The Rat Pack work tirelessly throughout the night hunting vermin, and they're desperately short of staff. If you're interested in joining, please dial 0800-RATTY on your telephone keypad for an application form.

"And now for some good news...This week's Hero Award goes to our Essential Service Volunteer Group. Thanks to them, we're enjoying an almost uninterrupted supply of gas, electricity and fresh drinking water. ESVG is run and managed by some hard working Golden Oldies and enthusiastically assisted by a large number of Bright Young Things! Please continue to be thoughtful in your use of essential services, and worry not, as we are investigating suitable alternatives.

"With regard to last Friday's phone poll, the votes have been counted and I'm pleased to announce we are unanimous in our desire to construct a wind farm on Hampstead Heath. If anyone knows anything about harnessing the power of wind to create electricity could they please call the Crisis Hotline immediately! Thank you.

"And now for the bad news…Not surprisingly, we had a poor turnout for the Sewage Disposal Open Day. Therefore, until further notice, please only flush your toilet when absolutely necessary.

"The Trafalgar Square Carless-Car-Boot-Sale had proved to be a huge success and is now open everyday. Please donate generously, and make use of the collection van when it passes through your area.

"Extra Recycle Centres are being made available in all neighbourhoods and will include an on-site wormery for organic matter. In a very short period of time, tiger worms will convert all of our household waste into rich compost.

"This brings me nicely onto the subject of fruits and vegetables…Another great, big thank you goes out to our team of gardening experts who, several months ago, came up with the bright idea of converting large sections of our parks and gardens into vegetable plots. Also, many of you took this urgent matter into your own hands and dug up your gardens in order to grow your own. I'm sure we're all relieved to discover that everything planted earlier this year is growing in glorious abundance. It would seem the Purple has had an astonishing effect on the soil, leaving it extraordinarily fertile. We're also in the process of making friends with a number of allotment keepers and out-of-town farmers. Everyone involved is expecting bumper crops this year…wheat, maize, barley, potatoes, broad beans, peas, onions, carrots, garlic, corn on the cob, runner beans, rhubarb, strawberries, plums, blueberries and apples…in fact…the list is endless!

"Covent Garden has become a fresh-produce-hotspot, where we can all buy, sell and exchange.

"You'll be pleased to know that a limited number of supermarkets have reopened. The majority of food on their shelves is fresh, locally grown produce and home-baked fancies. Three cheers to our Golden Oldies, for all their bread and cake making contributions!

"You don't need me to tell you that chocolate has become a rare and expensive luxury. Gram for gram, it is now worth its weight in gold. With this in mind, I know you'll be delighted to hear that a jumbo jet loaded with cocoa powder will be landing at Heathrow Airport sometime tomorrow afternoon. A further delivery of oranges, lemons and coconuts will be with us on Friday. Reserves of tea should last for several more weeks.

"Passenger flights remain suspended, and all aircraft use is strictly limited to the transportation of cargo. Likewise, the use of cars remains prohibited. Our public transport system is able to provide an improved tube and bus service and black cabs will continue to be available.

"The required number of fuel guards has been recruited and they're providing twenty-four hour watch at all petrol stations, bus terminals and airports. Please remember, if you wish to obtain fuel, you must be in possession of identification documents and a fuel ration card. There will be no exceptions to this rule.

"The vast majority of soup kitchens have closed, but our much awaited Drop-In Centres are now open in most neighbourhoods. They'll be manned twenty-four seven. At these centres you'll be able to get the latest news, advice and support on all matters. I'm delighted to announce that, cocoa permitting, hot chocolate and fudge brownies will always be available.

"And now, let's talk money...Those of you who lost savings when the computers crashed will be relieved to hear that the wait is almost over. Our team of financial experts will begin re-crediting your bank accounts next Monday. Also, starting next week, for your convenience, all wages will be paid directly into the new banking system. I'm sure you'll agree this is great progress!

"In order to raise awareness of money matters, we recently ran a competition encouraging everyone to think of a name for our new banking organisation. As promised, the winner was drawn at random and I'd like to congratulate fifteen-year-old Janette Baker from Brixton who not only came up with the novel name Greedy Pig Savings, but also designed this eye-catching logo."

Midge rummaged through her pile of papers until she found the picture of a fat, laughing, pink pig with a curly tail and pound signs in its eyes. She held it up to the camera for a few seconds.

"Greedy Pig Savings will soon have branches open across London and, once you've set up an account, you'll be issued with your very own Greedy Pig bank book and cash card. Greedy Pig staff will be delighted to take your money. Please note that an online banking service will become available when we've established a high-speed internet provider.

"Let's talk education…At present, school is only available to those aged twelve and under. However, in time, we hope to offer learning opportunities to everyone who wants them – no matter what their age.

"In our recent Education Survey, ninety percent of you circled 'highly unlikely' when asked of your intention to return to classroom learning. In order to combat this negative view, the DMC would like to scrap the current subjects taught and replace them with useful life skills. These are some of the suggested new subjects:

The Basics – that's reading writing and arithmetic
Computer Competence
Gardening
Cooking and Nutrition
D.I.Y.
Cycle and Moped Safety
Self-Esteem
Money Matters
Environmental Issues
Scuba Diving
Successful Relationship Skills
Look At Me! – that's dance and drama
Art and Design

"If you've any suggestions of your own, please let us know. New ideas are actioned on a daily basis, and thanks to your feedback, the under eights will soon be enjoying an afternoon each week dedicated entirely to glitter.

"Let's move onto other issues...The Mum Police have proved themselves to be an enormous success and a force to be reckoned with! They'll remain on our streets and can, of course, be contacted in an emergency by dialling 999.

"Miraculously, we all continue to remain free from illness and most of our hospitals have closed down or been converted into orphanages. Due to the ever-increasing number of moped collisions, many of our accident and emergency wards remain open. Please slow down or you may have your licence revoked.

"As you know, the Purple caused those who are helpless to fall into a protective coma, and our population experts assure us that many people and animals are still fast asleep. If you wake or discover anyone who is alone, unable or unwilling to care for themselves, please call the Crisis Hotline for advice.

"A great big wakey-wakey to those of you who have recently joined us! And let me take this opportunity to reassure you that everything's not as grim as it first appeared.

"Battersea Dogs Home is full-to-bursting with domestic pets so we urge you to take all stray animals to the zoo in Regents Park, where special facilities have been constructed. For those of you still looking for employment, please note: the Regents Park Animal Facility is now over-subscribed with volunteers.

"Don't forget to check London's daily newsletter, After Purple, which has a comprehensive and up-to-date job vacancy section.

"The Whistle Blowing Scheme is fully up and running and whistles have been sent to most addresses. Please continue to support your fellow Londoner.

"The Tucking-In-Service has been inundated with calls and is struggling to cope. If you wish to volunteer, you can call Babs on 0800-TUCK-ME-IN. Babs would like to apologise to everyone who has been put on standby during peak periods, and she thanks you for your patience.

"Thanks to our Communication Contraption Squad, our text-message-voting system is now free from glitches. When any issue requires your vote, simply text yes or no to the usual number and rest assured that all votes will be counted.

"Our one and only radio station, Heroic London Radio, has been broadcasting non-stop for eighteen weeks. On behalf of every Londoner I'd like to commend all those involved. Thanks to the friendly voice of Heroic London, many a lonely soul has made it through their darkest hour. Please continue to send in your requests and dedications.

"I'm thrilled to announce some good news for all you night owls out there! Starting this weekend, the cinemas in Leicester Square will be open around the clock.

"Due to popular demand one of the capital's most famous landmarks, the London Eye, is to be reopened. Also, an afternoon tea delivery service called Crumpet On The Run will soon be distributing affordable tea, cakes and a chinwag to those aged seventy-five and over.

"Many of you will have heard stories regarding recent sightings of the Purple, and I'd like to take this opportunity to dispel your fears. Despite lengthy investigations, not one of these reports has been proved. Inevitably, rumours and gossip abound so, although it's wise to stay alert, please try not to panic.

"You will no doubt have seen the striking purple and white posters on many of our billboards, and their slogan, encouraging us all to Remain Aware Proceed With Care, is one we should all try to follow.

"Mega gratitude goes out to our Golden Oldies...who've returned so enthusiastically to the workforce. Your wisdom and insight are invaluable. And to our Bright Young Things...we thank you for your guts and determination.

"Together we can overcome these difficult times!

"Together we can succeed!

"Thank you for watching."

Officially, that was supposed to be the end of *The Five O'Clock Announcement*, but a random idea popped into Midge's head.

"Oh, and there's one more thing...complimentary ice cream will now be available in all Booster Bars. Scoop Of The Day will be served at five in the afternoon and there'll be a different flavour every day of the week. Oh...and there's another one more thing...I'm desperately looking for the girl I ran into on my way to work this morning. We took a bus together and I got off at Westminster Bridge. Stranger, if you're out there, you know who you are…"

Midge dipped below the desk, grabbed the sandal from her briefcase and waved it at the camera.

"…maybe you have my other sandal…the one that hit you on the head? I think I left it somewhere on the bus and perhaps you found it? Even if you don't have my sandal, I really need to see you. There's something very important that we need to talk about. Stranger, I'll wait for you this evening outside the DMC HQ."

~ Fifteen ~

The Hounds of Love

The crowd in The Hounds of Love gave Midge a standing ovation.

"She's hilarious!"

"So much better than Penny!"

"Was that for real…the bleeding nose bit…or was it part of the act?"

"Love the comedy wig and glasses!"

"Free ice cream!"

"She's talking about me!" Ellie said.

"What do you mean?" Ping said.

Ellie opened her bag and pulled out the sandal. "I'm the stranger she's talking about!"

"You mean…"

"Yes! She's the girl I bumped into this morning."

"Oh my God," Ping said.

Ellie passed the sandal to Ping, then carefully removed the purple rose from her bag. "And…did you notice…she had a purple rose tucked into her buttonhole? It looked just like this one!" Both girls stared at the flower in Ellie's hand. "Ten hours without water and it looks like…like I just picked it!"

"Excuse me! Where did you get that from?" Ellie turned to face the boy who'd paid for the cocktails.
"Sorry...my name's Scott," Scott said.

"I...I...don't really know. My name's Ellie."

"I've got one too; I woke up with it in my hand this afternoon. And so did Marty..." Scott pointed to his friend.

"She's got the other sandal!" someone shouted in the crowd.

"She's the stranger!" another shouted.

The crowd lurched forwards and inwards, hands grabbed and pulled, and Ellie crashed into Ping.

"Let's get out of here," Scott shouted over the din of the music.

"Hold onto your hats, ladies!" Marty shouted.

The four of them pushed their way towards the door, and it took several minutes of nifty elbow work to clear a path through the unwanted attention. Eventually, they made it onto the pavement. The door banged shut behind them.

"What's happened to the light? It looks yellow!" Marty said.

Scott stared up. "The pressure's been building all day...the clouds...they're angry."

"Listen!" Ping said.

"I can't hear anything," Scott said, "not a single thing."

"Exactly," Ping said. "Even the birds have stopped singing."

"Something's coming!" Ellie said. "I can feel it in the air...I hope it's not..."

A colossal flash of lightning ripped through the clouds, followed by an explosion of thunder directly above their heads. Ellie lifted her hands up to her ears and a raindrop the size of a walnut shattered on her forehead.

"It's just a storm!" Marty shouted, tipping his head back to embrace the torrent.

Scott dashed over to the van, unlocked the doors, and waved for the others to join him. "I'll drive us there!"

A perfectly timed, second bolt of lightning grabbed their attention and a deep, rich rumble of thunder chased them across the road into the wind-rocked vehicle. Dripping, they squashed themselves onto the long front seat. The metal sign hanging outside The Hounds of Love somersaulted off its hinges, bounced across the pavement and clattered up the street.

Clutch, first gear, handbrake, accelerator, foot down, off.

On top of the dashboard, Ellie could see two purple roses. She reached into her bag, removed her own purple rose, and placed it down next to them.

Raindrops drummed the roof of the van making conversation impossible, but Ellie knew they were on their way to meet Midge at the DMC HQ. She pulled off her hat. Water trickled down her spine, cascaded off the end of her nose, and a smile, so big it made her gulp, opened on her face.

The wipers flicked at full speed, but could barely keep pace with the rain, and all around, thunder detonated like landmines. From the Kings Road they dropped down to the Chelsea Embankment, where they followed the River Thames until they got to Waterloo Bridge. Apart from the occasional moped casualty, who had been blown off the tarmac, the streets looked deserted. The van nipped to the left and the right dodging pools of water.

"Cool driving!" Marty shouted.

Within minutes they arrived at their destination.

~ooOoo~

When the broadcast finished, Midge immediately started to worry.

"You messed that up," a voice said in her ear.

Leave me alone, Midge thought.

"You should have done that better. I expect everyone's laughing at you."

I said leave me alone. Shut up.

"That was a disaster!" the voice insisted.

"Well, that was a disaster, wasn't it?" Midge said, switching off the equipment.

"Are you stark ravin' bonkers, darlin'?" Opal exclaimed. "That was bloomin' marvellous!"

"You've got a talent there, my dear, you could be the next big thing on TV," Pearl added. "But you need to sort out that evil, twisted monster."

"What?"

"That voice you can hear…it belongs to Doubt," Opal said. "We can see him sitting on your shoulder. Looks like he's got the upper hand."

"He'll twitter on for eternity if you let him," Pearl interrupted. She shook her head. "That girl doesn't know what she's capable of."

"You're telling me!" Opal shouted.

"Wait till Penny Treasure sees you tomorrow, you'll probably get the sack!" Doubt hollered.

Midge heard this last comment loud and clear, but tried her best to ignore it. She pulled off the hairnet then cautiously removed the tissue paper from her nostrils. Thankfully, the bleeding had stopped.

Opal crossed the room. "Come on, darlin', chin-up!"

Midge closed her briefcase then told a lie. "I'm fine."

"Have some faith in yourself!"

"Have you forgotten everything I told you this afternoon?" Pearl added.

"No," Midge said.

"Good, I'm glad to hear it. Now, come along, you've got things to do. Places to go to and fans to meet. Let's not have any more of this feeling sorry for yourself nonsense."

"You've given me the creeps," Midge said. "Can you actually see Doubt on my shoulder? Which shoulder?"

"Forget about Doubt," Opal said. "You've got more important stuff to worry about. The four pieces of the broken cup…the four minds that must come together to solve the puzzle…new friendships…a journey into the unknown!"

Midge looked down at the sandal in her hand. "Do you mind if I borrow these glasses until tomorrow?" I've got to meet someone outside the front entrance."

"That's the spirit!" the old ladies said in unison.

Wind and rain pummelled the building. Reluctant to go outside, Midge crossed the foyer and squashed her face against a window.

"There's a van parked outside! Two boys have just stepped out! And now a girl! This is amazing! She's here! It's the stranger I bumped into on the bus! Oh…no…there's someone else. That can't be right…there's only supposed to be four of us…four minds coming together…that's what you said?" Midge turned to Pearl and Opal.

"You're not part of the plan!" Doubt shouted. "You're not that important!"

"Don't worry, darlin', everything's working out," Pearl said.

"Trust," Opal said.

"They've come to return my sandal, and then they'll leave without me," Midge said.

Ellie was the first into the foyer. "Hi, Midge, remember me?"

Midge put on her best fake smile and tried to sound happy. "Hi."

"This is Ping, and Marty, and this is Scott."

Silence was followed by nervous laughter.

"You were great on TV, everybody loved you."

"Yeah, yeah," Midge said.

"No, really…you were."

"Was I?"

"She's just being polite," Doubt said.

"Thanks for coming over to drop off my sandal." Midge held out a hand to take the shoe and geared herself up to make some dull, polite chitchat.

Ellie reached into her bag, but it wasn't a sandal she removed.

Midge stared down at Ellie's hand, and then noticed each of the boys had a strikingly similar flower.

"Last night I had the strangest dream," Ellie said. "I dreamt I was lost in an incredible garden filled with amazing flowers, there was a wonderful smell of perfume; it was weird and magical all at the same time. A creepy, hooded figure chased me. My mum and dad were there. I picked a flower and when I woke up I had it in my hand. I'm not sure how or why it came to be there, but it would seem I'm not the only person around here who's got one."

"We think we know what you're talking about!" Marty spluttered.

"The flowers, the garden, the smell of perfume, we must have been there too," Scott said. "Although neither of us can remember as much as you can."

Midge stared down at the rose tucked into her buttonhole. She too had something to say, but escalating hysteria prevented her from getting the words out. She paused for a moment and remembered to breathe. "Yes, me too! Me too! I nodded off this afternoon and when I woke up I had this in my hand." She waved the flower through the air. "I don't remember many details. Flowers…friends. I'm not explaining myself very well. I woke up knowing I'd been somewhere truly awesome, surrounded by flowers and friends."

"And I got knocked off my bike a few hours ago," Marty said. "I'm not sure what happened to me, I was out of it for a while, but when I came round I was holding onto this."

Scott nodded enthusiastically. "The same thing happened to me, but that's not all, when I woke up my whole house had been cleaned...every, single room. I know it sounds stupid, but it's true...and there's more...all the spare rooms look like they're waiting for visitors, fresh sheets on the beds and towels laid out. I know you're probably thinking I've gone mental...that we don't even know each other...but I have the strongest feeling that you people are the guests I'm expecting. So...I suppose...what I mean...what I'm trying to say is...I think you should all come and stay with me."

An intense feeling of excitement surged in Midge's stomach; it rippled through her body, and gathered, throbbing, in her fingertips. For the first time ever, Midge suspected the voice in her ear...Doubt...could be wrong. Carefully, she returned the flower to her buttonhole. "Count me in!"

"And me!" Ellie cried.

"Me too," Marty said, "but one of you guys will have to test me on head lice and dandruff before tomorrow morning."

Scott laughed. "Don't worry, I'll help you and, anyway, I promised Dave and Dave you wouldn't be left on your own tonight."

"Head lice and dandruff?" Midge said.

"Dave and Dave?" Ellie said.

"There's loads we need to discuss!" Scott said.

Ellie turned to Ping. "You're coming with us, aren't you? I know you haven't got a flower, but that shouldn't stop you from being involved…in fact…you're totally involved…you're with me…you're my friend."

Ping smiled. "And you're my friend, thanks for thinking of me, but I'm going home."

"No, don't do that! I know you can handle being alone, but you don't have to be. You could be with us."

"I'm not sure if I can explain how I'm feeling," Ping said, "but if it were a headline in a newspaper it would probably be quite a long one and it would read something like…*Girl With Troubled Past Desperately Clings Onto Her New Life And Doesn't Want To Let Go And, At The Same Time, Hopes Her New Best Friend Won't Hate Her For It."*

"I have a headline for you," Ellie said. *"Best Friend Loves Girl With Troubled Past Unconditionally…And Always Will."*

"Sorry…I'm confused…does that mean you're not coming?" Scott said.

Ping looked back. "No, I'm not."

"Well, hang on a minute, at least let me give you a lift home."

"That's really kind," Ping said, pulling her hat down, "but it's not necessary. Covent Garden's just across the bridge…" Her voice trailed off as she disappeared through the revolving door.

"Will she be okay?" Midge said.

"Yeah, she'll be fine." Ellie sighed. "She knows how to take care of herself."

"So, it's just the four of us?" Midge said.

"Looks like it," Ellie said.

"Right, let's make a move," Scott said.

Midge turned to say goodbye to Pearl and Opal. "Did anyone see two old ladies?"

~ Sixteen ~

Marty's Leap of Faith

Marty had been living on the third floor of a multi-storey car park.

The van turned left onto Brewer Street and then right into a large, art deco style building made from pale stone.

"This must be it," Scott said.

"Yeah," Marty said.

"Radical," Midge said. "This place looks too smart to be a car park. I didn't know it existed. I'll bet it cost a fortune to park here in the good old days."

Ellie nudged Marty in the ribs. "Get you...with your Soho postcode!"

Marty didn't reply. The van circled its way to the third floor, passing endless abandoned cars.

"Here," Marty said.

Scott stopped the van and everyone jumped out.

"Wow, this looks amazing!" Midge said.

"Well, it isn't much, but it's what I call home." Marty smiled awkwardly and opened the driver's door of the clapped-out campervan. "It's got everything I need...a radio...a cooker...a light and a bed. Over there," he said, pointing at an exit sign, "is a deserted security guard's office. It's got a sink with working taps and a flushing toilet." Marty stared at his belongings. He scratched his head, disturbing the minute beads of moisture. "I'm real low on gas for the cooker, so I hope you Brits won't mind if I don't make you a cup of tea."

"Honestly," Ellie said, "don't worry. Not all us Brits put the kettle on every two seconds."

"And there's no need to worry about the gas," Scott said, "because you don't have to stay here any longer. You're coming to mine. It'll be great. I live alone in a massive house and there are five spare bedrooms."

"I'll have to bring my cat, is that okay?" Ellie said.

"Bring everything," Scott said.

Marty climbed into the camper van and sat on the floor.

"Mind if I join you?" Ellie said.

"No, jump in," Marty said.

"That's what I was about to say to you," Ellie said.

"Meaning?"

"I just said goodbye to Ping twenty minutes ago…she had the same look on her face that you've got…are we about to lose another?"

"You know, if you can read minds, you should tell people. It's only fair and polite."

"I can hear everything you're thinking!" Ellie said, mocking the style of a dodgy stage magician.

"Go on then…astound me…what's happening?" Marty tapped his head with a finger.

"Well, I reckon you're having second thoughts. You've got everything set up here and it works. You're wondering if we're a risk worth taking."

"You could make millions," Marty said.

"I hope so," Ellie said. "Thing is – I'm being serious – sometimes we have to jump. Even though we don't have a clue where we'll land, we have to trust that it will be on safe, solid ground and that everything will be okay. Have faith and then jump, that's what I'm about to do."

"But you seem so sure of everything."

"Maybe I'm not," Ellie said.

"Now you're confusing me," Marty replied.

"Do me a favour, close your eyes for a minute."

"What, right now?"

"Yes, right now, close your eyes."

Marty reluctantly did as requested.

"Now. Try to picture the three of us getting back into the van and driving away without you. Imagine how you'd feel. Do you feel relieved that we've gone, or do you feel slightly…anxious? What's the strongest feeling?"

It took less than ten minutes for everyone to pack up Marty's few belongings; all he owned was a handful of clothes, some toiletries, a football and a collection of hairdressing study books.

Before leaving he paused to say goodbye to an old friend. "Thanks for keeping me safe and dry." He patted the bonnet of the old camper van. "I'll miss you."

"Come on!" Midge shouted. "We've got two more suitcases and a cat to collect."

~ Seventeen ~

Secrets and Clues on Monday Night

Frank scooted around Scott's kitchen, poking his nose into every corner.

"I love animals," Midge said, "but we've only got a small balcony."

"It's a crazy coincidence," Marty said, "your apartment block on the same street as Ellie's house."

Midge nodded. "I know! It's wild! And so is the way you speak! Apartment block! It makes it sound so...upmarket! It's just a crummy block of flats."

Sitting at the kitchen table, surrounded by his new mates, Scott silently thanked whoever had sent them. "I'm just glad you're all here," he said. "It's nearly two o'clock in the morning, but I don't feel the slightest bit tired."

"Nor me," Midge said.

"How old are you?" Ellie said.

"I'm sixteen," Scott said. "What age did you think I was?"

"I wasn't sure, but I had an idea you were older than the rest of us. Where did you learn to cook? That pasta was gorgeous."

"Thanks. My mum taught me...she...she..."

Much to Scott's relief, Marty took advantage of the lull in conversation. "And just so you know...tonight's bath wasn't the first one in five months."

"So that's what the smell was!" Midge said. She waved a hand in front of her nose.

"Hey, I'm serious," Marty said. "I used to sneak in the back door of the Hilton on Park Lane. Under the cover of darkness, I got to use all of their mini soaps and shampoos. One time I nearly got caught by the Mum Police...they were always on the prowl."

"It's amazing," Midge said. "You hitched your way down to London and lived in that camper van all on you own."

"Yeah, I agree," Ellie said.

"I'll tell you what's amazing," Marty said, "this guy can cook, but more importantly, he can hear voices. What do they sound like?"

"Well, it's hard to describe." Scott thought about it. "Sometimes they sound like the hushed whispering in the cinema...you know...the sort of noises people make when the lights go down. The first sign they're coming is a screechy whistle, a bit like an old transistor radio that's not properly tuned-in."

"Wow," Marty said. "I know you feel weird about it, but you should try and make contact with them, maybe they could help us."

"I promise," Scott said. "I'll try tomorrow."

"Yes, tomorrow," Ellie said, "let's have a recap, to make sure we all know what we're doing." She picked up the notepad. "I'm going back to Mrs Mackay's to ask her about that photo."

"Yep, that's great," Midge said, "we need to find out if the garden exists in real life. And I'll hunt down Pearl and Opal; ask them about the four pieces of the puzzle. Hopefully, they can tell me how they fit together. I can't remember Pearl's exact words...but I'm sure she mentioned taking a trip to Scotland."

Marty drummed his fingers on the table. "I haven't got a clue what my part of the puzzle even looks like."

"Don't worry," Midge said, "it doesn't help to think about something too much. My mum used to say a problem's best slept on."

Ellie nodded. "My mum used to say it was a good idea to write your problems on a piece of paper before you turn out the light, then they'll leave you alone till morning." She gave a thumbs-down. "But, to be honest, I tried that loads of times and it didn't work, during the past five months I've had a billion sleepless nights. Every time I put my head on the pillow, it jammed with mad thoughts about what might have happened to everyone."

"Mine too," Midge said.

Ellie patted Marty's forearm. "I'm sorry you've had a crap time in this country. I don't understand why anyone would want to attack someone because they have an American accent."

"Or because your skin is black," Midge said, "I mean...who cares? In fact, I wish I was black. I hate having pale bibbly-bobbly skin that needs to be covered in factor 4000 sunblock every summer."

The others smiled.

"What's a bibbly-bobbly? I don't think we have that word in the States."

"Oh, it's a made-up word; it's what I call this red patchy skin on my arms." Midge pulled up the sleeves of her sweatshirt.

Marty leaned over and took her arm in his hand. "I can't see anything; you worry too much about nothing. You look great."

Midge blushed. "I'll tell you all one more secret, if my hair wasn't dyed Flaming Fox Red it would be plain ginger, and when it was, people used to take the mickey all the time."

"People make fun of anything that's different," Scott said.

Midge nodded. "Yeah, stupid, boring people with no imagination."

"I've got something for us," Ellie said. She put down the notepad and lifted something from her bag. "I wasn't sure if I should tell anyone about this, but if we're dealing in secrets, then I don't see why not. I can trust you all…can't I?"

"Sure you can," Marty said.

Ellie placed the flat, rectangular-shaped object onto the table. "Tah-dah!" was all she needed to say before the room erupted into cheers of elation.

"Chocolate!" all three of them shouted.

"Where did you get it from? I haven't seen chocolate for months," Scott said.

"Well, an old man called Mr Pink lives in one of my properties and he collects things and when I say collect, I actually mean hoard. His whole flat is filled with odd artefacts. He goes through phases of collecting different things, and as luck would have it, for six months before Purple Monday, his *thing* was chocolate. You name it, if it's made from chocolate, then he's got it by the box full: chocolate bars, chocolate buttons, chocolate drinking powder, chocolate oranges, chocolate bunnies, chocolate cakes, boxes of chocolate truffles."

"Wow! Totally cool!" Marty said.

"What else has he collected?" Scott asked.

"Oh, lots of things. For a while it was newspapers, that was really boring, then it was ornamental teapots, then it was kitchen utensils...you know wooden spoons, whisks, salad servers, cheese graters...that sort of thing."

"How ridiculous," Midge said. "No, actually, not ridiculous...just different and that's okay. From now on I'm not going to criticise anyone for being different."

"Nor me," Marty said. "In fact, we owe Pinky a big thank you. How did you talk him into sharing his collection?"

"Well, that was easy. Until the new banking system's up and running I'm supposed to keep a record of what rent and service charge people owe me. I told him if he gave me a regular supply of chocolate, I'd falsify his records and his bill would be zero. Of course he immediately agreed."

"Woo-hoo! You're a cool babe," Marty said. He leaned over and raised his hand above his head. "High-five, sister!"

Ellie lifted her hand to meet it, and much to everyone's amusement, their open palms slapped together perfectly. She divided the bar into four equal pieces.

Slowly, Scott swirled the chocolate around his mouth allowing the precious, gooey treasure to cover every part of his tongue. Lips closed, taste buds sizzled and saliva glands exploded with gratitude. He tipped his head back and closed his eyes. "I hate the silence in this house," he said eventually, "but that was different."

"There's plenty more where that came from," Ellie said.

"Are there ghosts in this old place?" Marty said.

"Ghosts? No. Only memories. Why do you ask?"

"Well, I don't mean to freak anyone out, but memories don't usually do the vacuuming. Someone cleaned this place for you today and you didn't see who it was?"

"No. I didn't."

"And what about the voices? I'm sorry, dude, but it sounds like ghosts to me."

Scott had to admit the evidence did point in a ghostly direction, but this wasn't a conversation he wanted to get into. "Well, yes, you're right, it does sound like a ghost, but…but…this house has been in my family for years, it belonged to my mum's mum and to her mum before that so, even if there is a ghost, which is unlikely, then it's bound to be a friendly one because it'll be a relative."

"Perhaps I could share a room with someone?" Midge said with a shudder. "Did your mum ever mention anything about ghosts or spooky goings-on?

I mean she'd be the one to know, she must know about its history."

"No, she didn't," Scott said, "she never mentioned anything about ghosts, but to be honest, we never had those kinds of conversations."

"No great granddad buried under the patio, or an old aunt bricked up behind a wall?"

"No, not that I'm aware of."

"There are lots of things I wish I'd asked my mum and dad," Ellie said, "but now they're gone, it's too late."

"Yes, I know what you mean, when my mum..." Scott stopped himself mid-sentence.

"When your mum vanished, was that what you were about to say?"

"Yeah...sort of..."

"Hey, it's okay, I feel the same too," Marty said. "You know, when I look back at what happened, I feel really bad. If I could turn back the clock I'd do things differently."

"What do you mean?" Midge said.

"Well, the week before Purple Monday I was really angry with my folks. I was fed up with us always moving around and I hated them for making me leave San Francisco. The last time I spoke to them we had a major bust-up."

"Oh, I see."

In a sudden burst of movement, Marty lifted his hands to his face to cover a sneeze. By the time he'd opened his eyes, the whole place had been plunged into darkness. "Oh hell, I'm blind!" he shouted.

The others dissolved into uncontrollable hysterics.

"No," Midge said, doubled up, "there's been a power cut."

"Oh, phew-wee!" Marty said.

Scott moved with precision, through the blackout, to a cupboard where he kept an array of candles. Slowly, he dotted saucers and eggcups around the kitchen and the room filled with a tangle of flickering shadows. Two grand, antique candlesticks made from twisted brass were given centre stage on the table. "These belonged to my grandma," he said, striking another match. "I thought we wouldn't need to use them, I thought they'd sorted out the electricity supply."

"Yes, so did I. But they did warn us this might happen occasionally," Ellie said.

Midge got up from the oak bench, walked around the table and placed a hand on Marty's shoulder. "Even if you had gone blind it wouldn't have been the end of the line. You've got us now and we'd look after you. That's what friends do." She walked a bit further. "And Scott, just imagine, when we find this strange garden we'll find your mum, your dad and your brother and sister. I mean, think about it, if the Purple managed to transport Ellie's mum and dad to that place then I don't see any reason why everyone else's family won't be there, too. We'll find them, don't you worry."

Scott stared into space. He grunted before looking Midge directly in the eye. "It's not that simple."

"What do you mean?" Midge said. "I know we don't know for sure what this is all about, but you have to admit we're onto something. We must be. I mean look."

She pointed at the four flowers, sitting in a vase, in the middle of the table.

Scott reached over and lifted one out. He looked at the rose for a few seconds before speaking. "My mum wasn't taken by the Purple...she died six months before it came."

"Oh," Midge said. She grabbed his hand and squeezed it tightly.

Scott sat down at the table.

Midge sat down next to him. "I'm really sorry."

Reassured by the presence of longed-for-friends and intoxicated by candlelight, Scott dropped his guard. "It was last summer...school sports day...maybe you remember it was really hot last July. My mum and brother came to watch and at some point during the afternoon my mum didn't feel well. She felt dizzy and had to sit down. Charlie, my brother, wanted to take her to the hospital, but I was running in the final of the eight hundred meters and so I persuaded them to stay. During the race she died of a brain haemorrhage. As I crossed the finish line an ambulance came screeching up onto the field and took her away. That was it. I never saw her again."

Marty shuffled along the bench. "Man, that's a nightmare."

Scott rubbed his moist eyes. "I keep thinking to myself that I should have let them go. I shouldn't have asked them to stay. I wanted my mum to see me running. I knew I had a good chance of coming first and I wanted her to see me win. If I hadn't insisted on them staying, then perhaps Charlie could have taken her to the hospital and she would have been okay. I wish I could go back in time and change things. I hate myself for doing what I did."

"It wasn't your fault," Ellie said, passing a tissue she'd found in her bag. "You mustn't blame yourself."

"You didn't do anything wrong, man," Marty said.

"When it's our time to go, then it's our time to go," Midge said. "Well, at least, that's what I've heard people say."

"But how do we know that for sure? How do we know that's true? I keep thinking, what if, all the time. What if she'd gone to see a doctor? What if I hadn't got into the final race? What if I hadn't asked her to stay? What if, what if, what if?"

"Have a good cry," Midge said, "crying definitely helps, but you should try to think about all the…um…good things…in your life. It might make you feel better."

Scott blew his nose then wiped his face on his sleeve. "Mm, good things, I'm sure there's lots of good things…can't think of anything at the moment though." He stared silently at the ceiling.

"Well…for a start…you've got some new friends," Midge said. "Also…you've got lovely hair…and…what was it? Oh yes, your arms and legs work and you're not blind!"

Scott cracked a smile through the tears. "Yeah, you're right, I'm definitely not blind and my arms and legs are in full working order." He pushed his fringe back. "This could definitely do with cutting."

"Well, that's handy, because I could do with some heads to practice on. You don't have lice or dandruff, do you?" Marty said.

Scott smiled again, desperate to pull himself together.

"Look!" Ellie said excitedly. "The storm's over."

Scott stood up, crossed the kitchen and threw the door open. The room exploded with a wet, woody smell and the noise of a hundred early birds. Frank purred his approval, performed an impressive dismount from the table and vanished into the misty morning.

Above the capital the heavy cloud cover had fractured, allowing the first faint patches of murky light to shine through. Scott checked his watch: four thirty. Daybreak had at long last arrived, bringing with it twenty-four hours of fresh hope and new possibilities. He stuffed the snotty tissue into his pocket. "Let's go onto the roof and watch the sunrise."

"That's an excellent idea," Midge said, reaching for a candlestick.

Minutes later, in the top attic room, Scott opened a small sash window and led everyone out onto a flat, leaded rooftop. Leaning against a chimneystack, far enough from the edge to be safe, but close enough to feel a tingle, he gazed in silence toward the horizon, where the sun had begun its triumphant rebirth. As the clouds continued to clear, a transparent line of fire sliced its way through the dawn, causing the wet roof tiles to shimmer like sheets of gold. As the minutes passed the intensity of colour grew, until the surrounding treetops ignited, each leaf flickering like a tiny flame. Thankfully, the brilliant rays warmed up his tired face and calmed down his fears. They reminded him that, no matter how long and bleak the night may be, light does eventually return.

Way above, the remaining storm clouds had lifted and separated, transforming into the shape of something that closely resembled an angel in flight; its colossal wingspan covering the length and breadth of the city. The left hand held what looked like a long, thin trumpet and the right arm stretched forwards, the index finger clearly visible and pointing north.

"That way to Scotland?" all four of them said at exactly the same time.

~ Eighteen ~

Is There Anybody There?

Eight-thirty in the morning and the top deck of the bus heaved with teenage commuters.

"What are nits?" Ellie held the book to her chest and waited for Marty's response.

"Nits are lice eggs; they look like tiny brown dots. Lice lay their eggs on the hair shaft close to the scalp, where the temperature is perfect for keeping them warm."

"Ooh yes! Well done!" Ellie said. "You gave me more than I needed for that question."

"I still can't believe I got mobbed at the bus stop," Midge said.

Ellie put the book in her lap and yawned. "See, I told you that you were good on the telly."

"I don't know why you doubted it," Marty said.

Midge turned her head quickly from side to side, peering at each shoulder. "Doubt…I'm fed up with him."

"You're fed up with who?" Ellie said.

"Nothing. Ignore me," Midge said.

"They need to get the bus numbers sorted out," Marty said. "Are we sure this one's taking us to the West End?"

"I haven't got a clue," Ellie said, "but if the driver doesn't slow down she'll take us to an early grave."

"I'm absolutely knackered," Midge said, laughing. "I could easily die from a lack of sleep."

"You know it all," Ellie said, "but if you want me to carry on, then I will."

Marty shook his head. "No, I think I'll be okay, and thanks for testing me."

"Could I have your autograph, please?" The stranger's voice belonged to a young boy sporting a yellow Mohican, standing in the aisle holding a pen and paper. The bus screeched around another corner and he stretched out his arms, much like a surfer on the crest of a wave.

"Are you talking to me?" Midge said.

"I hope your nose is all right now," he said.

"Yes, it's fine, thanks."

"Could you write it to Jack love from Midge? I want to show it to my mates at the office."

Midge took the pen and paper from the boy and did a quick scribble. "You'd better get back to your seat."

"If you survive this journey," Ellie said, "do you think you're gonna enjoy your new life as a celebrity?"

"Absolutely!" Midge said.

The bus came to an abrupt and final halt in Piccadilly Circus, the scene of Marty's almost-fatal accident the day before. The remaining passengers staggered out onto the street.

"I'm going to have to get a cab from here, otherwise I'll be late again," Midge said.

"Okay, we'll leave you to sign autographs! See you later!" Ellie said.

"Bye lovely new friends!" Midge screamed through the crowd.

Ellie and Marty waved goodbye and headed for Regent Street.

"It's great that we're not far from each other," Ellie said. "Can we meet for lunch if I'm back from Mrs Mackay's in time?"

"I doubt it. It's non-stop in the salon. We get lots of short breaks, but I haven't got a clue when they'll be."

"Oh, okay. Well, good luck today." She turned to leave, then turned back. "I hope I don't sound like a nag, but you must tell someone about your crash, you may have a concussion…it might be a good idea if you took things easy."

"Sure, sure," Marty said.

Ellie put her arms around Marty and gave him an enormous squeeze. "You need hug practice," she said.

~ooOoo~

After the others had left for work, Scott cleared away the breakfast things and did a quick tidy up. He switched off his mobile phone then sat cross-legged in the middle of the lounge. He didn't know how this would work, or even if it would work. He shuffled and fidgeted. He placed his hands on his knees, palms upwards. He took a slow, deep breath.

"Right, here goes," he said out loud. He closed his eyes.

A minute or so passed, but nothing happened. He opened an eye, had a quick look around the room, and then closed it. He waited, but no voices: just the ticking of the clock and distant traffic.

"Is there anybody there?" he whispered.

Immediately, the phone in the hallway rang. Scott leapt up and bolted out of the lounge. The phone continued to ring, so he reached out a shaking hand and picked it up. "Hello."

"Hello," a voice said, "is that Scott, as in Scott's Scooters? I got your number from the Mum Police, my motorbike has broken down and I need some help."

"Oh...you're a customer," Scott said.

The voice continued, "I really hope you can help me, you see I've been up all night working and I'm desperate to get home. I'm shattered and my animals will be wondering where I am."

"I'm a bit busy to be honest...where are you?"

"I'm on Waterloo Road, outside the station."

"Mmm...yeah...I suppose I can do that."

"Oh, you are a honey, thank you. I'm wearing black leathers and I've got short silver hair, but if you can't see me just shout for June and I'll find you."

"June, give me fifteen...I'll be with you."

It took Scott longer than expected to get to Waterloo Station because a fallen lamppost had blocked Clapham High Street. According to an upset pedestrian, an out-of-control bus had knocked it over twenty minutes earlier.

"Sorry I'm late," Scott said, jumping out of his van, "you must be June."

"Oh, sugar, you don't need to apologise, I'm just glad you can help me." June's green eyes flashed like polished emeralds. "I can't believe I've broken down, I've been around the world on this bike and never had a problem. Apart from the odd flat tyre in India, but that's to be expected when you're in and out of potholes, don't you think?"

"I suppose so, but I've never been to India so I wouldn't really know," Scott said.

"Oh, well, you should definitely take a trip there sometime; it's a magical place, so much to be inspired by."

Scott looked up from the engine. "Sorry to be the voice of doom, but it's a big job...I'm going to have to take it back to the workshop."

"Oh well, that's okay. I'll have to get the tube into work this evening and maybe Babs will let me drive home in the Smart Car tomorrow morning. I work for the Tucking-In-Service."

"I'll do my best to get it fixed within twenty-four hours."

"That would be great, but don't worry if you can't...I'll survive."

Once the bike had been safely loaded into the van, the two of them jumped onto the front seat.

"Where do you live? I'll drive you straight home, you must be exhausted."

"In Balham...and thanks...you're a star."

The van coasted along Waterloo Road. June started whistling, and Scott found the urge to join in irresistible.

~ Nineteen ~

The Man who Dropped Bombs

Marty turned the corner into South Molton Street and found it much busier than usual.

A few yards ahead of him, directly outside the salon, stood a large group of people. Many of them held banners and placards, which read POWER FOR PROTECTION! and STOP WASTING OUR ELECTRICITY!

Marty pushed past the demonstrators and into the salon. Miss Renee stood by the reception desk shaking her worried-looking head.

"What's going on?" he enquired.

Before she could reply, Mr Rupert came bounding around the corner. "We're witnessing the start of a hairdressing backlash!" he boomed.

"What? I mean, why? Sorry, I mean, I don't understand what you're talking about."

"Well, rascal, let me explain," Mr Rupert shouted, "this was handed to me this morning when I arrived to open the salon."

The old man pulled a letter from his back pocket and waved it in the air. Several more staff members came through the door: the reception area now a sea of concerned faces. Marty took the paper, smoothed away the creases, and read it out loud.

"The Power for Protection Movement is mounting a campaign to ensure we take the appropriate steps to protect ourselves.

We have evidence to prove that the Purple is about to return.

Our experts have devised a plan that will undoubtedly save all our lives.

Weapons capable of creating massive explosions are to be constructed.

In order to work effectively, these weapons will require massive amounts of power. Therefore, The Power for Protection Movement recommends that all wasteful use of electricity be immediately outlawed.

The Power for Protection Movement considers hairdressing salons to be an unnecessary drain on our precious resources of energy.

We will not rest until each and every one is shut down.

Voluntarily closing your business, as soon as possible, will prevent any hostility in the not-too-distant future.

For all our sakes, we implore you to think about this carefully and do the right thing.

Yours, in solidarity, The Power for Protection Movement."

A deathly quiet engulfed the reception area.

Marty turned to stare out the large front window. His eyes locked with the demonstrators and they began to shout, "WE DON'T CARE ABOUT HAIR!

WE DON'T CARE ABOUT HAIR! WE DON'T CARE ABOUT HAIR!"

Thankfully, the friendly ring of the telephone broke the hypnotising, rhythmic spell of their chanting. Andrea's hand hovered above the receiver.

"Well, go on, pick it up!" an unusually grumpy Mr Rupert shouted.

The receptionist looked flustered, but did as requested. Marty and all the salon staff waited with bated breath.

"Good morning, Renee and Rupert's Salon and Training Academy, this is Andrea speaking, how can I help you?" Andrea sung, the words *help you* shooting up to a higher key.

Andrea scratched her scalp with her pen until it became caught in her heavily highlighted fringe. She struggled to release it but, the more she struggled, the more it became impossibly entangled. When eventually forced to flick through the appointment book, she had no choice but to abandon the stupid thing and leave it dangling in front of her face.

"No, you'll need to get it permed, Mrs Kipper. The Curly-Wurly Poodle definitely requires a perm; it won't work on straight hair. Could you hold the line for one moment, please, Mrs Kipper, while I check to see when Miss Valerie has a free appointment." Andrea held her hand tightly over the mouthpiece and stared out at the crowd. "It's Mrs Kipper," she said with a face full of concern. "She wants to book in for The Curly-Wurly Poodle next week!"

Mr Rupert looked irritated. "Well, that's perfectly normal, after all, we are a hairdressing salon, aren't we?"

"Aren't...we...closing down?" Andrea said.

"We most certainly are not closing down!" Mr Rupert screamed. "Miss Andrea, please go ahead and book the appointment and let's all get on with our business. I'm calling a staff meeting at lunchtime, where there will be an opportunity for us to have an honest and open discussion about this ludicrous situation. And just for the record, I don't believe a word of this badly written letter. If the so-called Power for Protection Movement had any evidence to prove that the Purple was about to return, then I think they would have provided it, don't you?"

The reception area remained silent.

Mr Rupert marched over to the front door and poked his head out. "Where's your bloody evidence!" he roared. "Show me your evidence!"

The protesters completely ignored him.

"Mr Marty, meet me in my office in two minutes," Mr Rupert said, coming back inside. "And someone get me a pair of scissors...I'm going to have to give Andrea a fringe trim."

Two minutes later, and the door to the office had been firmly closed.

"I'm absolutely furious!" Mr Rupert yelled.

Marty watched in astonishment as the old man continued to whack a cushion with a tennis racket.

"Lion taming exercises!" Mr Rupert shouted through a cloud of dust and hair clippings. "Do you want a go, rascal?" He swiped the racket through the air returning an invisible backhand.

"Oh…no…to be honest, I'm feeling okay today."

"Are you?" Mr Rupert boomed. "Are you sure? This helps to release the anger you know." THUD! "Right, that'll do for now." Mr Rupert threw the racket onto the desk then collapsed in his swivel chair. He took a few breaths. "I knew it wouldn't last forever, rascal."

Marty sat quietly, waiting for Mr Rupert to continue.

"The Purple changed my life. I know this isn't what you want to hear, rascal, because you must be missing your mother and father, but I'm going to be honest with you…I'm glad it came. I'm old. I'm eighty-four years old. Five months ago I was struggling to get about, my arthritis was playing up and I was dead beat, but the Purple changed all that. It gave me a new lease of life. I've been feeling full of fun and free from pain. I've been feeling like my old self and loving every minute. When you get old, people ignore you, you suddenly become invisible. Nobody asks for your opinion or advice anymore and it hurts. You're seen as a nuisance. Not that long ago someone called me a stupid, old fart."

"I'm sorry."

"Oh, rascal, you don't need to give me your pity. I'm being selfish, after all, I've had my life, it's just that it went so quickly and I can't believe it's nearly over." He shoved a couple of fingers under his wig. "Don't half make your head itch, these things! Do you want to hear a story?"

"Sure, why not."

"It may surprise you to know, rascal, that years ago, during the Second World War, I was a pilot and I flew Lancaster Bombers. One night, whilst returning from a bombing raid, we were shot down over fields in France."

Marty sat with his mouth wide open.

"Out of the seven crew on board I was the only one who survived, but in the crash, amongst other injuries, I broke every bone in this hand." Mr Rupert held up his left hand before continuing. "France was occupied by the enemy in those days, but miraculously I was rescued by a compassionate farmer and his family. They managed to get me some medical treatment before hiding me in their cellar. However, despite their brave efforts I was eventually captured and taken hostage. For a year I was a prisoner of war and it was the worst twelve months of my life, but against all the odds, I survived."

The same, haunted look that Marty had witnessed yesterday returned to Mr Rupert's eyes.

After a prolonged moment lost in the past, the ex-war pilot continued. "When the war was finally over I came home a different person. I knew life wouldn't last forever and I was determined to do something meaningful with my time. I wanted to do something beautiful. I wanted to spread joy and happiness. Don't ever let anyone try to convince you that there is excitement in war. There isn't. There is only pain, loss and misery. And so, I became a hairdresser. Something I had always secretly wanted to do. People laughed at me. They thought it was ridiculous. From hero to hairdo, they mocked, how absurd, they said! But I'll tell you what's absurd: dropping bombs on innocent people! That's the most absurd thing ever! Over the years my business grew and I took great delight in giving pleasure to people, but as time progressed I began to experience trouble with my hand. Arthritis had set in where the bones had been broken, and eventually, I was unable to skilfully wield a pair of scissors like I used to. I had no choice but to bow out gracefully even though it was the last thing I wanted to do."

Marty seized the moment to speak. "Man! I had no idea you were a pilot in the war, that's an awesome tale, why don't people know that about you?"

Mr Rupert shrugged his shoulders. "Why would people know? It was a long time ago, and to be honest, I don't care to talk about it that much. Sadly, most of you kids think us old farts have always been ancient, decrepit and useless, but actually we've done a million and one fascinating things with our lives. We were once kids ourselves, you know! We went to school, we worried about exams, tried to make good career decisions and get jobs. If we were lucky we fell in love, got married and had children. We watched our parents grow old and sick and we said goodbye to loved ones. We went on holidays, celebrated birthdays, laughed at silly jokes and sometimes we cried ourselves to sleep. We kept on going through the best of times and the worst of times. On lots of occasions we got it right and sometimes we got it dreadfully wrong. For me, rascal, it has been a long and wonderful journey. A journey filled with an abundance of highs and lows and one that I wouldn't have missed for all the tea in China. I hope you will be as lucky as I have been and get to know what it feels like to have eighty-four years of memories. Can you imagine that, rascal, eighty-four years of memories?"

With only fifteen years behind him, Marty wasn't sure he could imagine that. He sat motionless.

"So, that's me and my life in a nutshell, rascal, and perhaps that story might help you to understand why I'm so grateful to the Purple…for all it has given me. For the past five months my body has been free from pain and filled with energy, and I've been able to return to the life and work I love."

Marty nodded his head. "I see."

"And there's more, rascal. The other thing I liked about this Purple mischief was the way it changed everyone's behaviour. It wasn't an enormous change; it was quite subtle. Did you notice it?"

"No. I don't think so…"

"We were suddenly nice to each other, rascal! People were friendly! I felt safe walking home at night. Passers-by stopped and chatted, folk came rushing to help if there was a problem. It's been a breath of fresh air, don't you think? But I always suspected this change wouldn't last forever and I'm annoyed with myself for being naive enough to hope it would." Mr Rupert cleared his throat. "I think the Purple cast some kind of spell across the planet, but I now believe this spell is wearing off."

"Mr Rupert, what are you saying?"

"Well, rascal, it was yesterday morning when I first began to suspect something was happening, because I woke up with a familiar pain in my left hand...and today it's getting worse. For the first time in five months, the aches and pains are back. My body's slowing down again. My youthful energy is fading. I can feel it slipping away."

"But you could be wrong? It may just be a passing sickness. Perhaps you haven't been getting enough sleep?"

"I admire your optimism, rascal, but unfortunately there's something else. As I was coming into work on the tube yesterday morning, nursing my painful hand, I couldn't help noticing a young girl stealing a handbag that didn't belong to her. Although it wasn't the crime of the century, it proved to me that this wonderful period of peace is coming to an end."

Marty sat speechless. He thought back over the past five months. Maybe Mr Rupert was on to something. Maybe it was true. Until yesterday, the people of London, and everywhere else for that matter, had been unbelievably selfless.

"Then, later in the day," Mr Rupert continued, "your spat with Miss Jive provided more evidence that things are turning sour. And then today I lost my temper with Andrea. I shouted at her and made her look foolish in front of her colleagues. Disappointing, rascal, very disappointing. Yes, slowly but surely, things seem to be returning to the way they were before Purple Monday. We're getting selfish again. We're all starting to squabble and fall out. There is no doubt about it, the magical purple spell is wearing off and I fear the situation can only get worse."

"This is unreal! What can we do? There must be something!"

"We need to take immediate action, rascal! Apologies and flowers might remedy our own poor behaviour, but my real concerns don't lie with the likes of us, they lie with that lot outside."

"You mean The Power for Protection Movement?"

"Exactly. Once I realized the spell was wearing off, I had a premonition that things would soon start to spiral out of control. I knew it wouldn't be long before someone had the bright idea to spend all of our money on weapons, some silly nincompoop was bound to come up with that plan; they always do. But mark my words, rascal...we're headed for big troubles. If The Power for Protection Movement succeeds in blowing the ozone layer apart they'll kill us all!"

The phone interrupted Mr Rupert.

"Hello, Mr Rupert's office, Mr Rupert speaking...what...oh good grief...thanks...I'll be up in a minute." Mr Rupert untied his kerchief and dabbed his forehead. "That was Miss Renee, trouble is definitely brewing. Apparently, our main competitors up the road, Sweet Talking Snips, have just had their front window smashed in. I have a feeling things are about to get nasty."

Marty shared the feeling.

"If we give in to these people's demands, rascal, we're sunk. Their intention is to scare us, but we will stand firm. In response to a crisis it's always a good idea to remain focused on normal, everyday routines, and besides," he laughed, "I can't for the life of me decide what our immediate action should be. At this moment in time I don't have a plan, but I'm sure I'll think of something." He reached his shaky hands into his desk drawer and lifted out a large pile of Midsummer Sunset leaflets. "Here we are, rascal, what do you think of these? I had them printed last night."

Yesterday seemed ages ago. Marty took one of the flyers and stared at it. "I've got something to tell you," he said.

After listening to every word, Mr Rupert's eyes had opened wider than saucers. "The fact that all four of you came back with an almost identical rose suggests to me that this garden could really exist!"

Marty nodded his head in agreement. "If we can find the garden...then...perhaps...I'll find my mum and dad. But not only that, if we discover the secrets of the Purple, maybe you'll be able to get rid of those aches and pains forever and we'll stop those people outside from destroying the ozone layer."

"Bull's eye, rascal!" Mr Rupert said, grinning. "I told you I'd think of something!"

"Apparently, this is like a jigsaw. My friend Midge says that the four of us each hold a piece of the puzzle, and when the pieces are put together we'll see the whole picture. But even though I've tried and tried to think what my piece is, I can't work it out."

Mr Rupert sat back in his chair, stroked his wig, and then leapt up. "I've got it, rascal! Often we humans have a habit of overcomplicating a problem, don't you think? Sometimes we're so busy searching the horizon we fail to see what's in front of us. I think what you're looking for could be directly under your nose!"

Marty stared around the room. "No, I don't see it."

"It's in your hand, rascal! It's printed on that leaflet in your hand. It's The Midsummer Sunset!" Without waiting for a response, Mr Rupert dashed over to the shelves. "My trusty Encyclopaedia Britannica. I know these things are old fashioned, but they still do the job." After banging the book down onto the desk, he flicked through its pages. "Here it is, rascal...Midsummer's Eve...June 24th. An ancient fire festival celebrating the middle of summer, when the veil between this world and the next is said to be thin, and when powerful forces are at hand. I'll bet everything I own, including my wig and false teeth, that you and your friends need to be in that garden on Midsummer's Eve at the very moment the sun is setting."

An electric current zipped through Marty's body. Had Mr Rupert cracked it? Creating that hairstyle had been a supernatural experience. The idea had come from nowhere...not to mention the ability. It *must* have been a message sent from a greater force. The Midsummer Sunset *had* to be his piece of the puzzle.

Mr Rupert stared down at his watch. "Today is Tuesday...it's June 23rd, rascal! You and your friends don't have much time!"

~ Twenty ~

The Winds of Change

After her goodbye hug with Marty, Ellie went straight to Great Marlborough Street.

The front door of the office was ajar so she raced upstairs, half expecting to come face to face with a burglar.

"Morning!" Ping said, busy licking an envelope.

Ellie blinked several times. "Are my eyes deceiving me? Is this a vision I see?"

"Ha-ha," Ping said, "this glue tastes awful, and no, it's not a vision…it's me. I told you yesterday I'd be on time today."

"I never doubted it for a moment."

"Liar, liar, pants on fire," Ping replied.

"Well, okay, I did sort of doubt it. How come you're here so early? Has something happened?"

"Not yet, but I'm a bit worried that it might do."

Ellie threw her bag on the desk. "Shall I make us both a hot chocolate?"

"You could do."

Ellie busied herself in the staffroom heating two mugs of milk. "It says three heaped teaspoons on the jar…but it tastes much better with seven."

Moments later, Ping came to join her; she leaned against the wall and bit a fingernail.

Desperate to lift the mood, Ellie opened the treasure cupboard and took out the box of after-dinner chocolate mints. "When we've finished these perhaps we could make a start on that chocolate Santa?"

"Maybe," Ping said.

"Okay," Ellie said, "talk to me."

"Well, I couldn't sleep last night. I've been up since five. I've got all this stuff spinning round inside my head. What's going to happen to me if you and your new mates find everyone?"

Ellie lost count of the spoonfuls. "I don't know. I'm not sure." She put five more into each mug, just to be on the safe side.

"It's okay for you lot, you want your mums and dads back."

Ellie stirred the drinks and dropped the teaspoon into the sink before turning to face her friend. "Maybe you could come and live with us? My dad could talk to the people at the care home and tell them you're my friend."

Ping looked cross. "But it doesn't work like that. Your mum and dad would have to apply to be foster parents and then fill out loads of forms and go for interviews. Everything would take ages. And even then, after all that, they probably wouldn't get to choose me. It's not like buying a kitten you know. There's no guarantee of anything."

Ellie took a sip of the chocolate and even though it burnt her tongue she didn't make a sound. The pair of them stared at their drinks.

"Yeah, you're absolutely right," Ellie said, breaking the uncomfortable silence. "There's no guarantee of anything…and that includes everything."

"What?"

"Well, there's no guarantee that we're going to find anyone, is there? I had a dream about a garden, I picked a flower, and I woke up with it in my hand. So what?"

"Mmm, yeah, that's true, but there's a lot more to it than that. The others think they dreamt about the same place, and you're convinced you saw your parents there. And what about that photo? The one at Mrs Mackay's."

"Okay, I have to admit there are some weird coincidences, and the truth is, I can't ignore them. I need to find out what's going on. I mean…how can so many people just vanish? How can it be that my mum and dad were here one minute then gone the next? It doesn't make sense. I need to know what happened to everyone, don't you?"

"Yeah, I suppose." Ping took a mouthful of chocolate and licked her lips. "Look, I'm not the world's biggest parent-hater, you know. I do miss my dad and my mum. But having them come back isn't going to make things right – not for me. It doesn't feel very nice, you know, when your mum deserts you and your dad gives you away because he says he can't cope." Her bottom lip started to tremble. She squeezed her hands around the mug.

Ellie reached up into the cupboard and took out the chocolate Santa. She tore off the silver foil then passed it to Ping. "Eat the whole thing. Go on, it's all yours."

Ping blinked back the tears and put her mug down. "Are you sure?"

"Yes, positive."

Ping held the chocolate Santa in her hands for a few seconds before slowly lifting it to her mouth. With her hand cupped under her chin to catch the crumbs, she bit off an ear. Ellie stood by, trying not to salivate. When Ping eventually opened her eyes, her chocolate-coated lips had lifted to a smile. She held out the remains of Santa's legs. "These are for you."

"Aww, thanks," Ellie said, and she licked them all over before Ping changed her mind.

Last week, when the internet flashed to life for an hour, Ellie did a search on chocolate and discovered it releases a chemical called serotonin into the brain. Serotonin makes people feel happy, the report said, and that's why it can be addictive. Ellie figured this must be the reason why so many people wanted to get their hands on some. Awash with serotonin, the girls went back into the office and put their feet up.

"I won't desert you. Never. Ever. No matter what happens. Even if tomorrow, everything goes back to normal, I'll come and find you. I'll do everything I can to help you, to make sure you're all right."

"Do you promise? Totally, completely and absolutely?"

"Chocolate Girl Makes Promise With Hand On Heart," Ellie said.

"That's the best headline so far," Ping said. "You'd better get going."

"Get going"?

"To Mrs Mackay's. Go and ask her about that photograph. I know that's what you're dying to do."

Ellie jumped up and grabbed her bag. "Thanks, you're a friend in a million."

"I know," Ping said. "I'll make a start on those after-dinner mints, shall I?"

After standing outside the office for several minutes, Ellie became restless waiting for a taxi. She raced around the corner into Argyll Street and came face to face with two boys arguing outside the London Palladium. One of them punched the other, and he fell backwards down the steps.

Instead of stopping to help, Ellie continued running. "Taxi!"

Thankfully, the driver spotted her in his rear-view mirror. "Where to, love?"

"Drayton Gardens, please, off the Fulham Road, as quick as you can."

"Hop in."

The taxi did a U-turn and drove directly past the boy lying on the ground. "Lovely day, isn't it?" the driver said.

"Err, yeah, I suppose it is."

Without warning the taxi came to a screaming halt, and Ellie flew forwards.

"You stupid idiot!" the driver screamed. "Can't you see where you're going?"

The cyclist picked up his bike then banged his bleeding hand onto the bonnet of the taxi. "It wasn't my fault!" he yelled back. "You should learn to drive properly. You could have killed me."

"Shame I didn't! You cyclists should be banned from the roads!"

Ellie lifted herself onto her seat and fastened her seatbelt. The driver mumbled some expletives before putting his foot down. As they sped away, she turned back to stare at the carnage.

The taxi zoomed west along Oxford Street, past a group of people waving banners and placards outside Bond Street Station. If they hadn't been going so fast, she might have been able to read what they said.

At Marble Arch, the site of a confusing one-way system, the bullyboy cab driver made mincemeat of several more cyclists. The aggressive driving continued through Hyde Park, and Ellie struggled to shake off a horrible, sinking feeling.

When the taxi pulled up outside Mrs Mackay's, Ellie threw the driver a handful of coins, jumped out of the cab and leapt up the steps. She had a key to Drayton Court but wisely decided it would be polite to ring the bell and wait. One quick press would have been sufficient, but she couldn't resist holding her finger on the button until she got a reply.

"Hello there," a familiar Scottish voice said.

"Hello, Mrs Mackay, it's Ellie, could you buzz me in, I need to talk to you about something."

"Of course, dear, come on in."

The door buzzed then clicked. An air of calm, a faint whiff of mothballs and Mrs Mackay greeted her in the hallway.

As well as the usual chirpy smile, tartan skirt and cream blouse, the old lady wore a double string of pearls and earrings to match. "Is there something wrong, dear? You look concerned. I hope you're not here with bad news. Do you need this place back already?"

Ellie attempted a smile. "No, it's nothing like that; you can stay here as long as you need to. Don't worry about moving." Mrs Mackay looked relieved and the two of them went inside. "I'm not here about the flat; I've come about something completely different."

"Would you like a nice, wee, cup of tea?"

Here we go again with the cups of tea, Ellie thought. Why do old people drink so much of it?

"You make yourself comfortable in the lounge, dear, and I'll pop the kettle on."

Ellie wandered into the lounge, threw herself onto the sofa for five seconds then got straight up. "I've come about that picture…the photograph I saw here yesterday."

Boiling water in a noisy kettle was drowning out her voice, so she went into the kitchen.

"What was that, dear? Did you say something about a picture?" Mrs Mackay had already wheeled out an ancient, faux-brass tea trolley.

"Yes, the photograph. The one I found on the floor in your old place. I know this is going to sound ridiculous, but the girl in it looks like me."

Mrs Mackay began opening several Tupperware containers. "Now, would you like a piece of fruitcake or perhaps a scone? Or maybe both?"

Ellie tutted and rolled her eyes then immediately regretted her behaviour. “That would be lovely,” she said, “both would be great.”

“Clotted cream or butter, dear?”

“Pardon?”

“On your scone, clotted cream or butter?”

“Oh, err, I don’t mind. Clotted cream.”

“Raspberry or strawberry jam?”

“Strawberry, please. But don’t open a jar especially. I’ll have anything.”

“Oh no, dear, nothing but the best for you. After all you did for me yesterday, I shall definitely be opening a new jar.”

Mrs Mackay turned her back to Ellie then emptied the kettle’s contents into the teapot and gave it a stir. “Now, where did I put that cosy?”

“It’s there,” Ellie said, pointing to the table.

“Now I had it this morning, maybe I left it in the lounge.”

“No, it’s there,” Ellie said again, only this time much louder.

“Did you say something, dear?”

“Yes, I said it’s there,” she pointed at it again, “didn’t you hear me?”

“No,” Mrs Mackay said, “I didn’t hear you at all…and…I can barely hear you now!” She stood for a second looking bewildered then walked across the room, opened a drawer and took out a hearing aid. She switched it on and fitted it to her right ear, ignoring the high-pitched squeal. “Och! Jolly good, the battery’s still working! Since Purple Monday I’d been enjoying the thrill of almost-perfect hearing, but for some reason, in that teapot-stirring moment, it vanished. Pass those spoons, would you, dear. You did say strawberry, didn't you?"

Ellie didn't reply.

"Don't look so worried, dear, I can hear just fine with this contraption."

"But..."

"It's always best to be like bamboo," Mrs Mackay said.

"Is it?"

"Yes, dear, it is."

Mrs Mackay spooned a large dollop of strawberry jam into a small china dish and then began to arrange the scones. Ellie resisted the urge to demand an explanation. Eventually, after the fruitcake had been sliced, it came. "Of all the plants in the garden, bamboo is one of the strongest, but amazingly, it's also one of the most flexible. If you ever watch it in a storm you'll see what I mean. It can be twisted, bent and pulverised by wind and rain, even hail, but it always bounces back. Once the storm has passed it looks just the same. Very rarely is it flattened."

"Oh, I see what you mean," Ellie said. She watched Mrs Mackay load all the cakes and fancies onto the trolley. "I do feel strong, I think, but I'm not sure I can be flexible forever. I have an awful feeling something's happening. Things seem to be changing."

"Nothing stays the same," Mrs Mackay said, "the winds of change never stop blowing."

Ellie stared across the kitchen, towards the fridge, and all-of-a-sudden, there it was, that photograph, stuck to the door with a magnet.

~ Twenty-One ~

Penny's Treasures

Midge strolled along the embankment in a daze, occasionally waving to admirers.

By the time she reached the DMC HQ, she'd created a future filled with fame, money and constant, loving attention from admiring fans. Before passing through the tricky revolving door she slowed her pace down – after all, she didn't want to go tumbling into the reception and make a fool of herself.

Yesterday the place had been deserted, but today people holding clipboards scurried in all directions. Midge walked across the reception, smiling politely at her gawping colleagues. When two curious creeps bumped into each other, she swallowed a laugh.

"Hello, my name's Michelle, but my friends call me Midge."

"Hello, dear," the ginger-haired lady behind the reception desk said, "my name's Eliza, but my friends call me Banana."

The laugh bubbled out. "Oh! Do they! Why's that?"

"Well, dear, I don't think I've got time to tell you just this minute, you're already quarter of an hour late…and Penny's waiting for you."

"Oh," Midge said.

"Top floor, dear, then go straight down the hallway. Her name is on her office door in gold letters, you can't miss it. Good luck."

"Thank you, Banana," Midge said.

"Oh, and one more thing," Banana said, "despite what she might have to say, I thought you were fabulous."

Midge gave a feeble smile in return and headed for the elevator. She'd brought her own glasses with her so, on the ride up, she put them on and double-checked her shirt had been properly tucked into her jeans. She'd fully intended to call in at Opal's stockroom and return the old-lady-style glasses, but that would have to wait.

Midge stared at the gold letters. She knocked. She waited. She knocked again. She waited.

"ENTER!" an impatient voice yelled.

Midge cracked the door and peeked in.

"COME IN! DON'T JUST STAND THERE!"

"Oh, right, sorry," Midge said. She closed the door and shambled across the room.

Penny's floral-print dress, round glasses, flat hairstyle and unusually large gums made her appear like a startled bush baby trapped in a treetop. She had perched herself, hawk-like, on the edge of her desk with a piece of dry toast in one hand. "My stomach's still not good," she muttered.

The window at the back of the office provided an amazing view of the London skyline, and a gigantic oil painting of a much younger-looking Penny rested against the right wall.

"You're twenty minutes late, young lady," Penny said, taking a seat, "and I've got lots to do, so I'm going to get straight to the point."

Midge hadn't been offered a seat so she stood, awkwardly, in the middle of the room and tried to appear relaxed. In the flesh, Penny looked surprisingly small.

"I have been presenting *The Five O'Clock Announcement* from the very beginning, and on every single occasion, I ensured they were delivered professionally and accurately. I'm aware that the entire population of London is watching and that it's vital for us to maintain the proper standards our public have come to expect. Yesterday, you not only made a fool of yourself, but also a fool of our entire organization. You have single-handedly turned the Decision Makers Council into a laughing stock. As head of this group I cannot and will not sit by and allow you to continue. You need to be closely monitored, young lady, and under no circumstances will you ever be allowed to present *The Five O'Clock Announcement* again. Do I make myself clear?"

"Well…actually…I think everyone quite liked what they saw yesterday. I've been stopped and congratulated by loads of people. Yes, I know I got a couple of things wrong…but…with some practice…"

Penny's face flushed hot-tomato red. "The subject is not open for discussion!"

Midge resisted the urge to run out.

"See, I told you. I said you weren't that good," Doubt said.

Oh no, not you, Midge thought. You're all I need. I was about to tell Penny about the autograph-hunting fans…

"I wouldn't bother," Doubt said. "Face facts, you've made a fool of yourself. Maybe that's why everyone wants your autograph? They want The Fool Of London's autograph!"

Midge's head jammed with confusion. Could Doubt be right? She went to speak, but discovered the words had done a runner. Nothing came out. She closed her mouth.

Penny smiled. "As I was saying, you need to be closely monitored, young lady, and in order for me to do this, I've arranged for your desk to be moved up here."

Midge's briefcase slid from her hand and landed on her big toe. Hiding the pain, she stared around the room.

"No, not in here! That would be ridiculous!" Penny snapped, "I do need some privacy you know. No…your desk is through there…in that small adjoining office." Penny frogmarched her across the room and pointed. "That's where you'll be working."

Midge poked her head around the door and saw what looked like a broom cupboard with a window. A desk had been squashed against the wall and on top of it sat a computer, a telephone, a large pile of folders and a spiral-bound notepad and pen.

Penny smiled again. "From now on, you'll be working as my personal assistant."

Hell! Midge thought. "Oh, okay," she heard herself say.

"Now…I'm not the only person around here with lots to do today so bring yourself and that notepad back into my office and I'll give you your orders."

Midge dumped her briefcase in her room, grabbed the pad and pulled a seat up to Penny's desk.

"Our first problem of the day is a big one. That jumbo jet loaded with cocoa powder has been delayed."

"What, no chocolate?" Midge said.

"Yes, that's right, no chocolate."

"Oh dear, people will be disappointed."

"Will you stop talking, young lady, and concentrate on writing!" Midge glanced up to respond, but Penny had swivelled her chair around to admire the city view. "Importing goods by air seems to be hit-and-miss at the moment, so I want you to get on to the Channel Tunnel people. Find out what they've got lined up for us this week. Ask them about oranges and lemons from Spain."

"What about coconuts?"

"What?" Penny said.

"Coconuts," Midge said again. "On the announcement last night I promised everyone coconuts by Friday. People get excited about that sort of thing these days. Will they be arriving?"

Penny snorted and waved her hand in the air. "Not interested. Can't abide them."

"Oh."

"Secondly, there's a group of old people in an old folks' home who've just woken up, apparently they were disturbed out of their protective coma by a silly buffoon looking for his grandma."

"Ahh," Midge said, scribbling frantically, "I wish I had a granny."

"Ahh nothing!" Penny barked. "That's another load of mouths to feed. You'll need to call the Camden Drop-In Centre and get them to deal with it. The information is in one of those files on your desk."

"Right you are," Midge said.

"Thirdly, we need to sort out this ice cream debacle you've created."

"Do we? What ice cream...debacle? How do I spell that?"

Penny groaned then turned her chair to face Midge. "Well, you seem to have conveniently forgotten all about that promise, haven't you? At the end of last night's announcement you told the entire population of London there would be free ice cream. Remember? Scoop Of The Day?"

"Oh yeah...I'd forgotten about that. I got...carried away...you know...in the excitement."

"Well, young lady, someone's got to pay for it. Ice cream doesn't grow on trees you know."

Oh, you don't say, Midge thought.

"If we withdraw the offer of free ice cream all hell will break loose. I'll have to speak to Willie Piles, the head banker from Greedy Pig Savings. We'll need to start taking a chunk of everybody's earnings to pay for things, and if anyone complains, I'll tell them it's your fault."

"From the stars to the gutter in the blink of an eye," Doubt said. "And what's more, when people discover they're going to lose some of their earnings, you'll get the blame!"

Penny hadn't finished. "But before you do anything, I want you to get hold of Brother Lewie the in-house handyman. I want him up here pronto to hang my portrait. I had it commissioned a few years ago when I was considering a move into politics. It's fabulous, isn't it?"

Midge stopped doodling on the pad and glanced at the picture. "Yes, I suppose so."

"That wasn't a question!" Penny shrieked. "It was a statement! Now off you trot."

Once in her office, Midge tried to make the best of what could only be described as an abysmal situation. She closed the door, opened the window and arranged her desk. Out of her briefcase came a collection of multicoloured highlighter pens, her own notepad with a picture of Amy Johnson glued on the cover, a ruler, a proper and rather smart-looking ink fountain pen, a pencil, a stapler, a mini dictionary, some post-it notes, a photo of her mum and dad (in the films, important business people always have photos of loved ones on their desk), two seashells from the beach in Cornwall (last year's summer holiday with Mum) and lastly, but most importantly, a bar of chocolate-covered marzipan. Midge kissed the bar repeatedly, whispered, "Thanks, Ellie," and hid it in the back of the drawer.

She picked up the to-do list. Get hold of Brother Lewie...how do I do that? I can't bear the thought of walking past Penny. I'll try the phone. Without knowing what number to dial she picked up the receiver.

"Hello. How can I direct your call?"

"Hello! Fantastic! Someone's there! Who's that?"

"It's the main switch board of course. How can I direct your call?"

"Oh right, yes, the main switch board. Um, could you put me through to Brother Lewie please...he's the in-house handyman...I think."

"Yes, I know who he is. One moment, please, whilst I connect you."

The phone rang for ages.

"I'm sorry, caller. Brother Lewie doesn't appear to be answering; you'll have to try again later."

"No! Don't go! I need to get hold of him straight away. It's quite important. Do you know where he might be?"

"Look, lady, I work on a switchboard not in a tent with a crystal ball, but if you were to push me for an answer I'd say he's holed up in his office."

"Oh right, thanks, and where is that exactly?"

"Where it's always been. On the ground floor, down the main corridor, at the end."

"Thanks," Midge said, "you've been a great help."

Midge replaced the receiver then braced herself for the walk past Penny. At least this errand would provide the perfect opportunity to pop in and see the old ladies, and if she got a move on, she might even have time for a cup of tea and a caramel wafer. Before leaving the office she searched through her briefcase for Opal's glasses, but they appeared to have vanished.

Thankfully, Penny was busy on the phone. "I'm just not happy about it, Willie. The name Greedy Pig Savings is awful...it...it sends out the wrong message…it could raise people's suspicions. Naming the bank should never have been a competition. I wish I'd stuck to my guns on this one…"

"Sorry to interrupt…hello…it's me…"

"What! What is it?"

"I'm off to find Brother Lewie."

"Just get on with it!" Penny screeched.

Midge closed Penny's office door then pressed her ear against it. After listening to several seconds of indecipherable mumble she gave up and took the lift to the ground floor. The handyman's name intrigued her. Brother Lewie, sounds like a monk; she imagined a wise old man with a circular bald patch dressed in an ankle-length gown holding a pair of stepladders under one arm.

At the end of the main corridor, Midge found one door. I must have gone wrong, she thought. This is Opal's stock room. Never mind, the old ladies will point me in the right direction.

Without bothering to knock, Midge opened the door and jumped in.

"Ay-up, luv, can I help you?" a northern accent said.

"Who are you?"

"I'm Brother Lewie," the northern accent said.

The wheels and cogs in Midge's brain crunched. The shelving that created the secret room had gone. So too had the Christmas tree, the record player, the armchairs, the upside-down tea chests and all the fancy tea-making equipment.

"Oh," she stuttered, "well, I've come to see Pearl and Opal but it doesn't look like they're here. Is this the right room?"

Brother Lewie scratched his nose. "Oh yes, luv, you've definitely got the right room, it's just that..." He started to laugh. "Is this a wind-up?"

"No. What do you mean wind-up?"

"What I mean is...are you having a laugh? Because, as I say, you've got the right room...but you're a bit late."

The wheels and cogs came to a grinding halt. "What?"

"Look, luv, have you been knocked on the head or something? Pearl and Opal used to work here when I first started, but they don't anymore."

"What's happened to them?"

"They retired."

"They retired? When?"

Brother Lewie folded his arms. "Well now...let's see...I reckon it must be about twenty years ago. Yeah, that would be right, twenty years ago. Then, about two years ago, they both died. Poor Opal she was the first one to go, it was her dodgy ticker that did it, and then Pearl quickly followed. I don't know what finished her off. Probably didn't want to stick around without her sister. Thick as thieves those two were. Did you say they were friends of yours? Are you all right, luv? You look like you've seen a ghost."

Midge lowered herself onto the floor. "I feel dizzy."

"You stay down there, luv...I'll get you a glass of water."

"Are you...sure about this?"

"Yes, luv. It's as true as my love for Manchester United Football Club. And let me tell you, luv, I love that team more than my wife."

"Oh right, thank you," Midge croaked. She took the glass and sipped some water. "I'll be all right in a minute."

"Take your time, luv...you don't want to faint."

Midge gazed up at the telephone on the wall. Several posters of Brother Lewie's cherished football team had been dotted around it. The letter Y poked out from underneath one. Midge put the glass down and forced herself onto her feet. Being careful not to tear the poster she gently unstuck one of its corners. Brother Lewie watched with interest as Midge revealed some old and faded graffiti.

REMEMBER STOCK ORDER FRIDAY

"I'm not going mad! I was here yesterday! I saw Pearl...and Opal...she wrote these words...you have to believe me!" Midge picked up the glass of water and steadied her hands.

"If you say so," Brother Lewie said.

Midge chewed the inside of her mouth.

"Maybe you need a cup of tea. Milk and sugar?"

"No. No, thanks," Midge said. "I haven't got time. I've got a whole list of things to do."

"Perhaps you should go home? Maybe take the day off? We've all been under a lot of stress lately."

"I don't need to go home. I'm not..."

"Shall I call the first aid team?"

"No, no, I'm fine…it's…it's. I'm all right. Let's just forget it. It was a joke, stupid one really."

Brother Lewie shook his head like he didn't believe her. "You've got a strange sense of humour."

"You need to hang a picture for Penny," Midge said. "That's why I came down here."

"A picture?"

"Yes, an oil painting, it needs hanging."

"She's a right madam that one. Got ideas above her station. I wouldn't trust her further than I could throw her, and if I did throw her anywhere, it would probably be into a cell at the Tower of London."

Midge managed a smile. "That's not a very nice thing to say."

"No, luv, it's not. But then she's not a very nice person. I remember a story about her that everyone else seems to have forgotten. Years ago, she was arrested on suspicion of helping herself to money that didn't belong to her, and I'm not talking about a couple of quid – I'm talking millions."

"Millions of pounds that didn't belong to her? Whose millions?"

"Her employees, I'm afraid to say. She ran into trouble with lots of her so-called business ventures…in order to save her own skin she stole all the money from the pension fund. Hardly any of the people that worked for her got their pension when they retired, but she always denied the whole thing and somehow managed to get away with it. I hope you haven't left your purse up there, luv."

"I don't have a purse; I keep all my money in my pocket." Midge remembered the bar of chocolate covered marzipan. "I'd better get going."

"Hang about, luv. I'll come with you."

Brother Lewie picked up his toolbox and foldaway stepladders and followed her up the corridor.

Penny pounced on Brother Lewie as soon as they entered her office. Midge sidled into her broom cupboard and closed the door. After a quick chocolate check, she closed her eyes and rested her head on the desk. I'm seeing dead people, she thought.

"Are you asleep on the job?" Penny sniped.

Midge jolted awake and sat upright. "No, I was just thinking."

"Well, don't," Penny screamed, "you might cause yourself an injury." She tipped her head back and roared with laughter. "I'm off to the canteen for a peppermint tea. You've obviously just had your break. I'll be back soon."

"See you later, then."

Midge waited a few minutes before checking to see that the hallway looked clear. Intrigued by Brother Lewie's story, and eager to find out more about this repulsive woman, she held her breath and opened Penny's desk drawer.

"You must be mental," Doubt whispered.

Information about the reopening of the London Eye, a menu and budget sheet for Crumpet On The Run, some diarrhoea medication and a letter, marked private, addressed to Leo the head chef telling him he was going to get the sack, left Midge feeling disappointed.

Systematically, she returned everything to its original place then leaned back in the boss's chair. Penny's snakeskin handbag, sitting under the desk, caught her eye. A brown envelope poked out from an unzipped compartment. The envelope, marked CONFIDENTIAL, hadn't been sealed so Midge swiftly removed its contents. According to one of the documents, Penny Treasure and Willie Piles were the Senior Directors of something called The Power for Protection Movement, and according to another, the suspicious pair had booked a Luxury Weekend Break in the Ashdown Forest! A letter confirming the booking promised a deluxe double room with glorious views and a complimentary champagne breakfast!

That woman's definitely up to something, Midge thought. She's in cahoots with the head of London's new banking organisation...and that's putting it politely!

On a high, but worried about the implications, Midge replaced the envelope and wondered who to call. She spun the chair, gazed out the giant window, and remembered the person she most wanted to speak to had vanished. London looked enormous. She felt herself shrink. She felt small and alone. "I miss you, Mum," she whispered.

Midge went into her broom-cupboard-office, closed the door and took out the bar of chocolate-covered marzipan. Halfway through licking off all the chocolate, she remembered Pearl's words from yesterday.

"You can see things that other people can't."

A fantastical realisation came exploding into Midge's head like a bolt of lightning. All at once, she realised her ability to see dead people was her gift of extra-special vision…and it had to be her piece of the puzzle!

~ Twenty-Two ~

Energy

June lived on the edge of Tooting Common behind a well-established beech hedge and an organised jungle of lush greenery.

Scott parked the van on the driveway of semi-detached paradise and immediately forgot he lived in London. When the back door of the house flew open, a plethora of animals landed on the patio. After running around in circles, two long-haired retrievers raced across the grass causing a group of wood pigeons to prematurely launch themselves. Not yet prepared for flight they noisily clapped their wings together, and for a second, it looked like a mass of clumsy feathers would crash land on Scott's head. He ducked and they missed him by millimetres.

June removed a feather from Scott's hair and then introduced him to the rest of her family.

"As well as Paddy and Max, I've got Nuts, the Jack Russell, and Bahloo, who's a woolly crossbreed." Bahloo reminded Scott of a dog he once had as a small child (except his one had four wheels and a handle). "This is Ariel and that's Athena," June said, pointing to two Siamese cats, "and, finally, over there, in that hutch next to the vegetable patch, a dwarf-sized black rabbit called Zeus."

June made a fuss of the animals around her feet, and Scott stood for a moment to admire the spectacular back garden. Two borders crammed with flowers ran up either side of the lawn, carrying the eye to an elegant, moss-covered lady who stood in the centre. An ivy-smothered wall enclosed the rear end of the plot, and through an archway there was another, equally spectacular, collection of flowers.

"Wow," Scott said, with Athena purring loudly in his ear, "it looks like your garden never ends."

"Some things never end," June said, "and some things are not what they seem."

Before Scott thought of a reply, June led him across the lawn and up to the statue. Ariel and Athena dug their claws into Scott's shoulders, but kept their balance.

June pointed to the archway. "Look closely and tell me what you see."

Scott scrutinised the scene. "I see a garden, and a wall, and another garden through the archway."

At that very moment, Nuts ran up to the archway, sat down with his tail wagging, and barked at his reflection.

"It's a mirror!"

"That's right," June said, "it's just a mirror on the wall, but it gives the impression of something else entirely. Very often we do that, don't you think? We see or hear something and then make an instant assumption about it."

"Well, yes," Scott said, laughing, "I suppose we do."

As they strolled towards the house, Ariel and Athena settled themselves into a comfortable, seated position. At the back door, June closed her eyes and took a deep breath. “Someone is here with us…I can feel the energy.”

The hairs on Scott’s arms stood up.

“I knew we weren’t alone as soon as the cats leapt onto your shoulders, they always do that to visitors who bring company; they like to look the invisible guests in the eye. I feel the all-powerful love of a mother for its child. I sense this love all around us.”

“I think it’s my mum! Sometimes I can hear her calling my name, but maybe it’s in my imagination. She died a year ago.”

June opened her eyes. “Don’t be afraid, Scott, your mum loves you and she desperately wants you to know something. I sense she can’t stay here for much longer, she has to go, she has to move on.”

“What do you mean? Move on where? Can you see her? Can you hear her?”

“There’s no need to worry, everything’s okay. Let’s go inside and I’ll make us some elevenses, there’s some things I need to explain.”

The cats leapt to the floor, Scott rolled his shoulders and June disappeared upstairs to change.

The interior of June’s house, stuffed with artefacts from around the world, looked like a gallery at the Victoria and Albert Museum. Scott wandered from room to room taking in all the sights: wooden sculptures from India, puppets from Thailand, paintings from Tibet, brightly coloured masks from Africa, blue glassware from Cairo, rugs from

Kazakhstan, wall hangings from Japan and silk cushions from China. On the mantelpiece was a well-used boomerang from the Australian Outback, and on the walls, countless pictures of beaches, deserts, jungles, rainforests, cities, sunsets and friends.

June reappeared, her black leathers replaced by a floating, white kimono. After feeding the animals she quickly rustled up a plate of hot buttered toast and two mugs of sugary tea. “Fifteen years ago my husband dropped dead as he was mowing the lawn. There was nothing I could do to save him. I was devastated, as I’m sure you can imagine, and for the first few weeks I wandered around in a daze.”

Scott put his toast down.

“Time passed by and still I struggled to get used to life without Alec. Then, one morning, nearly a year later, I went out to the vegetable patch to pull up some radishes and there, growing right in the middle of them, was his favourite flower – a dahlia. It had appeared overnight and it was beautiful. It was a deep, rich, red and in full bloom. But that’s not all, as I stood staring at the flower I heard music coming from inside. I ran upstairs to the bathroom and discovered that an old, broken radio had switched itself on and it was blaring out his favourite piece of classical music. It was an amazing experience because I had no doubt that these were signs from Alec. I could feel his love all around me. In that moment I realised that he wasn’t dead at all, I mean…how could he be…if he’d managed to send me these messages?”

Scott sat in silence, desperate to hear more.

"I had to find out all I could," June said. "I wanted to know what happens to us when we die. I wanted to know what had happened to my husband. For ten years I travelled the world searching for answers, and I felt his presence with me every step of the way. He led me to places and people who could help me on my journey of discovery."

June paused to take a bite of toast.

"Is he here with you? Is he with my mum? Are they both in this room with us now? Can you see her?"

June placed the crusts on the plate. "I like to save those for the birds," she said.

"I need to know! You have to tell me everything!"

"Alec isn't with me anymore, he's moved on to a new life. As for your mother, no, I can't see her. I don't have the ability to do that. I can only feel the vibration of her energy. After years of meditation and practice, I've taught myself to connect with the energies that often surround us."

"What do you mean energies?"

"There are some things that we will never fully understand, but that doesn't mean they don't exist. All I can tell you is that every living creature has an energy. Some people call it a soul, or a spirit, but I prefer to call it energy. When our bodies stop working this energy continues; in fact, this energy lives forever. This energy is who we really are."

"So, how do you know these…energies…are near you? How do you know about my mum if you can't see her?"

"Well, in order to make their presence known, an energy has to use a considerable amount of oxygen, so the first and most obvious sign is a sudden rush of air. In fact, if there were several energies in a small room, and all the doors and windows were closed, you may even struggle to breathe."

"Wow, really?"

"The second sign is much more difficult to explain, but it's a feeling I have now and again. A shivery sensation will rush through my body, alerting me that someone wants to make contact. Splinters of information somehow gather in my mind. I see pictures and images. Sometimes it's like a stained glass window. It's taken years of practice and I'm still working on it."

Scott shook his head. "You make it sound like you're learning to speak another language."

"Well, that's exactly what it's like, it's like learning a new skill, and you may be surprised to know that anyone can do it, all it takes is practice." She directed her luminescent eyes at Scott. "Of course, animals can do these things naturally and there are a few lucky people who don't need much practice at all. And some people, like you, can do more than sense a presence, they can actually see and hear things."

"So, when I said I could hear my mum calling my name, you believed me?"

"Of course I believed you. Those voices that you hear, they're not in your imagination, they're real. You have the wonderful ability to hear what most people choose not to, and with practice, you'll only get better at it."

June sipped her tea.

“So…what you’re saying…is that all animals…and some humans…can sense dead people’s energies?”

“Yes, that’s right. Although, to be accurate, I’d have to say it’s not just the dead. For instance, have you ever walked into a room full of strangers and been immediately drawn to some of them and repelled by others? If you have, then it’s because you are sensing individual energies and some of them you like and some of them you don’t. Maybe you’d understand this better if I referred to it as instinct? Instinct is partly the ability to tune into other people’s energies. And here’s another example, a few weeks ago my sister was staying with me and in the middle of the night my dogs woke her with excited barking. When she came downstairs to investigate, she found them wagging their tails by the back door. Ten minutes later I made an unexpected return home. Amazingly, my animals knew I was coming. They sensed my energy approaching.”

“Uh-huh. I think I get what you’re saying. But why do some people, like me, hear voices? And why do some people see things? Are these energies ghosts?”

“Yes, I suppose they are, but I don’t like the ghost word. Ghosts make people nervous. A ghost, if that’s what you want to call it, is just a dead person’s energy and some people have the ability to see or hear that energy in its old, physical form, they just don’t realise it.”

“Surely people would know if they were seeing ghosts, sorry, I mean dead people’s energies?”

"No, they don't. It's funny, really, because some people spend all day with a so-called ghost and then go to bed at night worrying about one turning up to haunt them."

"Yeah, you're right, that is funny, but what does happen to us when we die? Where does our energy go?"

"Well, that's the billion dollar question, and the honest truth is no one really knows the answer. None of us will truly know until it happens. But I believe this: when our physical body ceases to function, our energy is instantly released and it floats up into the atmosphere. Sooner or later it settles miles above the surface of the earth, where it may drift for months, sometimes years. Eventually, it will make a decision about what to do next. Some energies choose to come back to this world and are reborn into a new body and others choose to experience life on another planet."

"Another planet! How can you be sure of that? I mean no scientist has ever made contact with life on other planets."

June nodded. "Well yes, that's true, but no scientist has ever travelled the length and breadth of the universe. Did you know, Scott, there are more than one hundred billion galaxies in the universe, each containing millions or even trillions of stars and planets? Planet Earth, our home, is just one of those planets. In fact, many scientists believe that the universe is endless, that it goes on for infinity, and if that's true...well...the possibilities for life on other planets must also be endless. Out there, somewhere, there could be another boy who looks just like you, sitting in an identical kitchen, eating toast with a woman who looks just like me!"

Scott started laughing. "That sounds highly unlikely."

"But not impossible. Remember, an endless universe must mean endless possibilities. There is so much that we mortals don't know; things we don't have the slightest inkling about."

How can something go on forever? Scott considered the concept. Surely there must be an end to the universe? Perhaps, just like the flowers in June's garden, all the stars and planets come to an abrupt dead end by a colossal brick wall? But if they do, then who built the wall? And did the wall go on forever? And what was on the other side of it? He picked up another slice of toast and took a bite.

"And then some energies," June said, continuing, "like my husband's or your mum's, come back down to the Earth's surface because they have an important task to perform or a message to deliver."

"Do they?"

"Yes, they do, and then, when they're satisfied that all is well, they move on. You see we are all on an endless journey through eternity, always trying to strengthen our energy by experiencing love in many lifetimes."

"So, my mum has a message for me? That's what you're saying, isn't it?"

"Yes, I believe she does. But at this moment, I don't know what it is. Try to relax and be patient. When she's ready she'll tell us."

Scott jiggled his legs. “I’ve got another question for you.”

“Yes, I’ll bet you have. Fire away.”

“Well, you just said we’re supposed to strengthen our energy by experiencing love in many lifetimes, but that can’t be right. Some people don’t have much love. Some people just have crap lives filled with problems.”

June raised her eyebrows. “Yes, you’re right. Some people do have terrible problems and it’s a guarantee that everyone, you and me included, will experience their fair share of them, that’s part of being alive. Our challenge is to find a way to overcome them.”

“That’s easy for you to say! Sometimes it’s not possible to overcome them. Some things are huge. They’re even bigger than the Purple.”

A rush of air blew through the kitchen, disturbing loose papers and conversation.

June glanced at Scott then furiously scratched her arms and legs. “Like fleas nipping at me; all this information.” She closed her eyes and tipped her head back. She inhaled deeply then slowly released the breath. “She is here with us now, at this table.”

Scott sat in silence, almost too scared to breathe at all.

June’s limbs stiffened, her fingers arching like claws. Slowly her head rolled, her lips muttering inaudible words. Seconds later, she opened her eyes.

“What did she tell you? What was the message?”

June didn’t answer.

"Well, what was it?" Scott said, jumping up and running round the table.

June shook her arms then flicked her fingers through the air. "I need to release the energy. It was incredible…absolutely incredible."

"But what was it?"

"Let's go outside. You need to hear this for yourself."

Sitting on the lawn, at the top of the garden, with Ariel and Athena purring excitedly, Scott closed his eyes.

"I'm going to teach you how to tune in your psychic receiver," June said.

"My what?"

"Your psychic receiver. It's the part of your brain that picks up signals. Much like a radio or television set does."

"Oh. I thought that's what you meant."

June chuckled. "Do you trust me?"

"Yes."

"Right then; do as I ask. You should find this quite easy because it's obvious you have a natural ability. Try to concentrate on your breathing. Just breathe slowly, in and out."

Scott did as requested then turned his head to face the sun. The light from a burning star, 26,000 light years away, sent a swirl of orange colours to dance across his eyelids.

"Now," June said, "the brain is an amazing thing, but some people think we only use ten percent of it. I'm not sure if that's true but I do know something that is. We humans possess powers of various kinds that we habitually fail to use. Our brains and minds are capable of remarkable things, but in order to access this higher intelligence we must first quiet our thoughts."

Scott opened an eye. "So you want me to stop my mind from thinking?"

"Not exactly. Stopping your mind from thinking is virtually impossible, but what you can do is take control of those speeding thoughts and that's what I want you to attempt. I want you to imagine you're an air traffic controller."

Scott opened the other eye. "What?"

"Yes, I know it sounds strange, but that's what I want you to do. I want you to think of yourself as an air traffic controller who's in charge of a very busy area of sky. Do you think you can do that?"

"Err, yeah, I suppose so." He closed his eyes again.

"Good. Now let me explain. Because you tell every aircraft that enters your airspace to keep moving, none of them are able to slow down, crash into each other or land. Are you with me so far?"

"Yeah, I think so."

"Now, here's the best bit. The area of blue sky that you're responsible for is your mind, and every aircraft that enters it is one of your thoughts. As each new thought comes into your mind I want you to take control of it immediately. For instance, if you have a jumbo-jet-sized thought about what happened on the day your mum died, don't allow it to slow down; tell the pilot to give the engines more thrust. Keep it moving. If it's not allowed to slow down, it can't bother you."

"Okay. I'll try."

"For the next fifteen minutes you're in control. Be firm. Give your thoughts a definite and exact flight path out of your head. Insist that the sky is cleared. You'll discover that it feels great to have so much control. In that silent, clear blue sky of your mind, you'll find total peace and calm. If you were to ask an air traffic controller about their most relaxing days at work they'd tell you about the times when the sky wasn't crowded, and I should know that's true because I was one."

Scott opened his eyes. "You were an air traffic controller?"

"Yes, sugar, I was. I worked at Heathrow Airport for twenty years, and along with the knowledge I gained on my travels, I used my experience of that job to help create this powerful, mind-relaxation technique. And because I practice it myself, I know that it works. Now close your eyes again and take some slow breaths. Let's get to it."

Scott concentrated on his breathing, but questions roared in like fighter jets. Where was she? Was she nearby? Was she watching? Would he hear anything? Would her voice sound the same? Would she be angry with him? Would he cry and look like an idiot? Was this really happening? Was this all a joke?

Nerves highjacked breathing and heartbeat.

June held Scott's hands. Together they synchronised their breathing.

Adrenaline production slowed.

Butterflies landed.

Leave me. Leave me now, Scott thought. I refuse to acknowledge you. I am in control. My mind is clear.

Birdsong and bumblebees melted into the haze, and Scott realized he could no longer feel the grass beneath him. He let that thought go.

A crackling noise, like static, quickly elongated and changed pitch. His mum's voice was clear and unmistakeable. "This is what it sounds like miles above the surface of the earth, where blue fades into black. It's amazing here. It's total silence. It's bliss. It's ecstasy. Now you're up here, if you listen closely, you'll hear every word."

"Mum, is that you?"

"The school playing field, a crowd gathered around me, an ambulance. I can see you running. I can hear the siren."

"I remember. I'm sorry…I didn't know…"

"Listen! Listen! Forty-one years, six months, three weeks, five days, fourteen hours, seven minutes and twelve seconds. I had the time of my life – it was agreed before birth. I am happy here and excited about what comes next. You are not to blame. You have only my love forever and the time of your life to prize. This invisible thread will connect us for eternity and bring us together again..."

In a garden nearby, an annoying neighbour started a lawnmower and its buzz took Scott by surprise.

He fell back to earth.

~ Twenty-Three ~

Taking Risks

"It's me, dear," Mrs Mackay said, once she'd settled herself into her favourite armchair and taken a sip of tea.

"It's you? This is a picture of you? I thought it was me!"

"No, dear, it's definitely me; my father took it eighty-odd years ago. I was perhaps fourteen at the time. I meant to hide it away somewhere."

Ellie looked down at the picture. "I feel a bit stupid now. I had this whole story worked out in my mind. I thought someone had taken a picture of me in my dream...I thought...I thought you might know something about it."

"I haven't a clue what you're talking about, dear," Mrs Mackay said, picking up the teapot.

"Well," Ellie said, "this is going to sound really silly, but two nights ago I had a dream, an incredible dream. I dreamt I was in this amazing garden. It was filled with hundreds and thousands of flowers, there were flowers everywhere, just like this picture. There were walls around the garden and a clock tower, just like this picture. I must have picked a flower because, when I woke up, I had it in my hand."

Mrs Mackay placed the pot back on the trolley. She pulled out an embroidered hanky from her pocket and dabbed the corners of her eyes.

"Are you…okay?"

"Yes, dear, I'm fine."

"Maybe I've got this all wrong. What I've just said sounds ridiculous. Ignore it. You must think I've gone mental."

A solitary tear ran down the old lady's cheek. "No, dear, I don't think you've gone nuts. I dream about that garden myself. I have for years. I lived there, many, many years ago, in the house with the walled garden. It was my home."

Ellie dropped her scone onto the plate, and it landed cream-side down. "You what? What do you mean? So you *really* do know this place?"

Mrs Mackay nodded. "Oh yes, dear, I know it very well, it's the place where I was born. For hundreds of years my family lived on the Claremont Castle Estate in the Highlands of Scotland. The castle was built in 1600 and it was the most wonderful building, like something from a film. It had turrets, towers, a maze of endless rooms, a spectacular entrance hall with a vaulted ceiling, and stained glass windows. Around the castle were huge areas of beautiful landscaped parkland and some of the most amazing gardens you've ever seen. One of them was the garden in that picture. You look like you're catching flies, dear."

Ellie closed her mouth. "You lived in a castle?"

"Yes, dear, I did. It seems hard to believe, doesn't it? Sitting here in this wee flat, at the age of ninety-four, I sometimes find it hard to believe myself...but...it's true. Until the age of seventeen, Claremont Castle was my home."

"And why isn't it anymore? What happened? Did you sell it?"

Mrs Mackay laughed then screwed the hanky up in her fist. "No, dear, I didn't sell it, I left it. One night, seventy-seven years ago, when no one was watching, I slipped out into the darkness and disappeared. I never returned." She held out a hand and Ellie passed her the picture. "It's such a long time ago, but seeing this photograph has brought it all back."

"Has it?"

"Yes, dear, it has. They say time is a healer, but now I'm not sure." She shook her head. "No. I'm not so sure about that."

Ellie reached over and put her hand on Mrs Mackay's arm. "Shall I pour you another cup of tea?"

"Yes, dear, that would be lovely. Can you stay for a while? There's something I feel I should tell you."

"Yes, of course, I'll stay as long as you like."

"Well, it all started with plants. Plants and of course flowers. My great grandfather was a world famous botanist and that walled garden, the one you dreamt about, was also world famous."

"Really? Sorry, what is a botanist exactly?"

"Someone who specializes in the study of plants, dear. In those days botany was a very popular science. My great grandfather studied at the Royal Botanic Gardens in Edinburgh, and he risked his life travelling to the far-flung corners of the globe in search of new specimens."

"Gosh," Ellie said, "it's hard to imagine anyone risking their life for a plant."

"Well, yes, to you that probably does sound strange, but folk in the nineteenth century knew much less about this world than we do and they were desperate to learn more. Back then people were fascinated with plants and flowers from other countries, and expeditions to somewhere like Brazil could take months or even years to plan and execute." She took a sip of tea. "Of course, throughout time, there have always been brave adventurers willing to risk everything in order to gain knowledge."

The old lady took another sip, then another, and the antique clock on the mantelpiece struck eleven. Ellie listened to the chimes, watched the gold mechanism spinning in the glass case and turned to study the old lady's wrinkled face. The passing of time makes people look like walnuts with wigs on, she thought. She smiled to herself, grateful for the silly idea, and tried not to laugh out loud.

After a few seconds, the walnut continued. "My great grandfather went to all sorts of places…China, Japan, Burma, India, Africa, South America…by the end of his life that enormous walled garden was filled with some remarkable sights. There were monkey-puzzle trees, magnolias, orchids, tulips, dahlias, rhododendrons, primulas, roses and a multitude of palms and ferns. He had all kinds of apples and pears trained against the walls and in the glasshouses there were figs, grapes, melons and peaches. When he grew his first pineapple it caused a sensation. People had never seen anything like it before. Soon the place was overrun with visitors and they were amazed at the sight of these exotic new specimens, they didn't understand how they could survive in Scotland..."

"And why did they survive? Surely it's too cold up there?"

"Och-aye!" Mrs Mackay said. "That's what everybody else thought! But warm air currents travelling across the Atlantic from Mexico raise the temperature along the west coast of Scotland by several degrees...it's called the Gulf Stream. And because of it, it's possible to grow all kinds of wonderful things."

"Oh, I think I've heard of the Gulf Stream," Ellie said.

"Yes, dear, you probably have, but the Gulf Stream wasn't the only contributing factor. The air inside that walled garden would always stay warmer for longer because the walls would trap the energy of the sun. They acted like giant radiators releasing heat well into the night. Plus, at midsummer, up there in the north, the sun barely sets, there can be eighteen hours of sunlight a day." Mrs Mackay paused, obviously recalling the glorious, long lost days of her youth. "I used to love those never-ending summer evenings in that walled garden. Sometimes, it would be nearly midnight before it went completely dark."

An alarm bell rang in Ellie's head. The unbelievable collection of flowers! The heat trapped within the crumbling walls! The midnight sunset! This garden had to be the one in her dream. It just had to be!

"When my great-grandfather died, his three sons took over and opened The Claremont Castle Horticultural School. The gardens and castle quickly became the centre of the community, employing thirty-eight full-time staff. People came from all over Europe to study. Years passed by and its reputation continued to grow. By the time my father was born, gardening was in our family's blood and it was only natural that he would want to continue the good work. But in 1914, the year I came along, disaster struck."

"What happened?

"The First World War, that's what happened, and all the men who worked on the estate, including my father, signed up to fight. The War Office took over the castle and turned it into a convalescent home for officers. I don't remember any of this myself because I was too young, but according to my mother, the injured soldiers would sit for hours in the walled garden; they swore there was something magical about the place. They said that inside that garden the sights, sounds and smells of the battlefield would finally fade away, replaced by the gentle hum of the bumblebee, the heavenly sound of birdsong and the glorious smell of perfume." Mrs Mackay closed her eyes and inhaled deeply through her nose. "Ah, the smell of perfume in that garden, it was magnificent."

Ellie tried to shout I DREAMT ABOUT THAT PERFUME! But, because she had a mouth jammed full of fruitcake, it came out as, "WAHH DWAA ABA DAH PARWUM!" Sultanas and other chewed fragments peppered the tea trolley, but Mrs Mackay didn't seem to notice.

"People only expected the war to last for a few months, but the fighting went on for four years, eventually claiming the lives of seven million people around the world. Out of the thirty-two who left Claremont Castle only six came back. Luckily, my father was one of those men. Safely delivered from the pits of hell, that's how he always described it. Along with the five other survivors he set about restoring the gardens, and within a relatively short space of time they had been returned to their former glory. After the traumas of war, the gardens were more popular than ever and people once again flocked for miles to marvel at their splendour. Within a year it was business as usual. I think those early years were probably the best days of my life. I had the most idyllic childhood growing up on that estate."

Ellie smiled and nodded politely, even though she couldn't help thinking this story was going on a bit. She grabbed a napkin and began to clean up her mess.

"Little did I know that misery and loss were waiting for me just around the corner. Waiting silently and patiently to snatch away everything that was dear to me."

Ellie put the napkin down.

"By the time I was sixteen some of the original plants in the gardens desperately needed replacing and so my father decided to fulfil a life long ambition. He decided to retrace his grandfather's steps. As a thank you to the five loyal gardeners who had stuck with him through thick and thin he asked them to accompany him on a plant collecting expedition to India. Of course they all agreed to it immediately. Travel in those days was an expensive luxury, and a trip like that was a once in a lifetime opportunity. I remember the excitement of the preparations, and I remember waving them goodbye one overcast morning in early April. My mother went with the party, planning to travel as far as Darjeeling in the foothills of the Himalayas. The exact details of what happened still remain a mystery, but according to a local guide who was with them and survived, a tiger attacked the group as they trekked through an area of dense forest. One of them was mauled to death and the others ran terrified and screaming into the undergrowth. Night fell quickly and without sufficient survival skills or protection, the odds were heavily stacked against them. At first light, a rescue party was organised, but despite an intensive search, only bloodied scraps of clothing were found. What the tigers left behind, wild dogs probably finished."

Ellie winced, tried to think what to say, but couldn't. She desperately hoped this was the end of the story but, alarmingly, it wasn't.

~ Twenty-Four ~

Murder Most Muddy

"So...that was me...an orphan at sixteen," Mrs Mackay said.

Ellie wanted to point out that she had been made an orphan at fifteen, but she couldn't bring herself to say the words.

"I felt like my world had ended. I can vividly recall the first few months without my parents, they were bleak and dark, but I struggled on, doing my best to keep the gardens open. It was what my father would have wanted, but it was an almost impossible task. Eleven months later, a stranger turned up on the doorstep. His name was Harold Crinklebottom."

"Harold Crinklebottom?"

"Yes, Crinklebottom," Mrs Mackay said. "He was two years older than me and an ex-student of the horticultural school. Word of the accident had spread the length and breadth of the country and he arrived with condolences and the offer of help. He said he had worked closely with my father on several projects, and I immediately saw him as the answer to all my prayers. With his help, I knew we could get the gardens back on their feet. Overnight, he employed a small group to help him, and for the first time in ages, I had hope for the future. He worked all the hours

God sent and then, in the evenings, the two of us would walk together through the grounds enjoying the spectacular sunsets. Not only was he hard-working and good fun to be with, but also dashingly handsome…he had the finest set of teeth I'd ever seen. One night, out of the blue, he asked me to marry him. We'd only known each other for three months, but I said yes without hesitation. Looking back, it's easy to see it was a foolish mistake. I was young and naive and still grieving the death of my parents. I was lonely. Harold insisted that we get married immediately so, four weeks later, on August 29th, we tied the knot. It was a small ceremony with few guests. Deep down I had the horrible suspicion I was rushing into something I might regret, but like a fool I carried on regardless. Immediately after the wedding Harold changed. He became a different person…bad tempered and hostile."

"Oh no. I'm sorry," Ellie said.

Tears had cut lines in Mrs Mackay's neatly powdered face. She dabbed at them matter-of-factly then slipped the hanky up her sleeve.

"A few weeks after the wedding a man came up to the house to see me, his name was Arthur, he lived in one of the cottages on the estate. I recognised him immediately. He had been a good friend of my father's and he came with shocking news. He said that Harold had never been a student of the horticultural school…or even known my father. He said he was a dangerous impostor who had married me for my money! At first I tried to pretend otherwise, I told Arthur to mind his own business and to leave us alone, but, instinctively, I knew he was telling the truth. I was devastated. I couldn't believe I had made such a colossal mistake. I had jumped from the frying pan into the fire and of course there was no way I could turn back the clock. Divorce in those days was an almost unheard of scandal and, to make matters worse, I had just discovered I was pregnant. I struggled on, desperately hoping things would improve…but…of course…they didn't."

This story's beginning to sound like a costume drama, the sort that used to be shown on television on a Sunday evening, Ellie thought. "Crikey," she said.

Mrs Mackay began to splutter. Tears pooled in her red rimmed eyes. She clutched her pearls, took a deep breath then pulled out the hanky.

"It's okay," Ellie said, "you don't have to go on if you don't want to."

"No, dear!" Mrs Mackay exclaimed. "I have to tell you. I can't keep this a secret any longer." She blotted her face before stuffing the sodden hanky back up her sleeve. "Then, one day in early October, events took a terrible turn. After a blazing row I told Harold about Arthur's accusation. Harold ran from the house in a terrible fury and was gone for several hours. When he eventually returned, late that evening, he said the two of them had taken a long walk in the woods, he said they had had an honest chat, man to man. He said that Arthur had decided to move away, to go back home. I didn't believe it. I was instantly suspicious. There was earth on Harold's hands and under his fingernails. I knew something was wrong. I followed the trail of mud that had been left by his boots and it led directly to the stable yard where, after a few minutes of frantic searching, I found all the evidence I needed. A set of clothes hidden in an old sack and they were drenched in blood. There was a spade nearby and it was caked with fresh, damp earth."

A shaken Ellie went to clutch her own pearls, but of course she wasn't wearing any. "Murdered and buried in the woods? Is that what you're saying?" she whispered.

Mrs Mackay slumped forwards sobbing. "Yes, dear, that's exactly what I'm saying."

Unexpectedly, the clock on the mantelpiece marked the half hour with a single chime and Mrs Mackay cleared her throat. "Harold came charging into the yard looking for me, I remember his face twisted with anger. He lunged at me…his fingers inches from my neck…in a blind panic I picked up the shovel and swung it as hard as I could. It hit him on the side of the head. He fell to the floor. His legs were shaking then they stopped. I couldn't find a pulse."

For a split-second Ellie's mind flashed back to the hooded figure in her dream, its soil-encrusted fingers reaching to touch her.

The old lady continued. "Terrified of what I'd done, I packed a small bag and drove through the night to Glasgow. When morning finally came, I abandoned the car, pawned some pieces of jewellery, and caught the train to London. Once there, I hid myself away in an east-end boarding house until the child was born and then I did the hardest thing I've ever had to do…" Mrs Mackay gripped hold of the arms of her chair and tried to take a breath, her body shaking uncontrollably. "I…I…gave the child away…I gave up my own son for adoption."

The dam finally broke, and a flood of tears that had been building for seventy-two years came crashing out. For the good part of an hour, Ellie hugged, patted and stroked the old lady, passing her a succession of tissues.

Eventually, the water retreated.

Midmorning tea and cakes became cheese sandwiches for lunch and then, for the best part of the afternoon, Ellie listened, spellbound, to every detail of the old lady's life story.

"Life for single mothers in those days was a grim affair; there was no money or assistance available from the state. It would have been impossible for me to hold down a job and bring up a child. Besides, no one would have employed me."

"Why not?"

"Because," the old lady said, in a voice that sounded much like her old self again, "to be pregnant outside of marriage was not acceptable. Women like that were considered to be the dregs of society, given no more respect than a common criminal. I desperately wanted to keep the child, but I knew it was out of the question. With a loving family my son stood a much better chance of living a healthy and successful life. It was a painful sacrifice."

"You should be proud of yourself," Ellie said.

"Mmm, I suppose so." Mrs Mackay removed her glasses and polished them on a napkin. She lifted her handbag from the floor and took out a mirror. "Och, deary me," she squealed, "I look like a fright."

Ellie watched, in admiration, the meticulous re-application of face powder and lipstick. After blotting her lips on a tissue, the old lady continued.

"Completely alone in London, with all my life ahead of me, I made the decision to start anew. In order to avoid being arrested and hung for murder I got myself a new name. Thanks to a fake birth certificate, purchased on the black market, the orphaned teenager Mavis Brownlie and the unhappily married Mavis Crinklebottom were able to disappear forever. Next, I got myself a job as a cleaner. It was hard work, but I enjoyed the thrill of earning a wage, and with money in my pocket I was able to rent a bright and sunny room in Bethnal Green. Within no time I'd made new friends. I even ventured out on a couple of dates! In the back of my mind I always imagined that one day, when I had plucked up sufficient courage, I would travel back to Scotland, notify the police, and unburden my heavy conscience, but weeks turned into months and months into years. Then, in 1939, World War Two broke out and it changed everything. Just like the Purple, the war stole many people, and with most of the men off fighting, all kinds of work opportunities suddenly became available to us women. I threw in the cleaning towel and got myself a job as a bus conductor."

"A bus conductor!" Ellie laughed.

"Yes...a bus conductor...it was enormous fun! I got to know London like the back of my hand. Within a year I had been promoted to supervisor. Wartime in London was a dizzying mixture of high hopes and dramas and I remember, in particular, one night in December 1940, when much of the East End was flattened in the blitz. By a miracle, St Paul's Cathedral managed to survive almost intact. It was a glorious sight, that building standing tall amongst the ruins. It became a symbol of London's defiance against the enemy, and a personal symbol of my hope and survival. When the war finally ended, five years later, both of us were still standing." The old lady dropped her lipstick into her handbag then closed the catch with a satisfying snap.

"Go on," Ellie said, "then what happened?"

"Well, the end of the war was a time for new beginnings and so I enrolled myself at secretarial college. I quickly gained a certificate in shorthand typing and flitted from one temporary office position to another, before landing my dream job as personal assistant to Mr Tingle."

"Mr who?"

"Mr Tingle," the old lady said, "you know, the fizzy drinks man?"

Ellie shook her head.

"Tingle's Pop Drinks for Every Occasion!" Mrs Mackay sang. "You must remember the advert?"

Ellie grinned. "No, I'm afraid not, I think Tingle's Pop must have been before my time."

"Oh. Well, he was a successful businessman with a booming empire and a generous heart. Like everyone else, he believed I had lost my entire family to the horrors of war so, together with his wife, he took me under his wing. I worked for him for thirty years. He treated me like a daughter. The years continued to speed by and, with each passing season, Mavis Brownlie, Mavis Crinklebottom and the son I gave away became less like real people and more like fictional characters in a novel. Along with Claremont Castle and its wonderful gardens they became blurred, hazy shapes, lost on the horizon of time. That was until yesterday…until I saw this picture again."

A million questions bounced inside Ellie's head. She sifted them, trying to place them in order of importance. Did you never get the urge to try and trace your son? Have you never wanted to go back to Scotland? Who lives in the castle now? The only word that leapt out of her mouth was, "Sorry."

"Sorry?" Mrs Mackay said. "What are you sorry for?"

"I'm sorry for being rude and short tempered when I first arrived here this morning. I'm sorry for keeping my finger on the doorbell for ages and I'm sorry for sounding ungrateful when you offered me tea and cakes. But more than anything, I'm sorry for thinking I knew more than you."

Mrs Mackay smiled then tutted and rolled her eyes, much like Ellie had done earlier that day. "Och, don't worry about it, dear. We geriatrics are tougher than you think."

"Yes…I can see that now," Ellie said.

The old lady lifted herself out of her chair, took a moment to straighten her skirt, and walked across the room.

"A while ago, I hired a private detective, his name was Mr Russell…a friendly wee soul with a Liverpool accent…polite and inconspicuous. But despite turning the record office upside down, he never found a trace of the child I gave away."

"I'm sorry," Ellie said.

"Och, thank you, dear. I'm all right, really. It's just that I'd love to know what happened to him. I'd love to know how his life turned out. It's a strange thing you know, when something you love disappears forever."

"Yes, I know it is," Ellie said, nodding.

"Yes, of course you do, my dear, how stupid of me. It's a terrible thing this Purple." Mrs Mackay attempted a smile. "Well, at least there's one piece of good news."

"Is there?"

"Yes, there is. Mr Russell travelled up to Scotland for me and did some sniffing about…he came back with some fascinating information. It turns out I'm not a murderer after all."

"What do you mean?"

"Well, that blow to the head only knocked him out. Harold Crinklebottom died of natural causes ten years ago."

"Oh wow," Ellie said. She considered this for a moment before deciding it wasn't necessarily good news. "So, that means he got to live the life he planned. He got to live in Claremont Castle. He got everything that was rightfully yours. He stole your life!"

"Well, so it would seem, but not exactly. You see life has a way of getting its own back and it didn't take long for people to notice that Arthur and myself were missing. Harold was arrested on suspicion of murder, but despite a lengthy police investigation nothing was proved. They never found any bodies, you see. But unfortunately for Harold, that wasn't the end of it. In small communities folk talk and words travel quickly. The damage to his reputation was irreparable. Despite the law never finding him guilty, people came to their own conclusion. According to Mr Russell, Harold found it impossible to hold onto staff and his business ventures began to fail. Over the years his bad temper became legendary and, perhaps haunted by visions from the past, he slipped into insanity. For the last few years of his life he lived as a recluse. When he died at the age of eighty-six he was alone and broke, and because there were no known relatives the castle sat empty."

"But it's yours," Ellie huffed, "it's your family home."

"Yes, dear, you're absolutely right, and after several years of to-ing and fro-ing with some very expensive solicitors, I eventually got it back. I'm pleased to tell you that Claremont Castle Estate is now back in my name." She smiled, knelt down and lifted out an old shoebox from the sideboard. "You see, I always held onto my marriage certificate and my original birth certificate, I knew that one day I would want to prove my real identity."

"Fantastic! So what does the place look like? How many times have you been back?"

"Oh no, dear, I've never been back. I know that may sound strange, but I'm ninety-four, what do I want with a big house like that? According to Mr Russell the place has been sorely neglected, it's a shadow of its former self and I couldn't bear to see it like that. No, I'd rather stay here in London and remember Claremont Castle as it used to be. I've made provision for it to be passed onto one of my favourite charities when I die."

"Oh," Ellie said. She couldn't help thinking this sounded like a very unremarkable ending to a truly remarkable story.

Mrs Mackay took out a large bunch of keys from the shoebox and dangled them in the air. "But there's nothing to stop you from paying the place a visit, is there, dear?"

~ Twenty-Five ~

Invisible Threads

Scott woke at four in the afternoon, snuggled on the sofa with dogs, cats and cushions.

As he lay there, Paddy's wet nose pressed against his arm, he had a realisation: the panicky feeling that had been pounding in his chest for the past twelve months had gone.

"Good sleep?" June placed a glass of water on the table next to his head.

Scott took a large gulp. "Yes, thanks." He wiped the corners of his mouth on the back of his hand. "Amazing actually, probably the best I've had in ages."

"I'm not surprised. I expect you've been running on adrenaline for months. You needed to switch off."

"Yeah, definitely. I feel, I feel..."

"You feel peaceful," June said, finishing his sentence.

"Mmm, yeah, completely."

"Good," June said, "I'm so glad you feel that way because that's how life's meant to be. Over the years I've made contact with hundreds of energies, and all of them say the same thing. Don't forget to live your life."

"Don't forget to live your life?" Scott repeated. "Sounds funny, don't you think?"

"Yes, I suppose it does, but it makes perfect sense. Life is here and now this minute, it's not yesterday or tomorrow. Today is all we have so we might as well do everything we can to enjoy it."

"Yeah, you're right." Scott stretched himself out on the sofa and Nuts did a noisy yawn. "I know I've said it lots of times already, but thanks for helping me make contact with my mum."

"Oh you're welcome, honey, it was easy. Like I said, you've got a natural ability, and if you practice regularly you'll soon be making contact with other energies."

"What did she mean when she said this invisible thread will connect us for eternity and bring us together again?"

June settled on the arm of the sofa. "Well, I think she's talking about love…like a connection that will always run between you. It's a beautiful thought. Sometime in the future, maybe when both of your eternal energies are occupying different bodies, your paths will cross. And although you won't recognise each other at first, you'll feel the connection. It will feel like you're with an old friend. It will feel like this morning when we met."

"Wow! You felt it too?"

"Of course I did, sugar. I felt it as soon as I spoke to you on the phone. Maybe it was eighty years ago, maybe it was 800, but we've definitely met before."

"That's amazing," Scott said.

"And comforting. To know that your mum's not really dead, she's just moved on."

"But moved on where? I wish I knew the answers to everything."

"You and me both," June chuckled, "but that's never going to happen. You found out for yourself this morning that energies won't answer all your questions. They only tell you what they can."

"Mmm, I suppose so. If my own mum won't reveal the secrets of the universe, who will?"

"No one, I'm afraid, but try to look on the bright side…when you die…you'll find out for yourself."

"Thanks," Scott said, "that's really cheered me up!" Athena, who'd been purring loudly on Scott's chest, unravelled herself. "Do you think the animals know what's happened to everyone, you know, the people who vanished in the Purple?"

"Oh, that's a good question! Maybe they do, maybe they don't."

"Have you never made contact with any of them?"

"No, I haven't," June said, "but not through lack of trying. Sometimes I get the feeling there are a lot more energies in the air than usual, but they pass by in silence."

"Oh. So do you think everyone who vanished is dead?" Scott wasn't sure he wanted to know the answer to that question, but he felt it needed to be asked.

After a long drawn out silence, June replied, "I honestly don't know, sugar. I was going to ask you the same question."

"You were going to ask me! How would I know what's happened to everyone?"

"Because...I suspect you and your friends have made contact with them. That garden...the place where you picked the flower...you and your friends need to find it."

"If it actually exists. I'm desperate to hear what's happened to everyone today. We're all meeting at the Railway Inn on Clapham High Street in time for *The Five O'Clock Announcement*."

"Well, you'd better get a move on, hun, it's twenty past four...and so should I...I've got to be in work at six."

Scott lifted Athena onto the floor and began to tie his laces. "Aren't you really tired? Don't you want to ask for the night off?"

"What! Tell Babs I can't come in? She'd freak out! We're already desperately short of staff as it is. No, I'll manage. I've never been one to sit still for long. I always hated the idea of retirement. And anyway, tonight will be slightly less busy than usual because I can think of two girls who won't need tucking-in...now they've found some new friends to keep them company."

"You mean Ellie and Midge?"

"Yes, I do. As soon as you started talking about them, I realised who they were. I've been tucking them in for ages. And don't sound so surprised! Let me tell you something...tucking-in isn't just for toddlers...it's for all of us. No one should be alone all the time...unless they want to be."

Scott finished tying his laces then leaned back on the cushions. He brushed away the hair from his eyes and smiled. "I never needed to call the Tucking-In Service; I never had any problem sleeping."

"How wonderful," June said. "That's because your mum has been with you. You didn't see her but you obviously felt her presence. She's been keeping an eye on you for months. It must have been her voice you kept hearing, and no doubt she cleaned up the house for you, too. What an incredible energy! The love she has for you is gigantic."

"But now she's miles above the surface of the Earth…and soon she'll be starting a new life somewhere."

"But she still loves you, and that love will never die or fade away."

In his mind's eye Scott saw himself walking along the beach with his mum. "A holiday to remember," that's what she'd called it. Recollections of a California summer wrapped themselves around him like a pair of loving arms.

Back in the van he wound down the window, clicked in the seatbelt and started up the engine.

June passed him a paper bag. "Some sandwiches and there's some home baked biscuits in there, too."

"Thanks, I'm starving. I'll call you tomorrow, to let you know what's happening."

"Okay. Drive carefully." June leaned in and squeezed his hand. "It's been good to see you again, dear friend, after all these years."

"Yeah, it has," Scott said.

On route to Clapham, dodging mopeds and cyclists, a song popped into Scott's head: it had been an old favourite of his mum's. Singing out loud, he switched on Heroic London Radio. The exact same song burst through the speakers! Scott smiled and continued singing, his words in sublime synchronicity with the broadcast.

~ooOoo~

Ellie left Mrs Mackay's at quarter to four. In a desperate hurry, she took another taxi. After a quick and uneventful ride to South Molton Street, she paced the pavement outside Renee and Rupert's Salon.

A girl stuck her head out the door. "Are you Ellie? My name's Andrea, I'm the receptionist."

Ellie nodded.

"You're Marty's friend, aren't you? He saw you through the window. Why don't you come in and wait, they'll be finished shortly."

"That would be great!"

"I *love* your look. It's really cool...really...Marilyn Monroe!"

"Oh, do you think so? Thanks!" Ellie pouted and blew Andrea a kiss. Both girls laughed. "What's this?" Ellie pointed at the enormous picture mounted on a stand in the middle of the reception area.

"It's The Midsummer Sunset, our new style of the month. It's fantastic, isn't it? Everyone's gone mad for it, even the boys. We've been doing them all day."

Ellie studied the picture. "Yeah...it looks amazing."

"Your friend's clever, isn't he? None of us can believe he managed to do that on his first day."

"You mean Marty did this?"

"Ooh yeah, didn't he tell you? He's the golden boy. The Midsummer Sunset's tipped to be the next big thing in hair. It's perfect timing, really, because Midsummer's Eve is tomorrow. Mr Rupert's really excited about it."

Ellie turned back to gaze at the picture, and for a second all sound fell away. The glorious smell of perfume fleetingly replaced the sulphurous stink of perm solution. Ellie found herself standing in the walled garden, gazing up at the midnight sun.

Andrea's voice broke the spell. "Would you care for a hot beverage of your choice?"

"Pardon?"

"A hot drink. Would you like one? We've got real coffee."

"Oh…no thanks. I'm up to here with hot beverage." Ellie placed her finger on her forehead. She turned to face the salon floor, her attention grabbed by an elderly man wearing a wig.

"It's my signature manoeuvre! You should all have one! When styling is complete, I hand the customer a face shield, pick up the can of hairspray, and then…," he smiled and winked, "I execute a perfect pirouette on one foot!" The old man twirled 360 degrees, releasing a stream of lacquer. "Job done!" he bellowed. "You've all done very well today, rascals, I'm proud of you. It's business as usual for us…so we'll see each other bright and early tomorrow morning. No tests tomorrow, take the evening off.

And remember, we will stand strong against The Power for Protection Movement. We will not allow them to intimidate us. They're nothing but a shower of charlatans! And a charlatan, in case you're wondering, is a fraud...somebody who makes false claims."

The new apprentices nodded in agreement before dispersing.

Marty dashed straight to the reception area. "Ellie, I've worked it out! I think I know what my piece of the puzzle is!"

"And so do I! As soon as I saw this picture," Ellie pointed to the style of the month, "I had a vision. I could feel myself standing in the garden looking up at the sky."

"It's The Midsummer Sunset!" they said together.

"Exactly!" Ellie cried. "I think we need to be inside that garden, in time for the Midsummer sunset."

"But we don't even know if the garden exists, do we?"

"Yes, we do! I've had an amazing day at Mrs Mackay's, and just before I left she gave me these." Ellie pulled a bunch of rusty keys from her bag. "This beautifully crafted piece of iron is the key to the walled garden."

"Wow, this is awesome! But please don't tell me the garden's in Scotland...tell me it's nearby...someplace we can get to easily?"

Ellie shook her head.

"Oh man!" Marty said. "How are we going to get to Scotland by tomorrow?"

"I'll fly us there," a voice said.

Ellie looked up and discovered the man wearing the wig had a smile whiter than December in Lapland.

"My name's Captain Rupert Dodge. You must be Ellie. I've heard all about you!"

"You'll fly us there?" Marty said. "But when was the last time you flew a plane?"

Mr Rupert scratched his head. "Properly? About sixty years ago, but don't look so worried, until five years ago a friend of mine had a private pilot's licence and we used to go on jollies together. Sometimes he'd even let me take over the controls. It's just like riding a bike."

"Well no, I don't think it is," Marty said, "otherwise we'd all be doing it."

"Balderdash, rascal! Where's your Dunkirk spirit?"

"My what?"

"Your courage, your sense of adventure, your refusal to surrender."

"I've got this feeling in my stomach," Ellie said. "I've even given it a name. I've called it the Missing Feeling. It's agonisingly painful. I need to get rid of it." She thrust her hand towards Mr Rupert. "Yes, you're right; I'm Ellie, how lovely to meet you. If you think you can fly us to Scotland then I say yes, please, and thank you very much. When can we go?"

"Are you crazy?" Marty said.

"Throughout history there have always been brave adventurers willing to risk everything in order to gain knowledge, don't you think?"

"Bravo, young lady!" Mr Rupert said. "I couldn't have put it better myself. Now, all we need is an aeroplane."

"And some fuel," Marty said, "in case you've both forgotten there's a ban on all commercial flights, cargo only. Remember?"

"Ah yes, you're right about that, rascal, these days aviation fuel is rarer than hen's teeth."

"I didn't know hens had teeth," Marty said.

"I think that's the point," Ellie said, laughing. "Couldn't we use your friend's aeroplane?"

"Oh, he didn't own one," Mr Rupert said, shaking his head, "it belonged to a flying club miles away in Somerset, and anyway, it was only a small two-seater."

Andrea interrupted. "Excuse me…Mr Rupert…Miss Renee's just called from the staff room…she says Mr Cormac's done something highly irresponsible with a curling tong."

"What? Oh, for heaven's sake, I'll be right down. Now, rascals, I've got to go, but here's my home number. Please call me later. Let's have a good think about this. There has to be a way. There's an awful lot at stake here."

"Yeah, you're right," Marty said. He turned to look outside.

Ellie followed his gaze. "Who are they?" she said, staring at the screaming protestors. "I don't like the look of them at all."

"Neither do we," Marty said. "I'll tell you everything on the way to Clapham."

The Railway Inn heaved with bodies.

"I've got so much to tell you," Scott said, panting.

"Yeah, so have we," Ellie said, "although it's probably best if we wait until after The Announcement."

They ordered three mixed-fruit smoothies and looked up expectantly at the television.

"I wonder if she's nervous?" Marty said.

"Come on, Midge! You can do it!" Scott shouted.

The TV flashed to life.

"Welcome Golden Oldies and Bright Young Things! Thank you for tuning in. My name is Penny Treasure."

A groan of disappointment criss-crossed the room.

"No! It's not Midge!" Ellie said.

"And what's happened to Penny…she looks different," Scott said.

"She's got a big, fancy hairdo!" Marty said.

"And she's wearing make-up," Ellie said. "It's like she's had a makeover."

"Today's announcement is a serious one, so I ask you all for your undivided attention.

"Some of you may have noticed a group of protestors called The Power for Protection Movement protesting on our streets today, and no doubt, their message has caused anxiety.

"As leader of the Decision Makers Council it is my duty to set the record straight. I, therefore, wish to make the following statement:

"Reliable experts and advisors to the DMC have made an alarming discovery. They have located the Purple!"

The crowd in the Railway Inn took a sharp intake of breath.

"The Purple is lurking miles above us in the ozone layer, and it is planning to return to Earth!"

The room erupted into pandemonium, but frantic to hear every word it desperately tried to settle.

"Obviously we need to move quickly, and you will be relieved to hear that your trusted leader has taken immediate action.

"I have assembled a team of specialists, and they are in the process of building weapons capable of causing destruction on a massive scale. To help pay for these life saving weapons it will be necessary to take a portion of everyone's wages. Chief banker Willie Piles will, of course, organise all necessary deductions from your individual accounts.

"I understand this announcement will come as a shock, so in order to boost morale, we intend to honour a promise made to you yesterday. You may recall my colleague talking about Scoop Of The Day? If so, you will be pleased to hear that we will be using a portion of this money to provide free ice cream for all.

"Please try to remain calm. Please also be aware that it may be necessary for us to make personal sacrifices over the coming days. The creation of these weapons will require significant amounts of money and fuel.

"Trust that my team and I are doing our utmost to safeguard your future and the future of planet Earth. For further information and regular updates please tune in to Heroic London Radio where you can hear hourly news bulletins.

"I shall make another announcement tomorrow afternoon at five!

"Remember! Remain Aware Proceed With Care!"

The broadcast ended and, once again, the room exploded into chaos.

"Let's get out of here," Scott said.

Midge didn't get back to the house until after seven.

"Thank goodness you're here," Ellie said, opening the front door. "We'd started to worry."

"I got stuck at Kennington Station," Midge said. "The tube driver walked off, he made an announcement to everyone on the train, he said he wanted to go home and spend what little time he had left with his wife. I tried phoning, but I couldn't get through. Since the announcement everyone's gone mad. The networks are jammed."

"You're safe!" Scott said. "We haven't eaten yet, but it won't be long. Mushroom stroganoff with baked potatoes, is that okay?"

"Absolutely!" Midge said. "I'd be grateful for a slice of toast."

"Yeah, me too," Marty added, sitting at the table studying a map. "This guy really is amazing."

Ellie took a handful of cutlery and walked over to the table. "Have you worked out a route?"

Marty looked up from the road atlas. "I think the best idea would be to follow the motorways. The M1, the M6 and then the M74, that would take us to Glasgow. Of course we'd have to fly low enough to see them and clouds would make the whole thing impossible."

"What's going on?" Midge said.

Ellie dropped the cutlery in a crashing pile and picked up the bunch of keys. "Look! This is the key to the garden! I found out today that the garden definitely exists; it belongs to that old lady, Mrs Mackay."

Over dinner, and for quite some time afterwards, details of the day's events were swapped.

"I'm sort of having trouble understanding this," Midge said. "Do you mean you actually floated up into the atmosphere?"

Scott put down his glass of water. "No. I don't think so. I think it was just my mind. It's really hard to explain. All I know for certain is that my mum's energy is miles above the surface of the Earth, and for a few seconds we were up there together. It was incredible. She spoke to me. I definitely heard her voice."

"I believe you," Midge said, "honestly I do. I've never told anybody about this before but, a couple of years ago, when that sea lion swam up the Thames, it gave me a message. It didn't actually speak the words, but when there was a close-up of its face on the news I heard a voice in my head...it was loud and clear and it told me everything would be all right. And then, yesterday, I spent most of the day having tea and biscuits with two dead people."

"And I'm convinced I was Marilyn Monroe in a previous life. I know I've told you all before...I wish could explain…when I hear Marilyn's voice it touches me deep inside. She sounds so recognizable…like…like I'm listening to myself. Once, when I was watching her on YouTube, I knew exactly what she was about to say…I finished off her sentence before she did!"

"If anyone could hear us," Marty said, "they'd think we were a bunch of crazy people."

"Yeah, they would," Ellie said, "but you know what's brilliant? We don't. We totally respect each other's thoughts and beliefs. Not one of you laughed when I told you my deepest secret."

"Hey, sister! You got my respect! You know what I've learned these past five months? *Anything* is possible. And the frightening truth," Marty continued, "concerns Penny Treasure and her Power for Protection Movement because they define the word crazy."

"I exactly agree with you!" Scott said. "The Purple isn't up there. I know it isn't. We can't let her get away with this."

"And I don't trust her with my money," Marty turned to Midge, "not after listening to everything you just told us."

"Neither do I," Ellie said. "That's an awful thing to do, stealing money from pensioners."

"And there's something else that's bugging me," Marty said. "How come she's had her hair done?"

"Err, well, she wanted to look her best for today's emergency announcement. She said a makeover would give her maximum impact. She made me call Sweet Talking Snips and arrange for one of their top stylists to come over. I get the impression he's staying on as her personal hairdresser."

"Well, he probably is," Marty said, "now that he's got nowhere else to work. Did you know that Sweet Talking Snips had their salon smashed up this afternoon?"

"No, I didn't! No way!" Midge said.

"It's one rule for her and another for the rest of us! How come her organisation's campaigning to get every hairdresser in London closed down, whilst she gets her own personal stylist? Does that make sense to any of you?"

"No, it bloody well doesn't!" Midge said.

Marty banged a fist on the table. "I feel so angry! If that brainless woman was here right now...I'd smash my dinner plate in her face!"

"Dude! Take a chill pill," Scott said.

"Yeah...okay...I know," Marty said, "I need to cool my jets. Violence isn't going to help the situation one bit...and...I wouldn't do it for real. But honestly, guys, look what she's doing. The Power for Protection Movement hasn't provided one single shred of evidence about the Purple. They're using demonstrators to whip up a storm and send the city into a panic. People are going crazy out there. She wants to use the remains of our precious fuel supplies and a whole bunch of our hard-earned cash to build weapons...weapons that will blow the ozone layer apart! And on top of all that, she's trying to sweeten the deal with the laughable offer of so-called free ice cream, but it isn't free, is it? It's our money that's paying for it!"

"Yeah, you're right," Scott said, "and who knows what'll happen to my mum's energy and all the other energies that are up there. The damage she's about to cause will be huge."

"But why is she doing this? I don't understand," Midge said. "I mean what's in it for her? I expect she's got no idea about energies, but she must at least know that planet Earth without an ozone layer is a bad idea…even I know that."

"Money and personal glory," Marty said immediately. "I'll bet you my first week's wages that Miss Treasure *and* her good friend Willie Piles are helping themselves to some of our notes. And second, she wants to be a hero. She's an egomaniac."

"What's an egomaniac?" Ellie said.

"Someone who's consumed with their own self-importance."

"Sounds right," Midge said, nodding her head, "she's definitely that."

~ Twenty-Six ~

Doubt, Signs and Courage

After six attempts the call connected.

"Hello, and thank you for calling the Tucking-In Service," the recorded message said, "we are currently experiencing a high volume of calls. Your call is being held in a queue. Your call is important to us so please stay on the line and we will be with you shortly."

"But we don't need tucking-in...do we?" Midge said.

"Well, I don't think I do," Marty said, shrugging his shoulders, "but if that's what Ellie wants, then it's no big deal."

"No, I don't want tucking-in either," Ellie said. "I want an aeroplane..."

Before she had a chance to explain, a familiar voice came on the line. "Hello, Tucking-In Service, this is Babs speaking," Babs yelled, "may I have your postcode and house number, please!"

"Hello, Babs, it's Ellie, it's the house with large, black gates at the top of Cedars Road. I know we're not supposed to ask for anyone particular, but could you send June...as quick as you can."

"Now look here, madam!" Babs screamed.

Ellie put her hand over the mouthpiece. “Sounds like she’s having a nervous breakdown!”

“Have you any idea how busy we are tonight?” Babs continued. “Hysteria’s sweeping the capital! I’ve had to call in the Mum Police for backup! You’ll have to wait your turn like everyone else and make do with whoever turns up!”

Ellie heard the familiar, rasping flick of the cigarette lighter. “Oh. Okay. Sorry you’re having a bad night. Bye.”

“Good...” suck, pop, inhale of smoke, “...bye,” Babs hollered. The call disconnected.

Ellie put the phone down. “That’s annoying. We’re running out of time. We need to speak to June tonight.”

“Why June?” Marty said.

“Because according to Scott, she used to work as an air traffic controller and I thought she might know someone with a plane.”

“That’s brilliant!” Midge said. A loud knock spun everyone’s head. “Blimey, I wonder who that is.”

“Hello, is anybody there?” a voice shouted through the letterbox.

“It’s June!” Ellie said. She ran down the hallway and opened the front door. “It’s another one of those massive coincidences! I’ve just been trying to get hold of you!”

“Hello, hun,” June said, breezing in. “I wish I could say it’s because I’m telepathic, but actually, I was parked outside when I heard your call over the radio. Babs always forgets to switch the stupid thing off, especially when she’s under pressure. I drove round especially...I had to see those purple roses for myself. I'm in-between jobs, I can't stay long."

"Well, I'm sorry, but I don't know anyone who owns an aeroplane." June put her mug of tea down and picked up one of the dream roses. "I just can't leave them alone." She stroked the petals with her fingertips. "Wow! It's like holding a piece of heaven in my hands." She closed her eyes.

"Can you hear...or see...or sense anything?" Scott said.

"I feel incredible peace," June said.

"What about words...or visions?" Ellie said. "Can you tell us something more...more factual?"

June opened her eyes. "No, I'm sorry, honey, they hold no specific message for me. And...well...to be honest, I didn't expect them to. These flowers are nothing short of miracles and they've been manifested into the material world by all of you."

"Well, I can't hear anything unusual," Scott said. "And Midge...she can't see anything. They just appear like normal flowers to us."

Midge stood up and walked around the table. "Excuse me, but I've got to do this." She cupped her hands around June's face and patted gently. "Just checking...you know...to see you're real: flesh and bone, living."

"One hundred percent mortal," June said, laughing. "I promise. Hand on beating heart."

"So, what happens next? What should we do?" Ellie said.

"I'd go to Heathrow if I were you. I've got a friend who still works there. He's told me there's hundreds of aircraft parked on one of the runways."

"How come?" Midge said.

"When the Purple cleared they were sitting there. As far as we know, every plane made it safely onto the ground."

"Awesome!" Marty said. "So, are you saying we could use one?"

June shrugged her shoulders. "Maybe. It's worth a try. Trouble is, there's bound to be a fuel guard on duty."

"Couldn't we have a whip-round? Surely we could raise enough money to buy some?" Midge shoved her hands in her pockets and jangled her loose change.

"We'd never raise enough cash," June said. "Fuel's virtually priceless and, anyway, until my bank account's re-credited next Monday, I'm living hand-to-mouth."

"Until your bank account's re-credited," Marty repeated. He turned to Ellie. "Reminds me of a story you told us yesterday."

"Does it?"

"Yes...yes, it does. I can't believe no one's thinking what I'm thinking."

"Well, go on," Ellie said.

"Until the new banking system's sorted out, you're supposed to keep a record of what your tenants owe you...isn't that what you said?"

"Yes."

"And haven't you made a deal with one of them? You falsify his records if he keeps you supplied with something that's worth its weight in gold?"

The mist cleared. "Oh my God," Ellie said, "we can bribe the fuel guard."

"With what?" June said.

"Chocolate!" Marty shouted. "Ellie's tenant, Mr Pink, has given her stacks of it. She keeps it hidden in her office."

June threw her hands into the air. "Incredible! Truly amazing! We need to move fast. I think you need to fly up there tonight...under the cover of darkness."

"Tonight?" Midge said.

June nodded. "By tomorrow morning that ludicrous Power for Protection Movement may have already commandeered all the fuel...it'll be too late."

"Yeah, yeah, you're right...tonight's as good a time as any."

"Oh no, I've just had a thought," Ellie said. "Yesterday, Ping was alone with the entire contents of the treasure cupboard. I know for certain we ate a chocolate Santa, and then, when I left the office, she was halfway through a box of after-dinner mints. She could have wolfed the lot by now!"

June grabbed her keys off the table. "Action stations! Ellie, you come with me. We'll drive to your office first...and then...if the cupboard's bare...we'll head over to Mr Pink's...see if he's got anything left."

"I'll phone Mr Rupert," Marty said, "what should I tell him?"

“Find out his address. Now…let me think…tell him we’ll pick him up around midnight. And Scott, can you get your van ready to roll? Clear out the back and check to see you’ve got enough in the tank to get us to Heathrow. We’ll siphon some petrol from my Smart Car if we have to. Also, throw some duvets and pillows in there…bottles of water…any food you’ve got lying around…you’ll need things like that at the other end.”

“I’m onto it,” Scott said.

“I’ll load the dishwasher,” Midge said, “and hopefully there’ll be some space for an evil, twisted monster.”

“Huh?” Marty said.

“Nothing,” Midge said.

By eleven-forty, June and Ellie had returned.

An intoxicating array of edible treasure glittered on the kitchen table: three and a quarter boxes of chocolate-covered after-dinner mints, half a jar of luxury hot chocolate drinking powder, two and a half packets of chocolate covered peanuts, one “creme” egg, one chocolate orange and several bags of chocolate coins.

“I hope this is going to be enough,” Ellie said, “we stopped at Mr Pink’s on the way back, but there was no answer.”

“Well…it’ll have to be,” Midge said.

“I’m so excited for you all,” June said. “I have a feeling something incredible is about to happen.”

“I’m a bit scared,” Ellie said. “I keep thinking about that creepy, hooded figure I saw in the garden.

Maybe it's the ghost of Harold Crinklebottom, and – in case anyone's forgotten – he's a murderer!"

"Don't worry," Scott said, "no one with a name like that can scare me." He turned to June. "We'll be okay, won't we?"

"Yes, hun, of course you will."

"Can't you come with us?"

"I'd love to, but I've got my animals," June took a piece of paper from the pocket of her camouflage trousers, "and this is my work roster. I'm doing seven shifts this week. I haven't got a minute. You'll be okay...I promise. This is your journey, not mine."

The room fell silent. Ellie dragged a chair out from under the table: the grumble of heavy oak on stone floor giving sound to her feelings.

"Hey, come on! All of you! It's all about reading the signs."

"Signs?" Marty said.

"Yes, signs," June said. "Often, we have an intuitive feeling, and then, straight away, our rational mind tells us we're making a mistake. But if we pay attention, we're likely to see signs...they'll help us to know we're headed in the right direction."

"Can you give us an example," Ellie said.

"Yes! That's a good idea," Midge said. "I'd love an example. Thing is...we...we...might be about to fly in a plane. Driven, or whatever the word is, by some old bloke. Sorry, Marty, I'm not being rude, it's just that...I mean...the whole thing is a bit...a bit...extreme!"

"Signs come in all shapes and forms. They can be obvious and very dramatic, or they can be subtle.

Either way, they make us feel something here." June placed her hand on her stomach.

The four of them half-nodded, but none of them spoke.

"Oh, for goodness' sake! Do I have to spell them out to you?"

"Yes, June, you do," Midge said. "You have to be specific. We're all crapping ourselves."

"Right. Let me be detailed and explicit. You two crashed into each other on an empty bus at seven in the morning! You found a photo in an old lady's home that looks like a picture from your dream! You were visited by your mum's energy and given directions to Piccadilly Circus. You met Marty, who, by a strange twist of fate, ended up working in a hairdressing salon and created a hairstyle like the setting sun. The salon's owned by a man who's willing to fly you to Scotland!" June walked over to the table and picked up the vase containing the purple dream roses. "And then…there's these…the biggest sign of all!"

Midge started laughing. "Oh, those signs!" She placed her hand on her stomach. "I feel a bit sick."

"Well, you do have a choice. You could forget the whole thing right now and go to bed."

"No! That ain't gonna happen," Marty said.

"All the signs point to us flying up to Scotland," Ellie said. "Sorry, but you know they do."

"I know, I know," Midge said. She scraped the hair from her face then turned away. Slowly, she paced the kitchen floor. When she reached the door, she stopped and turned back. "We'd better get a move on, then."

"Yes!" Ellie clapped her hands together. "Everybody grab a toothbrush and a change of clothes…let's load up the van!"

"I'll open the gates," June said. "See you all outside in a minute."

Ellie checked her watch. "It's twenty past midnight, are we running late?"

"No, it's cool. I've phoned Mr Rupert. He said he'd meet us there. He said he had something important to do. He said don't worry, he'd definitely show up. He's gonna meet us outside Terminal Five arrivals around twelve thirty."

"So…that's us then…everything's sorted," Ellie said.

"Well, almost," Midge said, "but not quite. What about Penny Treasure? What about The Power for Protection Movement…and Willie Piles…and everyone's money? Surely someone needs to be here. She needs to be stopped…or at least closely monitored. She needs to be exposed."

"Are you trying to tell us you want to stay behind?" Marty said.

"No…I'm not…honest."

"Just as well," Scott said. "Each one of us has a flower, each one of us has a part to play. All of us must make this journey."

"But she does have a point," Ellie said. "Penny's out of control. Someone needs to get that information from her handbag."

"Someone brave…and with attitude," Marty said. "And, I mean, *big* attitude. I don't know anyone in this town who's qualified for that job."

"I do," Ellie said, grabbing her phone.

"You're not about to ring the Tucking-In Service again, are you?" Midge said. "I know Babs can be scary, but..."

"No! I'm not about to ring that lunatic woman, I've got a much better idea." Ellie tapped a few buttons. "Come on, pick up..."

"Hello...what time is it?"

"Sorry to wake you in the middle of the night...it's late. Twenty past twelve."

"Oh, Ellie, it's you...what's...is something wrong? Are you okay?"

"Yes, I'm fine. I need you to do something for me, something important."

"Yeah, sure, what?"

"Get a pen and paper...and Ping...while you're at it stick the kettle on...you're going to need a strong cup of coffee for this one."

~ Twenty-Seven ~

"Creme" Egg Vision

The whole moon had a ringside seat.

Silver light had oxidized the yard, coating everything in non-colour. Edges and boundaries looked blurred.

Midge threw her hastily packed rucksack into the back of the van then clambered in behind Marty. A rush of cool air danced through her Flaming Fox fringe. She turned and, for a split second, thought she caught sight of two old ladies. Scott slammed the doors shut behind her. She kneeled up, pressing her face against the window. Seconds later, the van turned left, obscuring her vision. The van headed north on Cedars Road. Midge sat back down.

"Are you okay?" Marty said.

"Yes, I think so." Midge pulled her backpack behind her head and made a pillow. She closed her eyes. A buckle poked into her neck, but she ignored it.

I need to unscramble my fears, she thought. I need to make a list of them...count them out...

Is death around the corner?

Is something evil waiting for us in the garden?

Are we blindly walking into a trap?

I feel sick...it's probably nerves.

Is Doubt going to have the last laugh?

Is it possible to die from a lack of sleep?

Did I just see the ghosts of Pearl and Opal, and if I did, why didn't they speak to me or give me some words of reassurance?

I'm still seeing dead people.

Who is this Mr Rupert and can he be trusted to fly us to Scotland?

What if the plane crashes? Bloody hell…death's a big feature on my list. Maybe I need to focus on the positive? I need to take control. I need to do what Scott did in June's garden. I'm clearing my mind…I'm making space for positive thoughts…I am in control. Think of two positive things…come on…there must be at least two. YES! HERE THEY COME!

1. I've never been in an aeroplane before!

2. Everything could go according to plan, and if it does, I'll discover the secrets of the Purple…I'll find out what happened to Mum and Dad! Why didn't I think of that before? That's the most significant thought of all! It's the reason for everything! It's the reason we're taking such a stupid risk! Brilliant…thank you…I feel slightly better.

The motion of the van jiggled Midge and her backpack from side to side. The buckle moved: no longer poking her in the neck. She took a calm breath. Moon and streetlight flashed through the windows. The whisper and mumble of friends' voices soothed her tired mind.

"We're here." Midge felt a hand on her shoulder. "Wake up...we're at the airport."

~ooOoo~

Starved of lighting, the black silhouette of Terminal Five reminded Ellie of a beached oil tanker. However, as they approached, a mass of gargantuan steel tubes and glass panels slowly revealed themselves. Signs for Short Term Parking and dozens of abandoned luggage trolleys put paid to the idea that this was anything other than an airport building. Suitcases, most of them ransacked, had been piled high at bus stops and doorways.

Ellie scratched the top of Frank's head. "He's turned himself into a furry ball of sulk."

"Don't worry," June said. "I'll take him home with me. I promise to love him like my own...till you get back."

Ellie lifted him onto June's lap. "Thanks."

Scott stopped the van by a no parking sign. "I've driven the length of the arrivals area, but I can't see Mr Rupert. Did he say anywhere in particular?"

"No," Marty shouted from behind, "he just said Terminal Five arrivals."

"I could do with some air." Ellie opened the window. "Someone's coming!" She leaned out. "I can see two figures...one of them's waving!" She heard Marty open the back doors.

"Rascal!" the waving one shouted.

"It's Mr Rupert!" Marty shouted.

The figures approached and Ellie immediately recognised the other. “Mrs Mackay?”

“I’m sorry we’re late everyone…but it took me an hour to persuade Maisie.”

Maisie Mackay gasped for air. “Heavens! I haven’t moved that fast in years!” She rested an elbow on the extendable handle of her wheelie bag. “We thought you hadn’t seen us.”

“You’re amazing,” Ellie said, “you look fantastic…the jacket…the headscarf…like a 1950’s movie star!”

“It’s classic Chanel,” the old lady said, “you can’t go wrong.”

“Whoa! Slow down! Rewind! This is crazy! How do you two know each other?”

“Aha! Good question, rascal! Allow me to enlighten you…earlier today…when we were in the salon…Ellie told us a Mrs Mackay had given her the key to the garden…and…would you believe it…by ridiculous coincidence…my sister Renee plays bridge with someone who goes by that name! As soon as I got home I gave her a call.”

“Yes, I would believe it,” Ellie said, jumping out. “It’s a sign! A sign that we’re on the right path!”

“Is it?” Mr Rupert said, grinning back. “How exciting. How very exciting!”

“Are you coming with us,” Ellie said, “you know…all the way to Scotland?”

“Yes…yes, I am,” the old lady said. “Captain Bossy here wouldn’t take no for an answer.” She reached over and patted Mr Rupert on the chest.

"Mind you, I've never been able to resist a man in uniform."

"You look awesome," Marty said. "Is it all original?"

Mr Rupert removed his officer's service dress cap. "Certainly is, rascal! The flying boots have perished a little, but the rest's as good as new."

"What's this?" Ellie said, pointing to the scarlet ribbon.

"It's the Victoria Cross medal," June shouted from inside the van, "my grandfather used to have one…they're awarded for bravery."

June, Scott and Midge joined them on the pavement and Ellie smiled at the obligatory round of polite handshakes, introductions and small talk. It amused her that a midnight rendezvous to steal a plane wasn't a big enough excuse to forgo manners.

"What we're looking for," Mr Rupert said, getting straight down to business, "is something gutsy and versatile. We need an aircraft that's large enough to carry the six of us safely, but at the same time, small enough to land on a sixpence. I'd prefer non-retractable landing gear, flight trim control via a moveable tail plane, an automatic fuel management system, clear instrument panel lighting and heavy duty brakes. According to Maisie, there should be plenty of parkland near to the castle and I want to be able to use it as a landing strip. I'm very familiar with modern planes, so I know what I'm looking for."

"The security barrier's to the left of the building," June said. "I'm afraid we'll have to negotiate it if we want to get airside."

Mr Rupert checked his watch. "The time is upon us! Courage everyone! Let's go plane hunting!"

June guided a handbag-clutching Mrs Mackay to the front seat of the van and Ellie lifted the wheelie bag into the back. When the van pulled off, her stomach flipped. Talking about bribing a fuel guard was one thing, but doing it was absolutely and completely another. She reached her sweaty palms into the carrier bag and lifted out a "creme" egg. This was it…no going back. They were minutes away from a negotiation that could end in failure and possible arrest, or supply them with an aircraft, filled with fuel, that would fly them through the pitch-black of night into the unknown.

Midge patted Ellie on the leg. "You all right?"

"Think so."

Midge rummaged through her pockets. "Don't suppose you've got an elastic band?"

"What?"

"My hair…it's all over the place."

"No…sorry…no, I haven't."

"Has anyone got an elastic band?" Midge enquired. When no one replied she scraped her fringe away from her face and muttered, "Flaming fox."

The van stopped short of the security gate.

"Best we take a moment to prepare ourselves," Captain Rupert Dodge said, his voice loaded with confidence. "Who's got the chocolate?"

"Me," Ellie squeaked. She coughed to clear her throat.

"If you feel up to it," he continued, "I think it should be you alone who approaches the fuel guard. If we go as a group…well…we run the risk of scaring him. A single female will appear unthreatening. What do you think?"

"Don't be scared, we're right behind you," Marty said.

"I'm not scared!" Ellie said. This time, her words pelted the air like machine-gun fire.

Without pausing, she picked up the bag of treasure, turned the lever, and pushed the door open. Night air, like cold, black water, rushed in and swallowed everyone. She stepped out onto the road and silently closed the door.

Not far ahead, in the illuminated security booth, solid arms and exceptionally broad shoulders filled a bottle green, short-sleeved shirt to bursting point. Above the muscles, an absurdly small uniform cap teetered on top of a fat, pink, shaved head. Moths, drunk on yellow light, crashed at the windows. Ellie took a few steps forward then stopped. Quickly, she tried to decide on an opening line.

Hello, I've come about a plane.

No, that sounded stupid.

Do you like chocolate?

No, that sounded completely stupid.

Trouble was, there were too many options. She couldn't think where to begin. Should she attempt to tell him the whole story? Should she start with the dream…then go on to talk about meeting Midge on the bus…and then explain about the photograph…the purple roses and the key to the garden? At that rate, she'd be there all night. Something bashed one of her ankles. She froze. A familiar purr turned fear into relief.

"You sneaky little thing! Who told you it was okay to get out of the van?"

Frank didn't bother to answer; he just made a run for it.

"No, come back!" Ellie shouted.

The muscle-bound guard jumped up, cupped his hands to the window and peered out. Ellie dropped to the floor, hopeful that strip lighting had reduced his pupils to nail holes. She watched him shrug his shoulders then turn and sit back down.

Frank continued to gather speed. In a desperate panic, Ellie picked herself up and chased after him. A small ramp provided the perfect launch pad, and Frank's leap across the handrail appeared effortless. Stretched out like a fur stole, his two front paws attached themselves to the door handle; muscles, claws and sinew working together in perfect harmony. The fluffy silhouette hovered in midair for a second then dropped. The door burst open.

The fuel guard leapt to his feet. "What the blazes…!"

Ellie, who'd tripped on the edge of the ramp and completely missed the handrail, crashed into the table. Flailing over the top of it, she grappled to catch the guard's radio. "Do you like chocolate?" she yelled.

"No, I don't," the furious guard roared. "I hate it!"

The veins in Ellie's head pulsated. With her full body weight on her hands, the piece of radio dug deep into her right palm. Remnants of a "creme" egg oozed between the fingers of her left hand. Slowly, she relaxed her arms, tucked in her head, and forward-rolled herself to safety. Clumsy, "creme" egg fingers slipped on surfaces. The distorted shape of the fuel guard glared across the table. Ellie closed her eyes and waited for the stars to fade.

"Well, would you believe it?" the distorted shape said.

"Believe what?" Ellie quickly processed the situation. She was standing in a very small room with a very large fuel guard who hated chocolate. She had broken his radio, scared him half to death and the only way out was behind him.

"It's Ellie, isn't it?"

Ellie had to admit his voice did sound strangely familiar. She opened her eyes and squinted. Harsh lighting and "creme" egg filling were giving her vision a run for its money. "Yes, it is," she said.

She rubbed her eyelids with the backs of her hands then blinked several times. Thankfully, the distorted shape reformed itself and finally came into focus. On the other side of the table stood the familiar punch-bag face of Big Bernard the Bulldog, Mrs Mackay's ex-boxer neighbour from the third floor.

~ Twenty-Eight ~

Your Nearest Emergency Exit May be Behind You

"Actually, I love chocolate, but usually it's made in factories which process nuts and I'm highly allergic to those." Big Bernard the Bulldog made a choking sound then clutched his throat. "One whiff of a peanut and it's curtains for me."

It fascinated Scott that someone so enormous, with muscles like meteorites, could be snuffed out by something so small and insignificant as a peanut. It didn't seem possible. He lifted the last piece of chocolate from the floor, placed it on the table, and watched Big Bernard's plump, sausage-like fingers wrap a bandage around Ellie's bleeding hand.

"So yes, that's all we want," Mr Rupert said, "a small aircraft and enough fuel to get us to Scotland."

"Just to get you there?" Big Bernard said. "Don't you want to come back?"

"Yes! We do! It's just that...well...we don't want to push our luck."

"Push it as far as you can," Big Bernard said.

"So...is there a plane we can use?" Scott said.

"I think we can sort something out," Big Bernard said. "Are you the driver of the van?" Scott nodded. "Well, you'll need to take us to Terminal 5B."

Following Big Bernard's instructions, Scott turned right and drove past a long line of British Airways aeroplanes.

"I say!" Mr Rupert exclaimed. "Look at this...the wing tips are almost touching! I've never seen so many in the one place!"

Holiday nostalgia came back for a hug. Last year Scott had flown to Los Angeles on a British Airways jumbo and now, as he drove past them, he couldn't help remembering. He wondered which one was theirs. Which one of these giant, steel birds had flown them halfway round the world for that final, happy holiday together? Which one had a piece of chewing gum stuck under seat 35K? The window seat, where Scott had watched movies for ten hours solid and eaten chicken casserole and trifle with plastic cutlery, served on a plastic tray, his mum sitting next to him.

"Turn right here. I said turn right here! Earth to Scott!" Mr Rupert tapped Scott gently on the shoulder.

"Sorry, what?"

"Turn right...here...after this last aeroplane."

"Oh, right...sorry...my head...it's somewhere else."

"No need to apologise," Mr Rupert said. "I recognise that far away look, I've caught it in the mirror. Memories highjack me, too."

"I'll bet they do," Scott said.

Scott parked the van and jumped onto the tarmac. Two colossal engines, suspended from a wing, dwarfed him. The contraption parked in front of the van looked hilariously small in comparison: like a toy.

It had five windows down each side and a propeller on the front.

"This is what I had in mind," Big Bernard said.

"Holy moly," Mrs Mackay muttered.

"Not getting cold feet, are you, Maisie dear?"

"Certainly not," Mrs Mackay said. "I've got my thermal stockings on."

Mr Rupert laughed. "It's perfect," he said between chuckles, "absolutely perfect."

"Great," Big Bernard said, "give me a few minutes and I'll be back with the refuelling truck."

Uneasiness engulfed Scott like a mudslide. "Are you sure this...little thing...can fly all the way to Scotland?"

Mr Rupert adjusted his cap. "Yes, I know it can."

"Oh good. Just checking."

"Courage! Conviction!" Mr Rupert said. "What I don't know about aviation could be written on the back of a postage stamp. I might be old, but I'm not an idiot. Do you honestly think I'd risk all our lives? Does anyone trust me to get us there safely?"

"I do," Marty said without delay.

"Thank you, rascal. Now listen carefully everyone and I'll tell you what I know. This Nixon 700 can easily get us to Scotland. It has an approximate range of 900 nautical miles which, roughly speaking, is nine hours of flying time. Cruising at top speed we should be there in four."

"Four hours!" Marty said.

"Yes, rascal, four hours, but don't panic, time passes quickly when you're having fun. We'll be eating haggis before you know it."

"Oh look, it's got a sliding door on the side," Midge said.

"Yes, it has," Mr Rupert said with a wink, "very handy if we need to parachute out."

Pillows, duvets, backpacks, Mrs Mackay's wheelie bag, bottles of water and several large Tupperware boxes of sandwiches (lovingly supplied by Renee) were stowed and secured.

June stood at the door and gave pre-boarding hugs. "Oh, you're travelling in first class today sir…let me show you to your seat!"

"Sorry I didn't get chance to fix your bike."

"No worries," June said. "I'll park the van in the yard and post the keys through the letterbox. They'll be waiting for you when you get back."

If I get back, Scott thought. He climbed aboard and took the seat directly behind Mr Rupert.

Big Bernard arrived in the refuelling truck. "I'll fill her up," he shouted. "That way you'll have enough to get you there and back, plus an extra hour."

"Like riding a bike…just like riding a bike," Mr Rupert mumbled in response.

Scott leaned over the old man's shoulder. "Shouldn't we wait till sunrise? Marty thought we could follow the motorways. He had a look at a map earlier…it's the M1, M6 then the M74."

"We can't wait till sunrise!" Mr Rupert turned to his dreadlocked co-pilot and squeezed his shoulder. "That information is impressive, rascal, but thankfully, this aircraft has a full navigational system. Even if it didn't I'd be using celestial navigation."

"Celestial what?" Scott said.

"Well, during the war, we used to track our position by measuring the angles between objects in the sky. The Lancaster Bombers that I flew had glass bubbles called astrodomes on the top of them, that's where the navigator sat."

"Cool as ice!" Marty said.

"I've located the North Star, so I already know which direction we should be headed in. Sunrise will be at approximately four forty, which means the last hour and twenty minutes of the flight will be in daylight."

Big Bernard's bald head appeared at the window. "I've checked all your doors are properly shut. It's a short taxi to the southerly runway. Once you're up you'll need to turn left...but I'm sure you know that already."

Mr Rupert nodded then reached his arm out the window and clasped hands with Big Bernard. It looked to Scott like a brotherly, comrades-in-arms-type clasp: the type he'd seen in films about the war.

"I owe you a free haircut my friend!" Mr Rupert quipped. He turned the key in the ignition. The propeller whirred to life, unleashing an onslaught of noise and vibration.

"Chocks away!" Big Bernard pulled the rubber blocks from under the tyres and the plane glided forwards.

As they bounced towards the runway, Scott pressed his face against the window. He waved a hand at June then checked to see his seatbelt was securely fastened. A finger tapped him on the arm. "Would you like a wee mint?"

"Oh, yeah, thanks." Scott took a mint from the tin then passed it back to the old lady. He sucked hard. Maybe sugar could coax his dry mouth back to life. He closed his eyes. *Mum, I don't know if you can hear me…get us there in one piece.*

~ooOoo~

The plane bounced along the taxiway and Midge chewed a piece of loose skin from a finger.

"Ladies and gentlemen," the captain's voice said over the PA system, "welcome aboard this Air Rupert flight to Bonny Scotland. We shall be flying non-stop at a height of 4,000 feet. In preparation for take-off please ensure your seatbelt is fastened, your seatback is in the upright position, your tray table is stowed away and that all baggage is safely tucked under the seat in front. Also, please take a moment to familiarize yourself with your nearest emergency exit."

The emergency word lassoed Midge's attention. She stopped chewing her fingers.

"Chief Stewardess Midge will now point out your nearest exit," the captain said.

"Who me?"

Unable to ignore the cheering, Midge reluctantly dragged herself to the front of the cabin. After hitting her head three times on the ceiling, she did a semi-squat.

"There is one emergency exit at the rear of the aircraft." Midge pointed to the rear and did what she considered to be a glamorous stewardess smile.

Everyone applauded. “There are two exits on the flight deck, one on the left and one on the right.” Midge tottered round, being careful not to headbutt the ceiling, and pointed a chewed finger in each direction. More applause. “And finally,” the captain said, “there is one sliding door to your right.” Midge turned back and pointed to the sliding door, but this time, in an attempt to mimic a game show host directing the audience’s attention to the star prize, she used both arms and did a mini curtsy. Cheering, foot stomping and several whistles drowned out the noise of the engine. “After take-off,” the captain continued, “Chief Stewardess Midge will be passing through the cabin serving you an in-flight meal which, today, thanks to an allergy-suffering fuel guard, will contain a large portion of chocolate. Please now relax, sit back and enjoy the flight.”

Buoyed by the attention, Midge did another curtsy and made her way back to her seat.

The plane paused at the top of the runway.

The engine idled.

Midge stared at the man in the moon.

The engine roared.

The plane lurched forwards. It picked up speed. A pair of invisible hands pushed Midge’s shoulders back against the seat. She stared up at the ceiling and gripped the armrest. She glanced down the aisle, towards the flight deck window. “I must remain calm,” she mumbled. Arghhh! We’re going really fast, she thought. The front is lifting! Whoa! The lights on the runway…they’ve vanished! Below her feet Midge heard a rumble, which sounded like the wheels falling off.

"That's the landing gear coming up!" a voice said.

Midge gulped, opened her mouth and her ears popped. Normal volume whooshed in. Shit! That was quick! It's happened already! I'm defying gravity!

The miracle of flight somersaulted through Midge's body. On the way down to her stomach it paralyzed her vocal chords. Her hot feet tingled with the vibration. She gazed, wide-eyed, at the blinking lights below. I'm up in the air, and that's my life down there. I live in a concrete box, with a balcony, in Clapham. I'm an ant…just a dot…a miniscule organism. If I died right now who would care? What difference would it make to the world? Who would miss me?

Ding! The seatbelt sign went off.

"Ladies and gentlemen," the captain said, "Chief Stewardess Midge will now distribute chocolate!"

That's me. Better get up. Be normal. Speak. Midge swallowed hard. "Good evening, Captain…I'd like to offer you first choice from the bag of treasure. No "creme" egg, I'm afraid…that got splattered."

"Oh, how marvellous, but I insist you ask my co-pilot first."

Midge turned to offer Marty some chocolate. "Sleeping?" she croaked. "How can someone sleep at a time like this?" She passed Mr Rupert two bags of chocolate coins. Mr Rupert didn't respond, but that suited Midge just fine: silence must equal deep concentration.

"Some chocolate?"

"Too right!" Scott said. "The chocolate orange…is that a bit greedy?"

"Not if you share it with me," Ellie said, stretching her hand across the aisle.

Midge noticed her mouth had turned unusually watery. "Sort it out amongst yourselves." She thrust the orange into Scott's hand. Ignoring the lump in her throat, she moved down the aisle. "What about you?"

"Och, just an after-dinner mint if you have one," Mrs Mackay said.

"You only want one? Have two," Midge said.

The old lady took the mints, popped one in her mouth and put the other in her handbag.

Midge dropped into the seat behind Mrs Mackay, clicked her seatbelt together and stared at the remaining chocolate in the bag. Ignoring Doubt, she opened a pack of chocolate-covered peanuts. She tipped a handful into her mouth. She didn't waste time sucking off the chocolate. She scoffed them in seconds then took another handful, then another. She shoved the empty bag into her pocket. Maybe a few chocolate coins? No one's looking…why not…

The plane banked sharply to the left. The man in the moon slid out of sight then bounced back. Midge's stomach rolled with him and her watery mouth returned.

Midge swallowed hard. She leaned forward and rested her head on the back of Mrs Mackay's seat. She crumpled the foil from the last chocolate coin. She took a desperate, deep breath. Her stomach contracted. It's coming! Frantically, she reached into her backpack and pulled out a plastic bag. Inside was

Jane Austen's *Pride and Prejudice*, but there was no time to remove it. All the chocolate peanuts, enough chocolate coins to buy a tank of petrol and the remnants of last night's mushroom stroganoff rained down on Mr and Mrs Bennet, their five children and the handsome Mr Darcy.

Midge scraped the hair from her face, groaned and then spat a mouthful of gunk into the bag.

"Ach, poor wee thing," Mrs Mackay said.

Midge peered up. Ellie and Scott had their noses buried in their hands. "Sorry, everyone..."

The old lady unclasped her handbag and rummaged through its contents. "If you can manage to swallow it, I think you should take one of these travel sickness tablets."

Midge licked the pill from her palm and took a glug of water. She dropped her head between her legs and closed her eyes.

"Here, have some tissues," Ellie said. "Are you okay?"

Midge took the tissues, but didn't reply. Drifting off, she heard a small Scottish voice whisper, "I think someone's had too much excitement for one day." She wanted to lift her head and say, actually it's too much chocolate, but she couldn't find the strength.

~ooOoo~

Marty had fallen deep.

He found himself jogging along a deserted road, fog clouding his vision. Above him, something towered in the low cloud. To his right he noticed a barrier, then a vertical pillar of red steel. He clambered up onto the handrail. The air, heavy with moisture, pulled down on his T-shirt. The soles of his sneakers squeaked and slipped on the metal. Below, white mist dropped to oblivion. Thick suspension cables stretched upwards, directing the way. Marty began to climb up over gnarled rivets and bolts; the colossal pillar of steel reminding him of a giant redwood tree. With an agility that Spiderman would envy, he tore upwards. Rugged determination brushed aside terror. Deep gulps, white nail beds, limbs aching, windpipe whistling, sweat dripping and then…finally…sunlight! Marty was standing on one of the towers of the Golden Gate Bridge. Down below, his hometown yawned: the upper floors of San Francisco's skyscrapers peeked through a bedspread of cloud.

Marty stared down at the football. He smiled. He knew he had acquired all the necessary skills to score the perfect goal. If he remained focused and kept his aim direct, he could achieve victory and send it spinning between the two towers at the opposite end of the bridge. With both eyes on the ball, he took two steps back. When his heel dropped lower than expected it sent a panicked signal to his brain. In an instant, he realized his error. Desperately, he grasped at nothing. He circled his arms to alter the balance. He screamed as he fell backwards. Rushing mist billowed his T-shirt like a tangled parachute. The rock hard surface of the Pacific Ocean ran towards him at eighty-eight miles an hour.

"Hold on!" a voice shouted. "Clear air turbulence!"

"Wow!" Marty said. "I was dreaming…I was falling…it felt so real!"

"Well, that's probably because we were, rascal. We must have dropped a couple of hundred feet."

"Uh?"

"Don't lose sleep, rascal, we hit an air pocket, it's a common occurrence, I just wasn't expecting it. Usually, that sort of thing happens higher up, somewhere between 7,000 and 12,000 feet."

"Radical," Marty said. He placed a hand over his thumping heart and stretched out a cramping leg muscle.

"Life is like a game of snakes and ladders, rascal…nothing's guaranteed."

"I must remember to keep my eye out for the snakes…"

"Sometimes it's impossible to dodge one, rascal. We roll the dice and we take our turn. That's life. Always remember the ladders are what make life worth living…and don't worry…there's plenty of them."

"If you say so."

"I do, rascal…look at me…I'm eighty-four…and I'm climbing one of the biggest ladders of my life! I feel like I'm twenty again, only this time round it's much better. I'm not on a mission of destruction. I'm not about to release a barrage of bombs, obliterating buildings and destroying lives. This time I'm part of a magnificent plan. I'm on a mission of love…one that may unite you with your parents. I'm flying high, rascal, and it has nothing to do with the aeroplane!"

Marty opened a bag of coins and removed the gold foil from two. After passing one to Mr Rupert, he placed the other on his tongue. He tried not to suck, grind or swirl, he wanted it to melt slowly, to last forever. He unpeeled another. He stared out the window and saw something amazing: his reflection, sitting in the cockpit of a plane, stars tangled in his hair. Not far from his own ghostly mirage, Mr Rupert's ethereal form floated in the black, his hands tweaking dials on the instrument panel. Marty watched in silence. In a quiet corner of his mind, he knew this hero from history was only on loan to the present day. He understood that the magical effects of the Purple were wearing off, and that the limitations of an eighty-four-year-old body would soon return. He opened his mouth to ask Mr Rupert about the condition of his arthritic hand, and then closed it. Instinct told him not to say a word. Marty realised that the very mention of the problem would cause it to grow. It would be like waking a monster. For now, the aches and pains appeared to be sleeping and, for everyone's sake, they were better left that way.

Marty thought about the last time he had flown. That flight across the Atlantic bore little resemblance to this one. The flight from San Francisco had been enforced. He had been a hostage. Freedom of choice had been withdrawn without notice. Hands, like cold, metal handcuffs had pinched his wrists. His parents had frogmarched him onto the plane, and he had hated them for it, but now, unbelievably, he was on his way to find them.

On the surface this seemed like a strange thing to be doing, but a quick search underneath the layers of sadness and anger easily revealed the reason: Marty had his own Missing Feeling. Although he couldn't forgive his parents for doing what they did, it didn't stop him from loving them. However, if, and when, he did find them, he knew things would be different. From now on they could never be the same. This experience had changed him forever. He had learned to stand on his own two feet. He knew how to create a life for himself, make friends, earn money and be happy. He had grown in knowledge and confidence. He had self-belief.

Ahead of him, the North Star shone like a beacon of hope.

Marty closed his eyes. Sleep wanted him back.

"Dream about ladders..." the old man said.

~ooOoo~

Ellie loosened her seatbelt and leaned across the aisle to speak to Mrs Mackay. "How are you feeling?"

"Honestly...to tell the truth...I'm terrified."

"Of what? Flying?"

"No dear, confronting my past."

"Of course," Ellie said.

"But I have to do it. If I don't do this now, I'll never get the chance again. It's time to exorcise the ghosts of yesterday. Time to let them rest in peace."

Ellie wished Mrs Mackay wouldn't use the word ghost.

"For years I've silently carried these memories, and now I need to set them free. Mr Rupert's right, going back to Claremont Castle will enable me to do that."

Ellie glanced down at the chocolate in her hands and realized it was beginning to melt; funny how holding on tight to something you love can cause it to spoil. She crammed five segments of chocolate orange into her mouth and chewed without reserve. She stared at the old lady and wondered if, perhaps, that's how life should be treated. Perhaps everything should be used and enjoyed immediately, before it withers.

"Not tired, dear?"

"Um, a little. Too busy thinking about stuff."

The old lady nodded her head. "Usually, things don't turn out as you expect. Years of life experience have taught me that. I hope you're prepared for the unexpected, dear. I'd hate for you to be disappointed."

"Well, if I'm honest, I'm hoping to find my mum and dad. I want to see them more than anything. Is it such a bad thing to have hope?"

Mrs Mackay shook her head. "No, dear, it isn't. Sometimes hope is all we ever have. Hope has seen me through some dark nights. But hope is not much use on its own, it needs fortitude and flexibility as constant companions."

"Flexible, like bamboo?" Ellie said.

"Well remembered," Mrs Mackay said, "always try to go with the flow…that way, life's challenges won't break you."

"And fortitude?"

"Endurance, strength and staying power; never give in, even in the bleakest of circumstances. If you were to ask me for one piece of advice, that's probably what it would be. Today is another step on your journey of life, my dear, but it may not be the step you're dreaming of. Remember, anything could happen inside that walled garden today."

Ellie nodded and tried to mentally prepare herself for anything, but it wasn't easy. "Do you think this is a bad idea? Should we have stayed at home? Played it safe?"

Mrs Mackay shook her head. "Absolutely not. We should be doing exactly this...following our hearts. Playing it safe is living half a life." She reached across and grabbed Ellie's hand. "I won't let you do that."

The old lady's charm bracelet dropped down from under the sleeve of her jacket; golden shapes twinkled as they danced in a shaft of moonlight. "It's you! It's your hand! You pulled me from the frozen water! I've seen this bracelet in my dream. I was trapped under ice...I thought it was death...but it wasn't...you were saving me from...from a life half lived!"

"That sounds wonderful, dear!" Mrs Mackay patted Ellie's hand.

"This is another sign! I know it is! They're getting easier to read. I'm so glad you're here. I think everything's going to be okay...everything's going to work out..."

"I think we should try and get some sleep, dear, don't you? We're going to need all our strength."

"Oh, okay, yes…maybe we should." Ellie sat back and tightened her seatbelt. Just breathe…that's what she said to me in my dream…that's all I have to do.

The drone of the engine had become little more than white noise, an unobtrusive hum in the background that foretold wonder. Ellie took a deep, reassuring breath and closed her eyes. A kaleidoscope pattern of hopes and fears shifted in her head. Moments later, a dreamless, dark sleep engulfed her.

Ellie woke. She stretched. She knocked the sandman from her eyes and stared out the window. Far on the eastern horizon, the day had also woken: its deep, red yawn like the mouth of a dragon. Ellie turned and stared across the aisle toward a dozing Mrs Mackay, her wrinkly face wrapped in a headscarf. Beyond the old lady, five round windows, like submarine portholes, locked out eternal deep blue. Scott's sleeping face had been painted unnaturally pink with sunrise.

The plane bumped over a succession of invisible air rocks. Mr Rupert waved a silent, reassuring hand. Ellie waved back. The world outside her window had transformed itself into a fancy cocktail: layers of orange and strawberry juice floating under a line of blackberry syrup, cloudy sediment swirling at the bottom of the glass.

Ellie checked her watch: one more hour and they'd be there.

~ Twenty-Nine ~

The Second Battle of Trafalgar

Meanwhile, on the ground in London, it was still dark.

Ping, dressed head to toe in black and high on adrenaline, re-read Ellie's instructions.

"Go to the office. Find the box file marked Penny Treasure. Take out the spare set of keys. Make a note of Penny's address and alarm code. Break into Penny's apartment and steal the brown envelope marked confidential (last seen in a snakeskin handbag). Take contents to offices of Post Purple News."

Finding the box file had been easy. On the way out of the office Ping poked her head into the treasure cupboard, hopeful that Ellie had left something behind. Not one mint. "Humph!" She stood in the doorway and adjusted the straps of her backpack. She stared down at the address in her hand: 66 Trafalgar Square, the most expensive property on the company books.

Ping shoved the address into a back pocket and slipped out onto the street. Anxious about time, she decided to power-walk. At the end of Great Marlborough Street, she turned left. Annoyingly, the streets buzzed with people. She dodged in and out of doorways, trying to keep a low profile. Someone had smashed a shop window. Showroom dummies wrapped in scarves, woollen jumpers and cobwebs lay in shattered glass. Ping dashed along Regent Street, shadow in tow, and cursed the full moon. When she reached the end of Regent Street she got the shock of her life: Piccadilly Circus looked like a regular Saturday afternoon!

An old man rushed towards her. "The Purple is coming!" He leaned into Ping's face, crossing the invisible line that marked the boundary of her personal space. His stale breath, warm on her skin, made her turn away. "You can run, but you can't hide!" he yelled.

All around, people gazed upwards. Many had binoculars or telescopes. Some had climbed the Shaftesbury Memorial Fountain. A figure clung, precariously, to the statue of Eros. Groups sat in circles holding candles. Ping lifted her eyes to the heavens and saw nothing but the moon and the stars.

"Don't leave us, child," a woman said. "Stay with us, pray with us. There is safety in numbers."

"Pray for what?"

"For protection…protection from the Purple."

Ping pulled her arm free from the woman's tight grip. "It's not the Purple we should be scared of right now."

"What do you mean?"

Ping shook the woman by the shoulders. "Hello? Is there anybody in there? Does the name Penny Treasure ring any bells? She's the mad woman who wants to blow holes in the ozone layer…"

The woman stared back at Ping. "We must trust our elected leaders…they've made a promise to save us!"

"But she wasn't elected," Ping said, "she appointed herself. And anyway, why should we trust her? She's a crook. She steals people's money!"

"You've got it all wrong," the woman said. "You're just a child, you don't know anything."

Ping resisted her urge to slap the woman. She didn't understand how people could be so naïve. She briefly considered explaining the situation, but then decided it would be a pointless exercise – a conversation with a fool would only swallow the remains of the night. The frantic impulse to stop Penny Treasure pulsated through every cell in Ping's body. It pounded in her heart and churned in her stomach. She pushed the woman as hard as she could and ran.

Despite its grand pillars, fancy ironwork and floor to ceiling windows, number sixty-six Trafalgar Square appeared unfriendly. The double doors, painted blacker than the night, loomed like the entrance to hell. Out of breath, Ping pressed a palm against the cold stone and gazed up at the penthouse on the fourth floor. She turned to face Nelson's Column. "Hello, Nelson," she waved a hand at the statue. "I don't remember the details…I was probably bunking off that day…but I know you lost your life in the fight for victory and I'm really sorry. Please don't let that happen to me."

The entrance to hell had creaky hinges. Ping inhaled musty air through her nostrils then slowly released it from her mouth. Thankfully, the moon had ignored her obscene remarks: instead of going away it had poured its remains through a skylight, and a cascade of broken moonbeams littered the communal stairway. “In and out in minutes,” she whispered. She wrapped her fingers around the polished wood handrail and began to climb.

A different key on the bunch opened Penny’s apartment door and finding it took an eternity. Ping fumbled with the lock for ages until it clicked. A monumental silence followed the clatter of keys.

Ping held her breath.

She strained her ears for the bleep-bleep of an alarm panel, but heard nothing. This meant one of two things: either Penny had forgotten to put the alarm on before she went out, or she was home and sleeping. A voice in her head, which she hoped belonged to Nelson, told her to assume the second.

Although poorly lit by fading moonlight, Ping could see that Penny’s entrance hall screamed money. An elegant console table, a vase of white lilies and a chaise longue with tasselled cushions could easily be the front cover of a glossy magazine. Even the wallpaper felt like fabric. Ping tiptoed across the intricate block flooring and into Penny’s sitting room, her torch picking out oil paintings on every wall. This place looks more like an art gallery than somewhere to crash and watch telly, she thought. Sunflowers in a vase…I’ve seen that painting somewhere before. Oh my God…I don’t believe it! There it is, sitting on the coffee table, it's the snakeskin handbag! I'VE FOUND IT!

Ping unzipped the bag and pulled out the brown envelope.

Should I use my torch again? No. It's too bright. Maybe if I head to the French doors…

In her dash for light, Ping tripped over a rug. Thankfully, the doors weren't properly locked and they burst open on impact. She landed face down on the balcony floor.

"Who the hell are you!" a voice screamed.

Ping rolled over and stared up at the figure in the doorway. "I…errm…"

"DON'T MOVE!" Penny shouted, "or I'll shoot." Penny had a gun in one hand and a phone in the other. She dialled a number, pausing after every two digits to redirect the gun at Ping's head. "Hello! Is this the Mum Police? This is Penny Treasure speaking, I want to report a break-in at my Trafalgar Square residence…hello…hello…is there anybody there? Damn it, I've lost the signal."

Penny threw the phone. After hitting Ping's forehead, it bounced across the floor. The screen flashed green for a second.

"Stand up!" Penny ordered. "Tell me your name!"

Ping lifted herself onto her feet. She touched her forehead, checking for blood. "My name's Ping, and I'm going to expose you for the cow that you are. I know what you're up to…the documents in this envelope prove it."

Penny glanced down at the envelope in Ping's hand. "They prove nothing!" She tipped her head back and roared with laughter. "But…now that you're here…as a reward for your recklessness…I might as well tell you the truth. I'm having an affair with Willie Piles…and yes…we've tricked the stupid people of London into thinking the Purple's about to return…"

"So it isn't?" Ping gasped.

"Don't interrupt me! Maybe it is…maybe it isn't. To be honest we've got no idea…we're speculating. Oh…but we have got hysteria and fear…and with their help we'll con the capital out of millions. Some of which we'll use to make weapons…better safe than sorry…but most of which we'll keep for ourselves."

"I always knew you were a con artist. I knew it the first time I saw you doing the announcements. You blink too much when you talk, that's what liars do."

"Huh." Penny shrugged. "Is that so?"

"Yes, it is! And I'm not the only person who doesn't like you. Loads of people think you're a thief."

"Ooh, we are getting our immigrant knickers in a twist…aren't we? If that's the truth then doesn't it make you wonder how I always get away with it?"

Ping didn't reply. She couldn't think what to say.

"You're one of the little people," Penny said, "and in the end, the little people always do as they're told."

"You won't get away with it this time," Ping snarled, "you ugly, evil, old rat!"

"Shut your mouth!" Don't say another word. I'm going to shoot you…and guess what? Dead people can't talk. I'll get away with murder, too. I can see the headline already…*Penny Treasure Thwarts Chinese Immigrant In Burglary Blunder*."

"Stop calling me an immigrant! I was born here!"

"I don't care," Penny said. "No one really cares about anyone. Let me tell you something, young lady. I grew up in a children's home. I was abandoned like a stray dog. Unwanted and unloved. I came from nothing. I clawed my way, tooth and nail, up the social ladder. I'm part of the elite now. I have influence. I am someone!"

"You've lost it!" Ping shouted. "You're planning to blow the ozone layer apart."

"Oh dear, what a shame, poor ozone layer." Penny's eyes bulged. "If you were remotely educated you'd know there's been a hole in the ozone layer above Australia for years. The scientists say it's already repairing itself..."

Penny continued to rant, but the words had become an undecipherable blur. Ping stared, wide-eyed, at the lunatic in the silk dressing gown. Oh my God! This could be me in fifty years time...old...bitter...lonely...bonkers! She lunged forwards, arms spinning. Penny screamed and pulled the trigger: the force of the blast knocking her backwards. The bullet whizzed over Ping's shoulder, a whistle of air racing past her ear. Penny jumped up and lashed out. Ping heard the rip of Penny's fingernails against her cheek, but felt no pain. Bleeding and furious, Ping grabbed the lapels of Penny's gown then spun her to one side. Penny skidded onto the balcony, staggering out of control, her foot landed on her mobile phone. The phone slipped on the tiled floor and Penny toppled backwards over the railings. For a second it looked like a perfect back flip. Ping dashed to the edge and reached down.

Penny's white and bloodless hands gripped the railings. "Help me! I'm going to die!"

"No! No, you're not! Grab hold of my hand! I'll pull you up!"

Penny's hand snatched the air before Ping managed to grab hold. She squeezed her fingers tightly around Penny's wrist. "I've got you!" HEAVE! This is impossible, Ping thought. HEAVE! No…I can do it! HEAVE! Isn't there a story about a mum who lifted a car off the body of her dying child? HEAVE! It was love that gave the mum her super-human strength. HEAVE! I don't remember who told me that story. I wonder if it's true? I don't love Penny. I don't even like her! I hate her.

"Arrrrgh!" Penny screamed.

"I'm sorry," Ping said, staring down into Penny's terrified eyes, "but if I hold on any longer you'll take me with you."

"Don't you dare!" Penny screamed.

"I dare," Ping whispered. And then she let go.

Penny's death plunge cry only lasted for two seconds. Ping dropped to her knees. Her hand clutched something hairy. She held it up to the sunrise. Penny's rich mahogany bouffant! It's a wig! Ping tossed it through the French doors then eased herself onto the floor.

Curled in a ball, Ping recalled the low points of her life. There's been screaming matches…even fights…but never murder! Murder! Oh my God! I've murdered someone! I feel dizzy. The wound on my cheek…it's burning. Is it murder? Could I have saved Penny if I'd really tried? What's that crackling noise?

"We're here to help you," a tiny voice said.

Ping kept her eyes shut and hoped the voice would go away.

"Please trust us," the voice pleaded.

"Leave me alone," Ping said.

"We can't do that," the voice said.

Oh my God, I'm hearing voices! Voices from where…beyond the grave…the other side…the past…the future? "I refuse to acknowledge your existence."

"Oh," the tiny voice said. "But we're outside the front door."

Ping opened her eyes. A green light flashed. She picked up the phone and put it to her ear.

"Now, listen carefully," the voice said. "My name is Deirdre and I'm not going away. We heard everything. We know you're not to blame. Please open the door and let us in."

Ping took the phone away from her ear and stared down at the screen. MUM POLICE. What an idiot! "I'm coming." She staggered through the apartment. She pressed the door entry button, eased herself onto the chaise longue and held one of Penny's over-plumped cushions to her cheek.

The Mum Police appeared in a second.

"My name's Deirdre," Deirdre said again. "This is Sonia. Do you need an ambulance?"

"No," Ping said, "just a plaster."

"And a cup of tea?" Sonia said.

"I don't like tea," Ping said.

"Oh," Sonia said.

"Is she dead? Is it messy down there?"

"Miss Treasure has a faint pulse," Deirdre said, "an ambulance crew are on the way."

"What happens now?" Ping said.

Deirdre took out her notebook. "We'll take you back to the station and get a formal statement, but there's nothing to worry about...as I said...we heard everything. We've already told the chief editor of Post Purple News to hold the front page. We need to get this story out as soon as possible. Hopefully, this town can get back to normal...whatever normal means. You're quite a hero."

Ping followed the ladies down the stairs and out into the early morning. She stared up at Nelson. Did he just wave at me? No...he couldn't have. Penny lay on the pavement, her mouth open in a silent scream, a ring of blood, like a halo, pooled around her head.

"That's ironic," Sonia said, "she's definitely no saint. I used to work for her years ago, and she stole all the money from my pension fund."

"I heard about that," Ping said. "Why do people like her always get away with it?"

"Because we let them," Sonia said. "The sad truth is most people think they're too small to make a big difference, but thankfully, you're not like most people."

Ping managed a smile. On the way to the station she tried to call Ellie, but no one answered. She sent a text message and prayed it would find its way quickly through the ether.

~ Thirty ~

Strangers in the House

When the plane bumped down onto the grass, Ellie opened her eyes immediately. “Oh blimey, we’re here!” She leaned across the aisle and patted Midge’s shoulder. “Are you still feeling rough?”

Midge lifted her head, grabbed the sick bag and dry-retched. “I’m dying,” she muttered.

A meadow of wild flowers had provided the perfect landing strip, the noisy propeller scattering sheep, like tumbling balls of wool.

“We made it! I knew we would!” Marty shouted.

“Let’s complete our post-flight checks,” Captain Rupert Dodge said.

“Oh yeah, sure thing,” Marty said.

Ellie undid her seatbelt, jumped up, slid the door open and inhaled the Scottish morning. Following a natural impulse she pulled off her shoes and socks then stepped her bare feet onto the dewy grass. “Whoo! Planet Earth! I’m glad we’re back together!” Wondering why no one else had joined her, she popped her head back into the aircraft. Mrs Mackay sat motionless, her seatbelt securely fastened.

Scott came to the door with a bag. “Once we’ve unloaded everything I think we should find a place for Midge to lie down. She needs to get some proper kip. Look at the state of her.”

Ellie nodded. “Mmm, definitely.”

Mrs Mackay had certainly been right about one thing: sometimes things don’t turn out as you expect. Ellie had imagined a very different arrival. She’d imagined them all leaping from the plane in a state of near-hysteria, and running like maniacs to the walled garden. She’d imagined them struggling with the key in the lock before kicking the door down, or climbing over the walls, SAS-style, with ladders and ropes they’d found in a nearby shed. She’d imagined them racing through the flowers, following sounds of laughter, to join their parents who were waiting at the end of a pathway, their arms open wide. She’d imagined this last bit countless times and usually it happened with a musical soundtrack, like the final scene from a cheesy movie, the type where everyone lives happily ever after. What she’d imagined was something completely different to the current, real life situation. She walked round to the front of the plane and thumped Mr Rupert’s window. “Did you see the garden? Did we fly over a walled garden filled with flowers?”

Mr Rupert opened the door. “Well, yes, I think we did but, to be honest, I was preoccupied with finding a suitable landing strip, these things don’t land themselves, you know.”

“I’m sorry…my bad…I’m *really* sorry. You’ve done a brilliant job getting us here. Amazing. Thank you.”

“No trouble,” Mr Rupert said. “So, here we are, that’s Claremont Castle…it looks incredible, doesn’t it?”

Ellie turned to face Claremont Castle and nodded her head in agreement. Built from huge blocks of streaky, gold sandstone it shone in the morning sun. At its centre stood an imposing battlement tower, surrounded by a series of leaded and tiled rooftops, countless zigzagging gables and tall chimneys.

Ellie ran back round to the sliding door. “Look! Mrs Mackay, you’re home!”

“Oh yes, dear,” the old lady said.

Scott passed the remaining supplies to Ellie. Midge staggered out with her sick bag, lowered herself onto the grass and clutched her stomach.

“What can we do to help?” Marty said.

“She won’t come out,” Ellie said, pointing at Mrs Mackay. “I think she’s having second thoughts.”

“Oh dear,” Mr Rupert said, “a firm hand may be required.” He leaned into the cabin. “Come along, old girl, shake a leg! You haven’t flown all this way just to sit and look at the place from a distance.”

“I’m staying in here.”

“Now, Maisie dear, you know as well as I do that the only way to conquer your fears is to face them head on. Everything will be just fine. The past is over…it has no control over you. You’re safe. There are no murderers here anymore.”

“It’s not just murderers! I’m terrified of seeing what should have been. This place should have been my life. It should have been my home. It’s where I was born. It’s where I lived with my parents. I don’t want to see everything and feel angry about what I never had. I don’t want the last few years of my life to be filled with bitterness.”

Mr Rupert sighed. "I never lived the life I wanted to, either. I never fell in love. Well, actually, that's not true, I did fall in love…I just didn't do anything about it…I let him walk away. Love became a missed opportunity that never knocked on my door again. I wasn't brave enough to take what could and should have been mine. Regrets, Maisie, we all have them."

"What's going on in there?"

Ellie walked over to the others. "Mr Rupert's talking about love and missed opportunities."

"Jeez!" Marty said. "They could be in there all day."

The three of them sniggered. Midge, who had her eyes shut, managed a groan.

Seconds later, Mrs Mackay emerged into the sunlight. "Sorry about that everyone…I just had a wobble…nobody likes a moaner…I'm fine now." She finished powdering her nose then dropped the compact into her bag. "Welcome to Claremont Castle everyone. Before I show you around my beautiful home, I'd like to lead us in three cheers. Well done to Captain Rupert Dodge for flying us here safely." She untied her headscarf and whirled it through the air three times. "Hip-hip-hooray! Hip-hip-hooray! Hip-hip-hooray!"

"Thank you. How marvellous," Mr Rupert said. "It was a pleasure. Now, I think what we need to do is take the supplies to the house and get settled in. Some of us could do with forty winks, and a spot of breakfast wouldn't go amiss. Sir Edmund Hillary didn't get to the top of Mount Everest on an empty stomach."

I'd like to try, Ellie thought.

The gravel driveway directly in front of the house crunched beneath Ellie's feet and some of the smaller stones got stuck between her toes. To the right of the battlement stood a grandly designed entrance porch with matching minaret towers. The head of a lion, green with lichen and stony-faced from years of waiting, stared out from the wall. Ellie gazed up at a pair of unicorns, a shield and some unfamiliar words carved into the stone. "*Ego sum peractio meus iter itineris.* What language is that? What does it mean?"

"I am completing my journey," Mrs Mackay said. "It's Latin." The old lady held out a hand, and Ellie passed her the keys. "I expect the inside may be a wee bit dusty. Do excuse the mess." After a burst of nervous laughter, everyone fell silent. "Oh," she said, looking back, "I've lost my nerve. Could someone do this for me? My hands are shaking."

Ellie and Scott jumped forwards at the same time. "I'll put the key in the lock, but you should turn it," Scott said.

The ancient device made a clunking-twang noise and the door opened effortlessly.

"Well done, Ellie!" Mr Rupert shouted. "I thought I'd have to run back to the plane and get some WD-40."

"What did you say?" Scott looked startled.

"WD-40," Mr Rupert repeated, "it's an anticorrosion spray, useful for all sorts of things. Excellent for bringing frozen locks back to life, I saw some in the aeroplane."

"No...no, that's not what I meant...did you hear something, Ellie? Did you hear that voice?"

"No. I didn't hear a thing."

"What about you?"

"No, dear," Mrs Mackay said. "But, to be honest, my hearing's not what it used to be. What was it? What did you hear? Maybe this isn't such a good idea after all."

"You know...it's nothing to worry about," Scott said. He shot Ellie a glance. "It was nothing. Just the wind blowing through an old building."

"Oh...yeah...right...that noise," Ellie said. "Yeah...I heard that...just the wind. Maybe there's a window open somewhere?"

"Get a grip of yourself, Maisie!" the old lady said. "You're acting like a ten-year-old! Where are my manners...come in, everybody."

Ellie followed the old lady into the main hall and decided it would be rude to comment on the rank smell. Oak panelling covered the walls, and an unfussy chandelier showcased ten years of cobwebs. Fascinated strangers peered down from a collection of gilt framed oil paintings.

Mrs Mackay threw her keys onto an elaborately carved table and tottered across the flagstone floor to the bay window. "Och, it's a wee bit fusty in here!" She swished back the floor-length curtains with the familiarity of someone returning from a weekend away. "I could murder a cup of tea and a biscuit!" After the laughter subsided she added, "There used to be a billiard table in here, but I expect it got sold.

Mr Russell did warn me that my nasty husband Harold auctioned off lots of furniture to clear debts."

"Hopefully, there's a bed somewhere," Midge said. "I'm really sorry…but I have to lie down…just a couple of hours. I'll be fine later."

"There's no rush," Mr Rupert said. "If you insist on pushing your body beyond its limits something will eventually snap." He lifted his hands up to his face, wiggled his fingers and winced.

"The bedrooms at the back of the house are south facing," Mrs Mackay announced. "They should have resisted the dampness. They'll certainly be warmer."

Ellie, Midge and Scott picked up bags, pillows and duvets and followed the old lady up the staircase, past a nine-panelled, stained glass window. The morning sun had grabbed a handful of stains and, without respect for design, thrown them back, higgledy-piggledy, across the wall. Colours jumped from peeling wallpaper to tired faces and back again.

The first room they entered had a bed with an oval-shaped black and gilt headboard, two bedside tables and a chest of drawers. Pale, water marked blinds at the window had turned the pink flowers on the walls several shades of caramel.

"This mattress looks a bit dodgy," Marty said. "Sleep on top of my duvet, at least you know it's clean."

"Oh, thanks," Midge said. She flopped down and pulled her own duvet up round her shoulders.

"I'll throw this sick bag out," Ellie said, "and I don't think there's much point in trying to rescue *Pride and Prejudice*."

"Oh, I don't care," Midge said, "it's totally predictable. Boy meets girl rubbish. There's a load of confusion, boy gets to prove how wonderful he is, girl falls head-over-heels and then, I don't know for sure cos I haven't got that far, but I expect they'll get married and everyone will live happily ever after. It's got nothing to do with real life. Well, not mine anyway."

"Nor mine," Mrs Mackay added.

"But don't go out, will you?" Midge said looking alarmed. "Promise you won't leave me in this place on my own."

"We promise," Ellie said. "We'll be right downstairs."

"In the dining room, next to the library, that's where we'll be." The old lady gazed round the bedroom. "I canny believe I'm back here. After all these years I'm finally home."

~ooOoo~

Downstairs, in the dining room, Marty had found a vase for the dream roses.

Mr Rupert had unpacked the sandwiches. "I brought a small camping stove with me, rascal, fancy a cuppa?"

"Err, yeah, why not. I mean, no thanks..." The stone lion's head at the front door had given Marty the jitters. "That lion we were talking about the other day, remember, the one that's angry and wants to taste blood, I think he's come back."

Mr Rupert gulped a mouthful of water. "Tell me what happened, rascal."

"Well, yesterday evening at Scott's we were talking about Penny Treasure and her crazy Power for Protection Movement, and I said I wanted to smash my dinner plate in her face. I couldn't help it, the words just came out. I was like a volcano going off and the scary thing is...at the time...I meant what I said."

Mr Rupert screwed the cap onto the water bottle. "Well, rascal, I've got some bad news for you about this lion...maybe I should have told you this before. The lion never leaves. He stays with you for the rest of your life."

"You're kidding me..."

"Just hang on a minute, let me finish. The news isn't all bad. The lion doesn't go, but with time and effort he gets better behaved. And if you really think about it, you'd realize it's impossible for him to leave. The lion is all the bad experiences you have in your lifetime...all the things that make you really angry. Of course, once you've had an experience, you can never un-have it. The secret to success lies in getting rid of the anger."

"How do I do that?

"You need to do regular lion taming exercises."

"Like hitting a cushion with a tennis racket?" Marty said with a smirk.

"You may think it's funny, rascal, but believe me, it works. Doing something physical gets the anger out...it helps to channel all that aggression. Hitting a cushion with a tennis racket is one way and so is kickboxing."

"Kickboxing!"

"Yes, kickboxing. If I were younger, I'd give it a try. If you fancy something a little more cultured you could take up ballroom dancing."

"Ballroom dancing? I don't think so."

"Well...okay...you could dance on your own to loud music when no one's watching...beat up some pillows...go running...join a football team...learn kung fu...jump about, scream, sing, shout..."

"I get the idea," Marty said, "honest, I do."

"Good, because I'm being serious. When you've taken away the lion's anger you're left with its courage but, more importantly, you'll be in control and that's the whole point. Either you control the lion or it controls you. But be warned...if the lion gets control...your destiny is out of your hands. Anything could happen."

"What's the worst that could happen?"

"A lifetime spent in prison or an early death, I suppose."

"Dude! Break it to me gently."

"No, I won't," Mr Rupert said. "If you were to smash someone in the face with a plate you'd do them a serious injury. And anyway, why stop with a plate? Why not use a knife or a gun? You could even get a gang together or convince the whole nation to support you...maybe you could start a war! Who knows where it might end. At the least you'll have lots of arguments and failed friendships, you'll spend most of your time being annoyed with people. My wartime experience locked a furious lion inside of me and for a while I couldn't get along with anyone. I bit heads off everywhere I went. But because that wasn't how I wanted my life to turn out I worked hard on calming it down. I knew for certain I didn't want it to have control of me."

"Maybe I will have that tea."

"Righty-O," Mr Rupert said. He took some matches from his jacket pocket and lit the camping stove. "Just consider it, rascal. When you're not angry, you're in control. When you're in control, you can achieve anything. And by the way, I'm not preaching to you, I'm not telling you what to do; you must do what you like...after all...this is your life."

Marty walked over to a window and stared out. Beyond the gravel drive he could see the aeroplane parked on the grass. The aeroplane that Mr Rupert had flown all the way from London! This old guy, Marty thought, he's totally amazing. I want what he's got...I've got ambition...maybe one day I could be a famous footballer...I don't want anything to stand in my way. He turned back to face his friend. "I'm seriously considering."

"Good," said the old man, beaming a shiny-white-toothed-smile. "Milk and sugar?"

~ooOoo~

Back upstairs, six feet tiptoed from the bedroom.

"I'll leave the door ajar,'" Mrs Mackay said in a whisper. "I don't want the poor, wee lassie thinking she's been locked away."

The three of them stood in the dark corridor. Scott thought he heard the faint sounds of laughter, maybe music. Did I hear that? I don't know. Usually, seconds before hearing voices, I get that screechy, whistling sound in my ears. This time, and the time before, I didn't. I'm knackered. Perhaps tiredness is doing something to my brain? I don't want to freak everyone out. I won't say anything now.

"Before we go downstairs I'd like to take a peek in all the bedrooms.

"This one used to belong to my parents." The old lady opened the door. Bare floorboards amplified the long, drawn-out creak from its hinges. "I don't believe it…everything's gone."

Apart from pigeon crap and feathers the room was empty. Scott walked over to the window with the sole intention of pointing out a missing pane of glass, but when he caught sight of the view outside his lungs expanded. "Look, there it is! It's the walled garden!"

"The garden?" Ellie dashed over to join him. "Wow! It's amazing! Just like I dreamt! There's the main pathway, twisting through the flowers. I remember a bumblebee, it hovered in front of my face…it mapped out a figure of eight. It must have been showing me a plan of the garden. Maybe it was telling me how to get out?"

"My goodness! It's spectacular!" Mrs Mackay said. "But someone must be living here! Gardens don't look like that without hours of backbreaking work."

Downstairs, in the main hall, Scott waited for Mrs Mackay to go into the dining room before grabbing

Ellie by the arm. "We're not alone…there's others. I can definitely hear them."

"I knew it! So there was a voice when I unlocked the door!"

"Yeah, it said, *she's here*, and a few minutes ago, upstairs, I heard laughter and music."

"Hell…this place is creepy. *She's here?* They must mean Mrs Mackay. Should we tell her?"

Mr Rupert poked his head round the door. "Come on, you two…there's a tower of cheese sandwiches waiting to be demolished."

Breakfast had been laid out on a table long enough to seat twelve. Scott immediately noticed the freshly laundered tablecloth. Dead animals' heads on the walls, some with gigantic antlers, gazed longingly at the food. Hanging at one end of the room was an almost life-size painting of several men standing in the walled garden.

"There's no dust or cobwebs in here," Mrs Mackay said, "even the light fittings are clean. And why is that picture on the wall? This doesn't make sense. Surely Harold would have taken it down? I don't believe for one minute he'd have been comfortable looking at my father and his team of loyal gardeners. Those men in that picture are part of a past he'd want to forget."

"Perhaps someone put it there?" Ellie said. "Maybe it's the same person who's looking after the garden?"

"Someone's in my house! I can feel it in my bones. We need to search the place. I canny sit here any longer. I canny rest till I know who it is."

"I've already been in the kitchen," Marty said, "there's definitely no one in there."

"I want to see every room," the old lady said.

"Let's go together," Ellie said. "I don't like the idea of splitting up. People always do that kind of thing in films…I find it really annoying. I never understand why. It's like asking for trouble."

"Yes, I know what you mean," Mr Rupert said, "it always strikes me as a ridiculous thing to do. Let's stick together."

A thorough check of the first and second floors revealed no hidden stranger. Scott nipped into Midge's room and found her sleeping soundly. A faint smile painted on her pale face was framed by a tangle of Flaming Fox hair.

Downstairs, the gunroom and the staff hall held no surprises.

For extra reassurance they stopped at the kitchen. "I love the old pots and pans hanging from the ceiling," Scott said. "A quick dust of the cobwebs and I'd be cooking."

"It's an original gas range," Mrs Mackay said proudly. "It was fitted in the 1920s. What's this?" The old lady pointed to the top shelf of a dresser. "The copper jelly moulds…someone's cleaned them!"

Scott had to agree. Not only were the jelly moulds sparkling, but someone had deliberately replaced them in order of size, from left to right, largest to smallest.

In the garden room, remnants of wicker furniture had been pushed against one wall. A line of marble statues, like shy people at a party with no music, stared across from the other side. Someone worried about drink and cake spills had rolled up the carpet. Scott closed his eyes and tried to tune in his psychic receiver. Nothing. He shook a disappointed head in Ellie's direction.

Despite struggling with every key, the door to the study wouldn't budge.

"Is there anybody in there?" Mr Rupert shouted. He drummed his fist on the door then cringed in pain. "I'll need to get that WD-40 after all," he said through a strained smile.

Unexpectedly, the lock clicked and the door glided open.

The curtains billowed in the breeze. A worn, leather armchair sat a couple of feet away from a desk and an antique globe was spinning on its axis. A sweet and smoky smell, that reminded Scott of cigars, percolated the air.

"Someone must be having a bonfire nearby," Mrs Mackay said, "best we get that window shut, we don't want the whole house stinking."

Bonfire indeed, Scott thought. He stole a furtive glance at Ellie and Marty.

Crammed full of books, but little else, the library had no obvious secrets to disclose.

Mr Rupert scanned the shelves. "How fascinating! Look at this one." The book's cover, shielded from years of sunlight by a row of loyal companions, had remained a richer shade of rust than its faded spine. "The Complete Works of Robert Burns," the old man said in a mock Scottish accent, "undoubtedly one of

Scotland's finest poets!" He flipped open the cover. "To my dearest father with best wishes for many happy birthdays love Maisie 13.10.1929."

"What poorly chosen words," the old lady said from the other side of the room, "he didn't get to celebrate another birthday, he died the following April."

Mr Rupert looked up from the book. "I'm sorry. I didn't mean to make fun of something so valuable."

"Och, don't worry," Mrs Mackay said, "it's just a book, but I'd forgotten all about it. To tell the truth there's so much I've forgotten about."

"It must be amazing to see all these things again," Ellie said.

"Yes, it is…and…I might as well tell you all now…I won't be going home with you to London. Now that I've made it back here, I can't bear the thought of leaving. I know you'll think me a silly, sentimental old fool but…you see…now that I'm here…I realize I am home."

Ellie crossed the room and gave Mrs Mackay a hug. "We can't leave you here alone…can we?"

"Well," Mr Rupert said, "she is her own person, so she does get to make her own decisions. But, Maisie, you really should think this one through. At least come back to London for a month or two…we'll get your affairs in order."

"Yeah," Marty said, "I think that's a great idea and we can help you pack."

"Yes, and Ellie can find a tenant to rent your flat," Scott said. "You'll be home before you know it."

"Well, yes, maybe that would make sense. I'll think it over." In silence she walked to the window. "You see that dense patch of woodland? I have a strong suspicion that's where Harold buried my father's friend Arthur. Would you accompany me on a walk up there, Mr Rupert? I'd like to pick some wild flowers and lay them as a mark of respect."

"Yes of course," Mr Rupert said.

"I'm so lucky," the old lady said. "I can see four beautiful faces, each one of them genuinely concerned for my welfare. Without friends, I have nothing."

~ooOoo~

Upstairs, in the bedroom, four faces stared down at a sleeping girl.

"I've told you already," one said, "it's not her."

"Are you sure?" another said.

"Yes, absolutely positive," the third said. "This one's called Midge. Ellie's the one you're after."

"Well, let's wake her up anyway. I'm sick of waiting."

"No! Don't wake her up, she looks so peaceful."

Two of the faces grumbled.

"Well, all right, she's got five more minutes...then her time's up."

~ Thirty-One ~

Have You Got the Information? Do You Understand Your Mission?

From the library, Ellie watched the far-off silhouettes of Mrs Mackay and Mr Rupert drifting in a sea of wild flowers. "We've searched everywhere...except the walled garden."

"We promised Midge we wouldn't go far," Scott said, "but I'm getting desperate. I hope she wakes up soon."

Marty joined Ellie at the window. "By the time the old folk get back she should be awake. We can't even think about going in there without her."

"Yeah, you're right," Ellie said. "And we need to tell Mrs Mackay and Mr Rupert what's going on."

"We're not exactly sure...are we?" Scott said.

"Well, you definitely heard a voice saying, *she's here*, then music and laughter. We can all see things don't add up. There's the picture in the dining room...the study door locked then suddenly opened...that strange smell and the globe spinning like someone had just been looking at it..."

"And some rooms look cleaner than others," Marty said. "It's like they've been lived in…like things have been moved."

"Why don't we go back into the dining room," Ellie said, "you can sit quietly under that big painting and tune in your psychic receiver. Maybe you'll hear something?"

~ooOoo~

"Mmm, I feel so much better," Midge said through a yawn. Floating between sleep and awake she'd sensed the door being opened, felt a rush of cool air pass over the bed. How lovely, she thought, someone's come up to get me.

Scott sat cross-legged on the dining room floor below Mrs Mackay's father and his team of gardeners. He closed his eyes, took a breath and cleared his mind of cluttering thoughts. "Is anybody there?"

Immediately, sounds of laughter somersaulted through his head.

Midge opened her eyes with a start. "What's so funny?" she said, before realizing there was no one in the room with her.

"I heard something!" Scott said excitedly. "I definitely heard laughter, did anyone else?"

"No," Ellie and Marty said.

Midge sat up in bed and glanced towards the door. She heard footsteps in the hallway and more laughter. She sprang out of bed. Her mouth tasted eggy. She fumbled in her bag for a piece of chewing gum then darted out into the gloomy corridor.

"Try again," Ellie said.
"Yeah," Marty said, "see if you can hear it again."

At the end of the corridor a door slammed shut; Midge raced towards it. The enticing sounds of music and chatter snaked towards her. Sounds like a party, she thought.

Downstairs, Scott closed his eyes and cleared his mind.

Midge made the end of the corridor in seconds and thrust the door open. Crossing the threshold, a wailing-bagpipe, cigar-smoky atmosphere walloped her round the head. A bare sole caught the edge of a loose floorboard. "Ouch!" She reached down, grabbed her foot and hopped into the embrace of a one-armed man with a chewed-up face. The music died.

Scott opened an eye. "I could hear voices and music...but suddenly it stopped. I'm not sure what they were saying. It sounds like people all talking at once. Like lots of people at a party."
"Keep trying," Ellie said.
"Yeah, don't stop," Marty said.

Midge wanted to scream, but panicked, shallow breathing wouldn't allow it. Gasping for air, she pulled in a concoction of stale smoke, death and fester.

"So, the wee lassie's awake at last!" the chewed-up face said.

In a falling glance Midge noticed the absence of a nose and an eyeball. She stared up in horror. The flesh along one side of the jawbone had gone, exposing a scatter of rotten teeth.

"One swipe of a paw did this," the chewed-up face exclaimed. "The wild beast ripped me to shreds in a second!"

"Put her down!" a familiar voice shouted.

"You'll scare the livin' daylights out of her," another said.

Midge hopped back in repulsion and saw a pair of brassy-blonde, bubble-perm hairdos: one belonged to Opal, the other to Pearl – never before had two bossy, biscuit-crunching, tea-sipping old ladies been such a welcome sight. A cloggy lump of fear, with the consistency of an un-chewed marshmallow, lodged in her throat. "Uhuluha," she said.

Behind the old ladies, five bedraggled men, in tattered, bloodstained clothing, held various musical instruments. Next to them stood a very glamorous woman: tall and elegant, she wore a heavily embroidered, floor-length, black dress. Billowing folds of cream chiffon around her neck reminded Midge of the froth on a vanilla milkshake. Draped over her shoulders sat a fox-coloured, full-length fur coat and, on her head, an enormous black hat that looked like a decapitated swan. After a double take, Midge noticed she only had one hand.

"We haven't got long, darlin', so you'd better listen carefully, we've got something to tell you," Opal said.

The man with the chewed-up face stared down at Midge. "You're a peely-wally thing!"

"I'm a peely what thing?"

"Peely-wally," the one handed, glamorous lady said. "He's saying you look pale, but don't pay any attention, it's just his way, he doesn't mean to be rude."

"I've been airsick," Midge said. "You're all dead, aren't you?"

"Aye!" the man with the chewed-up face said. "You can say that again. We've been dead for nearly eighty years and it feels like eternity."

"And I've been trapped in this old house watching it decay…waiting for this moment," the glamorous lady said.

"Oh," Midge said, suddenly concerned what this moment might bring.

"We've all been waiting for you," Pearl said, "every single one of us."

"Although to be fair," Opal added, "we've not had to wait half as long as this lot." She waved a thumb at the others. "And we've not been stuck in this run-down place. No disrespect, it's very nice and everything, but at least we had the warmth of the DMC HQ."

The glamorous lady scowled and adjusted the collar of her fur coat.

Opal winked. "But it's not been all that bad, me and me sister didn't get here till late last night and they made us really welcome. They certainly know how to throw a party these Scotch folk. We made jelly then rolled up the carpet. WOO! We were dancing till the small hours."

"I think you mean Scots," the glamorous lady said, "scotch is an alcoholic drink. We're Scots."

"Of course you are, darlin'," Opal said.

Midge nearly smiled.

"I even managed to do a bit of cleaning before you living folk got here. I would have done more, but I ran out of time." Opal gazed around the room and chuckled. "Ain't that ridiculous, been waiting for eternity then look what happens? At the last minute, we run out of time."

The others laughed. One of the men had a bagpipe, and when he used it to make a comical WAH-WAH sound, they all became hysterical.

Pearl fixed Midge with a beady-eyed stare. "Why don't you sit down, darlin'...I'll explain everything. Whilst I'm at it, I'll get that splinter."

Midge took a seat.

"This used to be my dressing room," the man with the chewed-up face growled, "but that nasty, evil, money-grabbing eejit sold all the furniture. If I ever get my hands on him I'll give him a thrashing he'll never forget."

"Donald!" the glamorous lady exclaimed. "Mind your language in front of the child."

Pearl prodded Midge's foot. The splinter popped its head into daylight and Midge had a revelation.

"Oh, I don't believe it! You're Mrs Mackay's dad, aren't you? You got killed by a tiger…that's why you look like you do!"

"Aye, that's right," Donald said, "and thanks for reminding me I've got a face like a lump of meat on the butcher's block."

The glamorous lady walked over to Midge. "Oh, do pipe-down, Donald," she said, "and I'm Jean, Maisie's mother. It's so lovely to meet you. And these men here, they're our team of gardeners. This is Calvin, Ewan, Fergus, Andrew and Blair."

"Good evening, missy," the men said, before nodding their heads politely.

"Oh, hi," Midge bumbled.

Jean put her one hand on Midge's shoulder. "How is Maisie? Is she well?"

Midge wasn't sure how to answer that question. "Erm…well, yes…she's okay. I think."

Jean tightened her bony grip and Midge searched for a fuller description.

"Well…she's ninety-four now…so she's quite old. She probably looks different to how you remember."

Pearl and Opal burst out laughing.

"I'm well aware of her age," Jean said, somewhat impatiently, "and I managed to catch a glimpse of her when you all arrived, so I do know what she looks like. But I've been so worried about her…you see, I haven't had proper contact with my dear, darling daughter for seventy-eight years. It's been awful. I've been going out of my mind."

"Uh?" a confused Midge said. "But you're an energy, you can see what you like, can't you?" The room erupted into moans and groans. “What? What did I say?”

“Hang about, hang about,” Opal said. “First of all you called us energies and none of us here really like that word...we prefer to stick with tradition...call us ghosts if you wouldn’t mind. And second, us ghosts find that sort of talk offensive. Everyone always assumes that death for us lot is non-stop fun and nonsense. People think ghosts can do what they like, but that’s miles from the truth.”

“Oh, well, I’m sorry,” Midge said. “I didn’t know.”

“Clearly,” Donald said.

“Well, why doesn’t someone tell me? I’m really interested.”

The ghosts fell silent, each of them looking to the other.

Jean took her hand from Midge’s shoulder and pulled a handkerchief from the pocket of her fur coat. “I’ll try not to get emotional...but I can’t promise.” She dabbed her eyes. “When we died it was most unexpected...I mean...can you imagine? One minute we’re happily trekking through the forest enjoying the flora and fauna when suddenly, out of nowhere, this happens.” She waved her stump at Donald. Donald, obviously sick of the unwanted attention, muttered something inaudible before taking a giant puff on his cigar. Clouds of smoke billowed from his gaping jaw. “Needless to say,” Jean continued, “I’d mentioned the risk of wild beasts, but of course no one listened. When it pounced we didn’t stand a chance. I won’t go into the gory details, but as you can plainly see, none of us survived. To tell you the truth I was absolutely furious, but then the most joyful thing happened…freed from our bodies…we floated up into the sky. We were so overwhelmed with the sudden realisation that death wasn't the end, we all burst out laughing."

Donald tipped his head back and chuckled at the memory. A perfect ring of smoke came drifting from his empty eye socket.

"Oh yes! I think I know what you mean," Midge said. "My friend June says that's what happens when we die, our energies leave our bodies."

"Oh, she does, does she?" Jean said. "Well, I can tell you from personal experience that it feels incredible, like nothing you've ever known. I still had my mind, you know, I knew who I was, I knew that Donald and the boys were with me…that we were together."

Pearl finally freed the splinter. She stared up at Jean and tapped her wrist. "Time, darlin'," she said, "you'll have to speed this up a bit."

"You'll have to speed this up a bit," Scott said.

"What?" Ellie said.

"You'll have to speed this up a bit," Scott repeated, "that's what I just heard."

"How weird," Marty said. "I wonder what that means. What should we be speeding up?"

"Maybe the voices are telling us to get moving," Ellie said. "Maybe they're telling us to hurry up and get into the garden. Do you think that could be the message? I really wish Midge would wake up. I think we should go up and get her, don't you?"

"And then," Jean said, "as we floated high above the surface of the Earth, we were given a choice. Something or someone gave us a message; it told us we could come back down and complete a mission. It wasn't an actual person who gave us this message, we didn't see anyone and we didn't hear a voice, we just knew. It's awfully hard to explain."

"Oh, don't worry!" Midge said, interrupting again. "I know exactly what you mean; I once got a message from a sea lion."

"Oh…how…lovely." Jean stared around the room open-mouthed. "If I could just be allowed to finish! When we were told what the mission was we knew we had to do it. We knew we didn't have a choice. It was to be the final act of love for our beloved daughter, and much to my delight the boys agreed to keep us company."

"And thank heavens they did," Donald said, "it's taken an excruciatingly long time trying to complete this task. Over the years I've traipsed up and down the country leaving endless clues. I've created countless opportunities for people to help us but, frustratingly, no one read the signs. In the end I just gave up."

OH WOW, SIGNS! Midge thought, I know about those. She went to speak, but a sideways glance from Pearl zipped her mouth shut.

"And then there's us," Opal said, who was busy trying to force open another window. "I'm a bit short of oxygen, is anyone else?" Everyone nodded. "Me and Pearl, we're Special Agents. When things go wrong, and people don't read the signs, we get sent in to help."

"You're Special Agents?"

"Yup, that's right. We were sent in to get this thing moving, to get it sorted out once and for all. We were given exact dates and times. We had specific instructions. In order to make sure Ellie found that photograph we broke a water pipe in Maisie's building, we wanted to cause a flood because we knew it would get her moving the furniture. Also, we knew precisely when you would be arriving at the DMC HQ and we were told you were one of the small minorities of people who have the gift of extra-special vision. Twenty percent of people who can see ghosts can also hear them, and thankfully, you fall into that category. We were thrilled about that because it made our jobs so much easier. We needed you to stay with us, in the building, until five o'clock...for the announcement...so...I'm sorry to say...we popped a little sleeping pill into your tea."

"You drugged me?"

"Yes."

"I knew something was going on." Midge shook her head. "I don't usually nod off in the daytime."

"Well, we're sorry about that," Opal said. "But when you woke up, you passed our test with flying colours."

"Test?" Midge said.

"The *food test,*" Pearl said. "You ate the tripe and brawn sandwiches...at least you swallowed a couple of mouthfuls."

"Argh! Those sandwiches…I nearly threw up!" Midge said.

Opal smiled. "You showed us you've got true grit and determination…we knew then you wouldn't fail us. Also, we made sure you met up with Ellie and the others by deliberately contaminating that bag of frozen prawns…because everyone was off sick you got to appear on TV."

"Oh, the prawns!" Midge said. "But poor Leo, the chef, he got the blame for that. He got the sack. I saw a letter in Penny Treasure's drawer."

"Unfortunately, he was the fall guy," Pearl said, butting in. "There are always winners and losers in this game. Our assignment was to get you up here…to give you the information. Once you've got the information, and understood your mission, these lovely people can get on with their lives. Sorry, I should say, their new lives."

"Me? I've got a mission? What is it?"

Opal took over. "Don't panic, darlin', it's straightforward. All you have to do is introduce Maisie Mackay to her living relatives. That's what this lot here were supposed to do. They were supposed to put Maisie in touch with her son, but unfortunately he died before they found a way to do it."

"It might have helped," Jean snapped, "if I'd been able to leave this house. Why was I trapped here? Even the boys were allowed to leave. Donald's clueless when it comes to leaving clues."

Donald looked furious. "Well, thanks for the support! You've got no idea how difficult it's been. It was almost impossible to find anyone who could hear me, let alone see me, and when I did find someone who could see me they took one look and ran a mile."

"Obviously you didn't try hard enough. You didn't use your imagination. It was my idea to get that picture down from the attic and hang it up in the dining room..."

Pearl interjected. "All right, Jean, keep your wig on."

Jean exploded. "It's not a wig, it's a hat! And to be honest, the constant jokes about it are wearing thinner than the air we're struggling to breathe."

"Blaming won't help," Pearl said calmly. "You know as well as we do that rules are rules and it's impossible to deviate from them. It was strategic planning. There had to be a relative of Maisie's in this house at all times, in case anyone with the gift of extra-special hearing or vision showed up. Unfortunately, that ghost happened to be you. The boys had their own instructions."

Midge didn't want to inflame any more tempers, but there were answers she desperately wanted. She forced herself to ask a question. "Where's Harold Crinklebottom?"

"He's dead!" Jean spat the words out like they were poisonous berries she'd swallowed by mistake.

"Yes, I know that, what I meant was, where is he now? Where's his ghost?"

"How should I know?" Jean's lips curled into a snarl. "All I know is, when he was alive, I spent every dead moment I had scaring the living daylights out of him. I made his life a misery, and when he tried to sell this place and leave, I did everything I could to frighten off any prospective buyers. He got trapped here with me…and I'm pleased to announce…by the time he died…I'd driven him insane!"

"Oh right," Midge said. She nodded politely. Bloody hell! Some of these ghosts have quite a temper.

"Love for her daughter," Pearl said.

"What?" Midge said.

"I know what you're thinking and I'm trying to explain it. It was Jean's love for her daughter that caused her to behave in that way. It fuelled her. Love sometimes wears a disguise."

"And there is always retribution," Opal stated.

"Retribution?" Midge wasn't entirely sure what that meant.

"Justice," all the ghosts said.

"Yes, justice," Opal repeated. "No one gets away with anything. It may come in this lifetime, it may come in another, but there will always be a reckoning. The scales must balance."

"Any more questions?" a grinning Pearl said. She tapped her watch again then pinched Midge's big toe.

Yes, loads, Midge thought, but I'm too busy remembering the times I shoplifted on my way home from school.

"Feeling guilty?" Opal said.

"Sticky fingers?" Pearl said.

"I only did it to get a buzz. It was always stupid things…things I didn't need. An ice cube tray, a tin of pineapple chunks, a bottle of food colouring. Will something happen to me?"

"You'll lose something of equal value," Opal said.

"Oh...that's not so bad." Pearl tapped her watch for a third time and Midge reluctantly focused her mind on other matters. "There's something I'm not quite understanding. Where's the ghost of Maisie's son? Surely, if he was here, he'd know who he was...there wouldn't be a need to tell him he's related."

Moans and groans filled the room once again.

"I said *living* relatives," Opal repeated. "That's the whole point of this mission, to put Maisie in touch with her descendants. That way Claremont Castle will remain in the Mackay family."

"Oh right, of course," Midge said, trying to follow the plot. "So, where do I find these relatives? I hope it won't involve another long journey by air?"

Pearl shook her head. "Are you trying to tell me you ain't worked it out yet?"

"Err. Well. No. Not really."

"The penny's got stuck in the machine!" Pearl said.

"The lights are on, but no one's home," Opal said. "Why are you here?"

Midge, who was beginning to feel like an unprepared contestant on Junior Mastermind, gazed up blankly from her chair. "Because Mr Rupert flew me here in a plane." She knew she was clutching at straws with this answer.

"Don't try my patience, lady. What I mean is, why this place in particular? Why this house?"

"Oh, I see. Well...we all had a dream. And when I say all, I mean my friends and me. That's Ellie, Marty and Scott. We all woke up holding a purple rose. Do you remember? I woke up with mine after you *drugged me* in the secret room?"

"Keep going," both the old ladies said.

"But actually, I'm not sure if Marty had a dream, he got knocked unconscious, he could have been hallucinating or something. Ellie definitely had a dream…I know that for a fact…June gave her some kind of dream-enhancing potion. She's the only one who can remember the details. She remembered being in a walled garden surrounded by flowers and there was a clock tower nearby…"

"Go on," Opal said, "you're nearly there."

"Well, you already know the next bit. The next day she went to Mrs Mackay's house to help with the broken water pipe and saw that photograph, the one hidden behind the chest of drawers, the one that looked like it had been taken in her dream. The girl in the photograph looked exactly like Ellie, but it turned out it wasn't Ellie after all, it was Mrs Mackay…" Before Midge had finished her sentence the penny dropped. "Oh my…no way! I don't believe it!"

"Well, you'd better believe it," Pearl said, "cos it's true. Ellie looks exactly like Mrs Mackay because they're related. Ellie is Mrs Mackay's great-granddaughter."

"So, now you know, we can all leave," Opal said with a smile.

"Hallelujah!" Donald shouted. "Although I'll be sad to say my final farewell to Claremont Castle."

"I won't!" Jean cried. "I'll be glad to see the back of it. And I'll tell you something else I'm looking forward to…getting out of this dress. I'm sick of the sight of it.

I hope in my new life my parents wrap me up in something soft and comfortable."

"Tell our daughter and our great-great-granddaughter that we love them…won't you?"

"What? Yes, of course. I'll tell them everything. But you're not leaving right now, are you?"

"Yes, darlin', we're off to some place called Kyoto," a fading Opal said. "Donald found it on the globe for me…it's an ancient city in Japan."

"Look after that lovely hair of yours, won't you?" Pearl said. "And when you find yourself tempted to have it cut really short, resist the urge. I've seen a few years into the future…for several months of it you've got a head like a sheep's arse."

"OOOH! I'm going all shivery," Jean shrieked. "It's like someone's tickling me on the inside."

Midge jumped to her feet, urged up by the sound of deflating bagpipes. "No, don't go yet!" she shouted. "There's a load of questions I haven't asked you. What about the purple dream roses? What about the walled garden? I need to know who the hooded stranger is."

"That's not part of our mission," Opal said, her voice warbling, her body see-through like a hologram.

"And Doubt? You know…the evil, twisted monster…you saw him sitting on my shoulder…I need to get rid of him."

"Everyone has Doubt," Pearl said. "You take him too seriously, darlin'. You need to make friends with him…he'll keep you safe…prevent you from doing something stupid."

"We'll meet again, don't know where, don't know when, but I know we'll meet again some sunny day…" Opal's singing faded to silence.

A second later, apart from two chairs, a set of bagpipes some drums and a flute, the room was empty.

Buffeted by the breeze, a thin purple haze did a showy last dance with tumbling clouds of cigar smoke. Colours, like the dying moments of a spectacular firework, circled the room before exiting through the open window. Midge knew in her heart they'd gone for good.

For a short while the magnitude of what had just happened caused time to freeze. The past and the future vanished. Midge felt nothing but the present moment. Calm and comfortable, she stared into space. Dust flickered in streams of light.

Ellie, Marty and Scott tore through the door, shattering the stillness.

~ooOoo~

"I know," Ellie said, "we heard downstairs, well, actually, Scott heard it. He heard one of the voices saying I was Mrs Mackay's great-granddaughter. I can't believe it! I just can't believe it!" She walked over to the open window. "I wish I'd seen them all. I wonder, if I'd been in the room with you, would I have seen or heard something?"

"I don't know," Midge said.

"And now things make sense. I remember my dad once telling me that my granddad had been adopted as a baby. And I remember the story of how Mrs Mackay met my dad. It was weird. The residents of Drayton Court were looking for a new management company but couldn't find one they liked. Then, one morning, Mrs Mackay lost her handbag in the supermarket and my dad found it. He went round to her address but she wasn't in so he left his business card."

"Cool," Marty said, "coincidences and signs. Not only did she get her bag back, and a company to manage her apartment block, she also got to meet her grandson. How strange, that for all these years, they didn't know they were related."

"Wait till you tell her," Scott said. "I can't wait to see her face."

"You'll be able to call her granny from now on," Midge said, "and what's more, one day all of this will be yours." She opened her arms. "One day you'll inherit Claremont Castle!"

Ellie started laughing. The whole thing seemed unbelievable, almost ridiculous, like a headline in a newspaper...*Girl Reunited With Long Lost Relative Becomes Property Millionaire Overnight!* In her mind she played out the story, fantasized how her life could be.

She leaned out the window.

To the far right, on top of the stable block, she saw the clock tower: the same one from her dream. It had the same flinted stones, the same rusted weather vane, the same shiny gold hands and roman numerals on a sky-blue face. It was nearly twelve...nearly midday on Midsummer's Eve. Beyond the clock tower a wall, with honeysuckles and passion flowers peeking over the edge, summoned her: its call tearing holes in her fantasy.

Ellie turned to face her friends. “It’s time for us to enter the garden.”

~ Thirty-Two ~

Words Have Wings

The door to the garden wasn't locked.

The glorious smell of perfume rushed towards all four of them. It surrounded them. In seconds, thousands upon thousands of molecules invaded their nostrils. Minute atoms held together by unseen chemical forces passed through slimy membranes, like ghosts walking through walls. The scent of perfume slipped into their bloodstream and linked arms with adrenaline. In pasty mouths it mingled with the vinegary taste of fear, giving their saliva a sweet and sour flavour. Ellie, Marty, Midge and Scott stood in stunned silence and stared at the spectacular forest of flowers. Insects buzzed past their ears. Transformed by shimmering heat, the tops of the walls wobbled like jelly. The air felt thick, almost solid. Directly above, in a honey-coloured sky, the sun had rolled to a standstill.

"What do we do now?" Midge whispered.

"I don't know," Ellie said. She passed her rose from one hand to the other.

"Everything looks perfect," Scott gasped.

"Yes, yes it does," she replied, "and look...this must be the purple rose bush...the one we picked our flowers from." She reached out and touched a leaf.

"Guys, look at this," Marty said.

Running the length of the wall behind them were several glasshouses, their timber frames freshly painted. Unlike some of the windows in the house, none of the panes were broken.

"There's fruit growing inside," Midge said. "Looks like hundreds of peaches."

Soothed by the glorious sight of Mother Nature's tastiest work, everyone's breathing settled.

On the ground, next to the door of the glasshouse, sat a blue, rectangular tin with the word ESSO embossed on its side. Scott broke ranks and picked it up. "This is an old petrol tin, I recognise it. My dad has one just like it in the workshop. I'll bet it's for a lawnmower."

"But whose lawnmower?" Marty said. "Who's doing all this?"

A solitary squeak answered his question. It flew through the air like a stone propelled from a sling.

Four hearts nearly stopped.

"I heard that noise in my dream," Ellie said. "I thought it was rats, but I didn't see any."

Another squeak followed, only this time it was much louder.

"What is it?" Midge cried. "I'm getting nervous."

"I don't know," Ellie replied. "I remember turning around and there he was...standing right behind me."

The squeaks grew loud and frequent.

Ellie's leg muscles twitched.

Marty's eyes couldn't blink.

Scott clenched his fists.

Midge held her breath.

The thing rounded the corner. It moved slowly. It came into view. It stopped.

"A wheelbarrow?" Midge said.

"With a squeaky wheel?" Scott said.

"Who are you?" Ellie shouted.

"My name is Harold Crinklebottom."

"Can you see him, too?" Midge's barely audible question received a nod from Ellie, Scott and Marty.

Harold Crinklebottom stood only a few feet away. His shroud, encrusted in soil and tied roughly round the middle with a piece of rope, covered the entirety of his withered body. He pulled away folds of material to reveal a colourless face. Sad, sunken eyes that had retreated into dark circles, stared out from either side of an angular nose. The lips thin, almost shrivelled. Wasted skin and bone, with the occasional wisp of white hair, he looked exactly like a dead man who'd been dug up.

"I didn't think it would be you," Ellie said. "I was told to expect the unexpected and at first I expected you, so then I got to thinking it wouldn't be you." I'm talking rubbish, she thought. She closed her mouth.

"I'm exhausted," Harold said.

"You're a murderer," Marty said.

The others couldn't believe he'd said it.

"Yes, that's right, I was a murderer, but I have paid the price, and now I am a guardian of the truth."

"Where's my dad?" Scott shouted. "And my brother and my sister? Are they in this garden?"

"Yes, they are here."

"They're really here?" Ellie said.

"Yes," Harold replied. "You are holding them."

Midge stared at the rose in her hand. Her legs wobbled. "What do you mean?"

"The life force that once flowed through your loved ones is now in these flowers. Around the world it is the same, in gardens such as this everywhere."

"I don't understand," Ellie said.

"Minute atoms which once formed the human body separated, sent to every corner of the cosmos, leaving nothing behind but the glue that holds them together." Harold lifted a cane from the wheelbarrow then leaned forward and pushed it into the soil. "That glue is the very essence of who we are and it is known by many names. Energy, Life Force, Spirit, Soul." Using twine he began to tie up a drooping foxtail lily, his scrawny fingers shaking with the effort. "Once these energies had been released into nature, they were free to do whatever they chose. Not surprisingly, all of them rushed to experience life as a flower."

"Flowers…why?" Marty said.

"Well, take a look around. What could be more blissful than a lifetime spent doing this? No fighting, no arguing, no stealing, no murdering, no hatred, just the opportunity to enjoy the thrill of being alive. These flowers live together in harmony. They are in heaven." Harold grimaced then clutched his back. "Ah, my old bones!" he rasped.

Scott shook his head. "So the Purple…it scattered the bodies of our loved ones…it transformed their energies into flowers?"

Harold scowled. “No! You are not listening! One person’s energy appears transparent, you could never hope to see it, but when you bring together the energies of many…something amazing happens…the one colour reveals itself.”

“Purple,” Ellie said.

“Yes, that is correct. Purple is the colour of our eternal energy. It’s the colour of the soul. Underneath this costume that we call our bodies, we are all Purple. How funny it is to witness your panic. The terrifying, howling fog that you all fear is nothing but concentrated life energy. It’s pure love, the most powerful force in the universe. That’s why it healed the sick and protected the weak. It gave renewed power to the old. It even enriched the very soil you walk upon. For a short while it brought you peace because for a short while you remembered you were all the same.”

Harold stopped to catch his rancid breath and a butterfly, indifferent to the situation, danced around his head.

Midge’s mouth formed words. “Who made this happen?”

Harold smiled. “You did.”

“What do you mean?”

“You wished them away.” Henry started laughing.

“You can quit the screaming skull act,” Marty said. “Start talking…we need answers.”

“That’s just stupid,” Midge said. “You can’t wish someone away.”

“You can wish for anything,” Harold said. “Words have wings…and so do thoughts. Perhaps, if everybody asks for the same thing, at exactly the same time, it will happen."

"So, we got what we wanted," Ellie said. "Is that it? You're saying it's *our* fault."

"It's no one's fault. There's no blame. You did not know this would happen."

Scott took a step forward. "You said everybody…who do you mean by *everybody*?"

"Aha! Someone's listening. Yes, that's right, *everybody*. Not only did you wish them away…they chose to leave. Your precious loved ones had grown tired of the struggle. They no longer enjoyed the human experience. The people with power and influence knew, deep in their hearts, they were close to destroying each other and planet Earth forever."

Ellie took two steps forward. "So they killed themselves? They're all dead? I'll never see my mum and dad again, is that what you're telling me?"

"Energies never die," the dead man said, "they simply take on a new form." He gazed around the garden at the multitude of flowers. "But the answer to your question is yes. You will see your families again."

"How do we know you're telling the truth?" Marty said.

"Because the truth is all I have left to give you," Harold replied, his smile fading. "A month after my physical death, I woke to find my eternal energy had been forced back into my decaying body. For ten miserable years I waited in limbo, trapped like a prisoner within the walls of the stable yard. For what felt like forever I gazed up at the house that used to be mine. In the cold and damp I waited and waited. Then, five months ago, I was released to tend this garden, I knew to expect an abundance of flowers and I have worked relentlessly to make everything perfect for them, to make amends. Today my work here is done. These lost souls have renewed themselves. They have rediscovered a meaning for life. They are ready to return. By sunset today this garden will be nothing more than dried stalks, withered leaves and dead petals."

"And then what?" Ellie said. "Will everything go back to normal? Will things be just like they were?"

"No," Harold croaked. "For a short time there will be harmony, but lasting peace is not a guarantee. You have already witnessed for yourself that greed has a habit of creeping back. Unless you make a conscious effort to unite, the fighting will resume."

"So…what should we do for the rest of our lives?" Although spoken in hushed tones, Marty's words resonated with deep concern. "Should we stand around like flowers being nice to everyone? Is that what you're saying? I don't get what this means. What about all the things I want to do with my life? I've got ambitions and dreams."

"Ah, yes, dreams," Harold replied. "We all have them and it's right that we should. You dream of becoming a legendary footballer, don't you?"

Marty took a step back. "How…do…you…know?"

"And you," Harold pointed to Midge, "you want to be on television, you've had a taste of fame and you like it. And what about you, Scott? I think you aspire to owning a chain of garages?" Scott nodded. "And you, Ellie, my own flesh and blood, maybe you dream of building a property empire, amassing a fortune in bricks and mortar just like me?"

Ellie shuddered and wished herself away.

Marty wished himself away.

Scott wished himself away.

Midge wished herself away; away from Harold, the all-seeing, all-knowing, talking, rotting carcass.

"Well, my friends, all of this is good. Fulfilling your desires is a part of being alive; it's a part of evolution. It's important for you to chase your dreams, but remember not to cause destruction in the rush to find them. Taking without giving will never bring lasting happiness."

A monumental silence crept through the garden, touching the birds and the insects.

A gentle breeze followed in its wake. Rolling down the path, it caught everyone's attention. It blew strands of hair into Midge's mouth. Fresh and unexpected, it infused the garden, sending a rhythm of energy through vegetation.

Flowers swayed on a crowded dance floor.

For seconds it enthralled, but then it grew in intensity, it gathered itself together, it called in every detail of its power. For a silent moment the stems of every plant leaned in one direction. Then, without warning, a rotating column of air thrashed through the undergrowth. Leaves and flower heads scattered. Before Harold managed to speak it enveloped his entire body. The funnel of wind peeled away layers of skin in seconds, tearing an expression of pure pleasure from a shrunken face. It separated bone from gristle and nerves from sinew. It drew the water from muscles and organs, turning flesh to powder. When the life force had been sucked from his body, Harold's dehydrated heart fell to the floor and crumbled to dust. Ellie, Marty, Midge and Scott breathed it in and blinked it out. Ribs and femurs clattered onto the pathway. A skull rolled to their feet.

And then the wind came for them.

"Run!" Scott shouted.

Three of them turned and ran, but Midge went forwards. On her way she kicked Harold's skull into a flowerbed. The wind's effect on her was immediate. It lifted her feet from the ground then rotated her body. She went to scream, but the twist made it impossible.

Ellie dashed back to help, but felt herself being swallowed immediately. Tumbling upside down, like she'd been hit by a wave of water, she lost all sense of direction. As her energy ripped from her body, her physical self disintegrated. The minute atoms that formed a fifteen-year-old girl exploded outwards and there were more of them than all the stars in the universe. In her mind she saw herself like a handful of glitter thrown in front of a wind machine. A second later, after a loud popping noise, she flew free. Free like a bird that slips through a hole in the cage.

It wasn't her brain that understood because she no longer had one. Nor was it her five senses. She had no eyes, no ears, no mouth, no fingertips and no nose to smell with. The part of her that understood everything, including where she'd come from before birth but had forgotten by the time she could speak, remained untouched.

She flew up into the air. Marty on her right, Midge to her left and Scott somewhere just above. Their energies intermingled, making communication automatic.

They rocketed fifteen miles in thrilled silence. With the weather below, they continued upwards, passing through the ozone layer, until the curve of the Earth's surface revealed itself. They hovered in elation on the edge of space watching white puffs of cloud bubble over the Atlantic.

From this vantage point their connection with each other became clear. They knew each other's thoughts and they understood how, without the clumsy restrictions of the human form, doubt and fear no longer existed. Freed from the tyranny of constant worry, they enjoyed an unblocked flow of instinct and intuition. The same intelligence that keeps the Earth spinning in perfect orbit with the sun, that creates gravity and changes the seasons, flowed through them.

In that moment, they realized there is no such thing as coincidence. Nothing happens by chance because everything is connected.

Scott saw a glittering, purple thread crossing hundreds of miles, and he tugged it gently. His mum's life force, residing in the body of an unborn baby in Rio de Janeiro, immediately returned the signal. The pulsing vibrations caused the unsuspecting mother to throw-up her breakfast.

Burning bright with knowledge they re-entered the earth's atmosphere, swooping down and skimming over the surface of the ocean, over islands in the ocean, towards white cliffs. They made land on a pebble beach, pebbles and chalk crunching in waves. They heard the sounds, tasted the salt. Up onto green grass, over fields, rivers and roads, elements, minerals and chemicals coming together. Senses returning. Wind on mucus. Spinal jelly. Intestines. They followed the contour of the land, tearing through valleys, villages and small towns.

The bare bones of Ellie's right foot hit the ground first. Intense pain seared upwards through her legs and pelvis then through each vertebrae, which reappeared in perfect time to encase her spinal cord. Teeth forced their way through bleeding gums, and hair sprouted in the wet blink of a newly formed eye. Skin wrapped tight, like cling film. The fibres of her brain fused together in an incredible explosion of light. By the time her left foot made contact with the pavement her entire body had been reformed. Ellie stared at her hands, each finger perfectly straight and immaculate in every detail. The Missing Feeling was history.

A deep humming, which she knew to be the sound of the earth turning on its axis, faded from her ears. She stamped her feet on the pavement and felt gravity.

~ Thirty-Three ~

Notes for Tomorrow

Ellie stood on Clapham High Street, close to where she'd been knocked off her feet two days ago. She checked her watch. Twenty-two minutes past nine: sunset on Midsummer's Day.

She stared up at the sky. The sunset looked heavy with human energy; deep plum melting into glittering violet. Apart from two children and a pensioner, the street was empty. She'd made it back to Earth before everyone.

She stood rigid, desperate to hear birdsong. Nothing. A puff of wind against her cheek had the same effect as a starting gun. She sprinted down Clapham High Street, past the Railway Inn.

Their unspoken, wordless communication had ended, but an invisible purple thread, spun from the fibres of loving friendship, had them securely connected: Ellie knew where her friends were headed.

Midge had decided to materialise on a beach in Cornwall, she would wait at the water's edge paddling her feet in the cool Atlantic. She understood, without doubt, that her mum would meet her there, at the scene of their last, shared happy moment.

Marty was on his way to San Francisco; perhaps he'd arrived already? He'd left too early, his parents had pulled him off the intended path and now he had to go back. He had to realign himself. He had to find *his* direction. Maybe he would stay for the rest of his life in the city by the bay, where the fog rolls in under the Golden Gate Bridge, or maybe he would return to London. Instinct is poised to give him the answers.

Scott would be just around the corner, sitting in his big, old house waiting for his family to return. In ten days time there'll be a party to celebrate his brother and sister's nineteenth birthday. Scott planned to bake a cake, probably three layers tall. Hopefully, there'd soon be chocolate and coconuts and lemons and almonds, all the things he'd cooked with in the past.

Ellie turned the corner into Gauden Road. The wind whipped up. Deep plum dropped from the heavens, pushing a haze of mauve into the streetlight. She leapt up the steps, two at a time, then realised she didn't have her key. She kicked open the gate at the side of the house, nearly knocking it off its hinges. She grabbed the spare key to the patio doors from under the plant pot.

It's coming! I can feel it! The air pressure's changed...my ears have popped.

Once inside, Ellie darted to the lounge.

She dropped to her knees by the window. "I don't want to miss a thing, I want to see it all, in as much detail as possible."

Leaves and papers scuttled up the road, running for their lives. "You don't need to be scared," she shouted. "It's the Purple! It's not what you think! Everything's going to be okay." The light changed again, dark and rose-tinted, like looking through a lens. Ellie wondered if they'd appear on the top or bottom step. Will they know where they've been? Will they remember?

A spark of panic ignited in her chest. Will I remember? Last time, when the Purple came, it did something to me! It put me into a walking, talking trance for months! I don't want that, I don't want to forget anything. She grabbed a pen and paper from the table by the phone and scribbled some words.

i've floated on the edge of space!!!

i'm not scared of dying!!!!

instinct points me in the right direction

intuition tells the truth

marty midge scott

the walled garden

claremont castle

mrs mackay my great grandma and mr rupert they must still be in scotland i MUST go back for them

ping

"PING!"

Ellie pulled her phone from her pocket and switched it on. Before she managed to make the call, a text message bleeped onto the screen.

penny treasure is dead! i crept into her apartment. she had a gun. she fell off the balcony. i couldn't save her. the mum police say it wasn't my fault. she was a fraud and a liar. dont be scared about the purple coming back. DMC LEADER IN DEATH

PLUNGE HORROR! how about that 4 a headline? did you fly? did you make it? call me!

Ellie pressed the call button. The phone rang twice before the signal failed. Ellie tried again, still no signal.

The windows rattled. A tsunami of swirling Purple came crashing over the houses and landed in the middle of the road. Ellie dropped the phone on the floor. Howling wind saturated with human life force bounced up from the ground and splattered the glass. Ellie pressed her palms and face against the other side of the pane, forcing her eyes wide open. She watched the Purple swirl and squash then squeeze through the gaps in the wooden window frame. It rushed down the chimney. It exploded up, through the floorboards. The room filled with a million screaming, shapeless people. Ellie fell backwards, and laughing, stared up at the forms of her parents floating down from the ceiling like a pair of radiant, ridiculous, peace-loving sunflowers high on nothing but life.

grahamjsharpe.com

Printed in Great Britain
by Amazon.co.uk, Ltd.,
Marston Gate.